To Christine, Charlie and
Chelsea, for encouragement.
To Jayne, for reading.

The three men exited the doors of the Old Bailey into a dark November afternoon. A light rain was falling, which mirrored their feelings. They turned right and walked up the slight hill towards Newgate Street. The man in the middle, who was forty-seven, stood just over 6 feet tall and wore a dark blue tailor- made overcoat that came to mid-thigh. His suit was Italian and his black shoes were made-to-measure. His head was shaved and his blue eyes stared ahead as they walked.

On his right walked a man who was at least 4 inches taller, his dark skin shone as the rain slid down his features. He was wearing a hoodie that clearly showed his muscular frame underneath and his faded jeans and trainers completed the street look – at thirty-five he still liked to play the wide boy.

On the left walked a man dressed in a crumpled suit that had seen better days. He was forty-one and stood at 5 feet 8. His hair was just past his shirt collar, which was fraying at the edges, and his shoes were scuffed and unpolished.

The three men reached the top of the road and came to the junction. The traffic was crawling slowly past as they stood waiting to cross. The lights suddenly changed.

"What a crock of shit," said the man in the hoodie.

The man in the middle turned to him, "Don't worry, our turn will come. You know those boys will cross our path again sometime, and anyway Jordan, we did our bit. The cock-up wasn't ours."

Detective Sergeant Jordan Rhodes turned to look at his boss, "Still fucks me off, though."

The smallest of the three men, Detective Chief Inspector Harry Davis, said, "He's right boss. Someone, somewhere gave a few names out and messed this case up."

The boss, Chief Superintendent Charlie Smith, Head of

the Central Murder and Serious Crime Squad, said, "It happens boys. It's happened before and will probably happen again, but always remember we never give up and, like a roundabout, our chance will come again to nail them."

The case they were discussing was the trial of two brothers, who they had arrested and charged with the murder of three men shot in a club. The trial had failed when two witnesses had suddenly forgotten all they could remember – they were supposed to have been in police protection, but someone had clearly got to them or their family.

They crossed the road, turned left as they reached the other side and walked down Snow Hill towards the police station. They went up the three steps together and pushed open the doors and into an entrance that looked like it had not changed for a hundred years.

"Open the door," Jordan said.

The constable behind the counter looked up and was about to say something, when he recognised the three officers stood looking at him. He quickly reached the buzzer to open the doors.

"Thanks," said Jordan.

They turned right into the corridor and then went up two flights of stairs to the first floor.

"Are we going to meet up with the rest of the team boss?" asked Harry.

"Get our files together from the office, box them up and arrange for them to be picked up and taken to base. I'm just going to see the station commander to say thanks for putting us up. I will meet you at the back in ten minutes."

With that, Charlie Smith turned and carried on up another two flights of stairs to the next floor. He noticed that the tiling on the walls looked like something he had seen on the *Antiques Roadshow* – it probably was, as he knew nothing had changed much at this police station. He went left as he reached the second floor, passing three doors before he came to the one with 'Station Commander' on it. He knocked and heard the order to come in.

He entered and saw Commander Roy Evans seated in full commander's uniform behind his desk.

"Charlie, how did it go?" he said as he looked up.

"One that got away," Charlie replied.

"How?" asked Roy. "You had everything tight; the evidence was solid."

"Had a couple of cases of witness amnesia, so the crown prosecution said we had to drop the case," Charlie said.

"Sorry mate," Roy said. "What now?"

"I just came to say thanks for putting up with my team running around your station," Charlie said. "I know they can be a strange lot and take some getting used to."

The commander leaned back in his chair and smiled. He had known Charlie for over ten years, meeting him first when they were both in the Drug Squad and had liked him since. "They always say the team is a reflection of their leader and they certainly follow after you."

They both laughed.

"You want a quick drink before you go?" asked Roy.

"No thanks, mate. I'm going to meet the rest of the team for a bite and a drink. Try and cheer them up," Charlie replied.

Roy stood up, leaned across the desk and shook hands. "Well, drop in anytime – maybe not with your entire mob in tow next time. We can have a good catch up. I will keep my ears open, in case I hear any whispers about your witnesses."

"Thanks Roy."

Charlie left the office and made his way down the stairs to the ground floor. He noticed the pile of boxes marked with his squad's name on them at the bottom. *Someone will have an accident with those there.* He poked his head round the door of the desk sergeant.

"Sarge, can you get those boxes moved somewhere out the way till they're picked up? I think one of my boys left them there by mistake."

The sergeant looked up.

"Okay, Sir," he said, in a vaguely patronising tone.

With that, the chief superintendent turned and made his way to the back of the station, pushed open the doors that led out to the police car park and was met with the cold rain that had now started to fall more heavily.

Just outside the door, in a cloud of cigarette smoke, stood Jordan and Harry.

"You can put those out – I am not having the car stinking of cigarettes. Who left the boxes at the bottom of the stairs?"

"That was me boss," said Jordan. "I was hoping that arsehole of a sergeant would fall over and break his neck."

"You make friends so well. Now, put those out and let's go. Have either of you two rung the rest of the team?" Charlie asked.

"I did," said Harry. "I told them we'd meet at The Ruby and go over everything."

"Okay, let's go."

They walked across the car park towards the back corner where the chief superintendent's two-month-old, metallic silver-blue Bentley convertible was parked. "I take it we're not having the top down?" Harry asked.

***

The prime minister had called his most senior ministers and party officials to a meeting at Number Ten. They were all seated at the table, which was normally used for full cabinet meetings.

"I want to thank you all for coming at such short notice," the prime minister said. "As some of you know, for the last few months I have not been too well. I thank you all for taking on some of the work I should have been doing. Yesterday, I had a meeting with my doctor and a senior consultant. They have told me I need to have an operation and then complete rest for six months."

There were surprised looks from those around the table who did not know how ill the prime minister had been.

"I have sat down with the chief whip and the party chairman and talked over the situation, and have decided to stand down. We have a large majority in parliament so there's no need to call a general election. The party is pretty settled and so we think, in line with party rules, that an election amongst all our MPs for a new leader who would then become prime minister is the best solution. We are still doing well in the polls and have some important legislation coming up, so we don't want a long drawn-out fight for the leadership. The best solution would be a consensus, so we don't risk any in-fighting. I ask you all to bear that in mind; please let's not get into briefing journalists against each other. There will probably be some who are not at this meeting who will wish to stand. The party chairman says the rules state that anyone wishing to stand must have the backing of thirty-five elected MPs, with signed nomination forms backing him or her. I will be holding a press conference tomorrow morning to make my announcement. The chief whip will say a few words now."

The chief whip stood up, "I am sure that we all hope the prime minister has a speedy recovery," he said.

All around the table nodded.

"During the election of a new leader, we must not let our main functions of government slip. The prime minister pointed out there are important bills before the house in the coming weeks – none more important than the new terrorism bill that the home secretary is proposing to bring into law. We have managed, just, to keep a majority on this, but we know it's contentious and not all – even in our own party – back it. Also, some of the newspapers oppose it. Let's make sure we don't give any ammunition to our opponents that could be used to stop it becoming law."

The chief whip sat down.

"Thank you," the prime minister said. "I have asked the party chairman to call a meeting of all our MPs to inform them of what is planned and how the election will work. Now, I dare say rumours will start to do the rounds before my press conference tomorrow, but I ask that if you are contacted to just say you have heard nothing. I will be calling a full cabinet meeting in the morning before I go into the press conference to explain what's happening to the rest of our colleagues. I shall not be putting my support behind any one candidate for the leadership. The party must decide. Thank you all again for coming at such short notice, and I will see you again in the morning. Now, I have a few more things to discuss with the chief whip and the party chairman."

The rest of the people round the table rose, bade goodbye and left the room.

"How do you think the leadership contest will go?" the prime minister asked.

"I would think that only three people are in a strong position," the chief whip said. "The foreign secretary has been in government a long time, knows his way round and has many contacts; the health secretary has made some good impressions on her running of the health department; and the home secretary has built up a good following amongst MPs with his stand on terrorism and the work done in other departments."

"I would agree with the chief whip," the party chairman said. "There is not a lot to choose between them and it will come down to personality. The home secretary is well liked and has made a good impression – not just in our party, but with the public in general."

"I think that it could be a risk in any future election though," the chief whip said. "The public might not wish to see a Muslim prime minister, regardless if they agree with our broader policies."

"The home secretary does not beat on about his religion and I have never heard him use it in any way to further or excuse anything he does," the prime minister said.

"It's the perception amongst the public but the people in the press might use his religion as a tool against us," the chief whip replied.

The prime minister turned to the party chairman, "Do you think the same?"

"Well, it could be a problem," the party chairman said, "but the home secretary comes across as a good, honest man and always scores highly with the public in opinion polls."

The prime minister stood up, "We will see how things pan out over the coming days. I want both of you to keep me informed on the feedback you get from our MPs and if you see any potential problems that could damage the party standing. We must get the right person."

After leaving Number Ten, the chief whip turned right out of Downing Street and headed for the Houses of Parliament. He got on his mobile phone and spoke to his office, gave them the names of three MPs and said to ask them to come to the Whip's office in an hour for a meeting. He then called a journalist who he had gone to school with and invited him round for a drink that evening. He enjoyed working with the prime minister and had not had too many disagreements with him, but this opportunity – to make sure the next leader would fully appreciate his talents and for a reward of high office to come his way – was too good to miss.

★★★

An hour later, he was seated in his office. There was a knock on the door and his secretary came in, telling him that the three MPs he had asked to see were now waiting outside. He said to send them in.

The three MPs came into the room and stood in front of his desk. He always felt his position gave him the power of a headmaster, and knew that the MPs would stand there until he told them otherwise. Looking up eventually, he said,"Please take a seat."

The three sat down opposite him.

"Now, I have invited you to this meeting because of discussions I have had with you all at one time or another about the direction the party should be taking. I want to take you into my confidence about some news that will be announced tomorrow and I want you to start preparing the ground for it."

The youngest of the three, who had only been in parliament three years but was ambitious to move up the ladder, asked, "Is it a new policy or an about-turn on an old one."

The chief whip looked at him. *He's an arrogant so-and-so*, he thought, but he had used him a number of times to plant awkward questions to ministers when he wanted to exert pressure over party policy. In contrast, the other two were much older, had only ever held junior posts in government and he knew they felt their talents had been overlooked.

"No, neither of those." He waited a few seconds while all three of them lent forward. "The prime minister will be announcing tomorrow that he is stepping down."

The three in front of him all involuntary sat back.

The chief whip spoke again before they could ask a question, "Now, I am taking you into my confidence because I feel we all want the party to go in the same direction."

They all nodded.

"With a new prime minister, we can achieve that. I want to hear who you think is of the same mind as us."

None of them spoke, but looked at each other, waiting for someone to comment.

"Come on," the chief whip said, "I want to hear your opinions."

It was the youngest of the three who spoke first, "Do you know yet who will be standing?"

"I expect about five, but two of them hardly have any support and will just be doing it to get their names in the papers. I would think it's between the foreign secretary, the health minister and the home secretary."

"They all have support in the party," the MP in the middle said, "but I would back the health secretary. She would bring the party back to its roots and stop the drift to the middle."

The chief whip nodded. "What about you two?" he asked.

The younger one nodded in agreement, while the other said, "I agree, but I don't think she would have as much support as the other two. They have lots of backing amongst MPs."

"I agree with you," the chief whip said. "I too feel the health secretary would be the best for the job, which is why I asked you here. I will be arranging a private meeting with the health secretary and want to be able to tell her she has the support of many in the party – that's where you come in…" He pointed at them. "We have to do our best to make sure our fellow MPs understand why she would be best for our future. I am sure if she did become prime minister, she would reward those who helped her." He didn't need to say what those rewards would be. "When I speak to her, I will advise her on who she should recruit to help organise her campaign to become party leader."

"What about the other two? The foreign secretary has a lot of friends in and outside of the party," the youngest asked.

"I think with the prime minister stepping down due to ill health, it might be discreetly pointed out that the foreign secretary's age is older than that of the prime minister – rumours may even start about his reported health. I am sure a journalist overhearing a conversation about his rumoured health problems would report it in the papers, and telling our fellow MPs we don't want to go through another party election again soon could sway them from him."

The one in the middle said, "The home secretary is well liked in and out of the party too, and some of the reforms and laws he has seen through parliament have been well received."

"I think the home secretary would be favourite," the chief whip said, "but his new bill on terrorism, which he is trying to get through parliament, does not even have the backing of everyone in our party – even a number of papers have come out against it. We have to ask, would his religion hold the party back at a general election?"

"I don't think his religion has come up before," the youngest one said. "He gets good ratings in opinion polls with the public."

"That may be the case now," the chief whip replied, "but if he was leading the party into a general election, I think his religion would come into play and could cost us many seats. I have seen some internal polling done privately for the party and it could be bad."

"So, how will we counter him if he runs for the leadership?" the young one asked.

"Start to whisper into your fellow MPs' ears that you heard polling with him as leader would cost us a lot of seats," the chief whip said. "I will make sure that news gets out to a few papers. You can ask around if anyone has heard the rumours of his family being mixed up in a tax scandal, and I'm sure some journalist might pick that up and run it."

"Which members of his family were mixed up in the tax scandal?" the younger MP asked.

"I haven't heard that there is a tax scandal, but we can put it around that there is. Let him get asked questions – you know the public hate MPs who don't pay their full taxes," the chief whip said. "Now, I have to remind you that I must be seen to be impartial in the coming party leadership election, so no word must get out about this meeting. I will keep you informed of any news that comes across my desk if I think it would aid our campaign. When I have spoken to the health secretary later, she will probably be in touch with you about joining her campaign. For now, we have a head start on the others, so get out and start to sound out other MPs on who they would support if the prime minister were to step down. I want to know who they say – maybe I could apply some pressure on certain individuals to change their minds to suit us. Remember, be discreet."

The three MPs all stood up and left the office. The chief whip sat back. *The first part is in motion,* he thought. He would call the health secretary in for a meeting later; she was a bright woman, ambitious, and he knew she would love the chance to become the second woman to become prime minister. He would ensure he got his rewards when she did.

★ ★ ★

They arrived at a pub in East Ham thirty-five minutes later. It was known to them as The Ruby, though it was called The King's Head on the signs outside – it got its nickname because it did the best curry in East London, as far as they were concerned, and was run by the cousin of one of the team.

The three of them entered. There was no carpet, just polished wooden flooring, and the paint on the walls was a cross between green and yellow. It was quite crowded, but they pushed their way through to the far corner where they saw the rest of the team seated. The team consisted of Detective Constable Danny Kane, twenty-six, 5 feet 8, with long, dark hair; his nickname was Hippie, like his boss, he had spent some time in the Drug Squad. Seated on his left was Detective Constable Manjitt Virdee, twenty-nine, whose cousin ran the pub. She could have been a model, just over 5 feet 11, with long, jet-black hair and Bollywood star looks. She was a whiz with computers, but as hard as nails – being a sixth dan in karate – and had proved herself in a few rough arrests. She had been destined for the Fraud Squad, but had been seconded to the boss's team. There, she had found a home in the police that she hadn't felt before, so had turned down the Fraud Squad and with it a certain promotion to stay with the boss's team. The last of the group was the smallest; standing just over 5 feet 5, Detective Constable Oscar Hernandez was thirty, olive skinned – his parents were from Brazil – and known as Pelé after Brazil's, and one of the world's, greatest footballers.

Ironically, he had never been any good at football, he preferred his samba music and was great on the dance floor.

"Hey, boss," they said, almost in unison as they saw the boss approaching. "How's everyone?" Charlie said. "Let's get the food and drinks and then we can talk."

They sat down beside the others. Manjitt waved a hand and within a few seconds, one of the bar staff was there to take their order.

"Tell Malkitt we will have our usual." She looked around at the team and they all nodded, "Put it on the boss's bill."

The team cheered and the boss smiled.

"Right, let's go over everything," he said.

★★★

It was late that evening when Chief Superintendent Charlie Smith turned off the A12 in Essex onto a small country road. He had left his team still sitting and talking in The Ruby – he was on standby this weekend and planned to see to a few things and enjoy a night out. Harry was senior officer on duty and would call if anything came up.

His Bentley purred along the country road in the direction of his house. He had the news on Radio 4 on in the background. It looked as though the rain was just starting to ease off.

He came to a small junction and turned left past a sign that said 'Private road. No through traffic'. It wound its way for half a mile past tall trees on both sides of the road, which kept the light out even in the summer. At the end of the road, he came to some tall iron gates, pressed a button on the key fob and the gates started to open. As soon as they did, security lights came on and illuminated the area. He drove through the gates and looked in the rear-view mirror as the gates started to close behind him. He drove 30 yards and stopped in front of a small cottage. The lights were on downstairs and the front door opened as he pulled up. A man in his late fifties came out and walked to the car. Charlie pressed the down button on the window.

"Evening, Charlie," the man said.

"Hello, Mike, I should be here most of the weekend unless anything comes up. How's Maggie?"

"Fine thanks, just doing dinner. She said that the dogs have been okay and they're currently out back. She put some mail on the table in the hall for you."

"Thanks, Mike, see you tomorrow."

He pressed the window up, put the Bentley in drive and continued on his way.

Mike and Maggie Reynolds had worked for him for over eighteen years. Maggie as his housekeeper and Mike kept the grounds and garden looking good. They also let the dogs out to run around when he wasn't there. The road bent slightly to the right on a long curve and his house came into view. It could not be seen from any of the roads that went round his 50 acres of land. It was one of the reasons he had bought it – he liked the solitude and privacy. It was a large Georgian house with six bedrooms, four bathrooms, three en-suites, three reception rooms and a lovely, large, country style kitchen. It was far too big for him on his own and had cost £2.5 million, but he loved the place and occasionally the team would come down for Sunday dinner, which Maggie would cook for them.

He pulled up in front of a barn to the left of the main house, pressed the fob on his keys again and the barn door started to open. He had had the barn converted to a large garage space a month after he bought the house. He now drove the Bentley into the garage and parked it beside a Land Rover Discovery, which he had because the roads in winter around his house needed the four-wheel drive. To the side of that was a red Ferrari Daytona, which had cost him over £300,000. He had probably only driven it a dozen times and had put only a few hundred miles on the clock, but it reminded him of his dad and it looked stunning.

He left the barn, the doors closing slowly behind him, and pushed open a gate to the side of the house. He then went round to the back of the house, walking on the small shingle that crunched under his shoes. As he came to the corner, he stopped; in the garden, chasing and playing, were his three dogs. He watched them for a minute before turning the corner, but the dogs had seen him and came running towards him. The three greyhounds leapt up and ran around him. He bent down and patted and stroked them.

"Come on, you three. Let's go in."

The dogs followed him to the back door, which was open. Inside, along one wall, were three dog beds, water and food bowls. The door was always open, so that the dogs could still come and go as they pleased when no one was in the house.

He went to the proper back door that led to the kitchen, got his keys out and unlocked it. As he opened it, the dogs pushed past him and ran inside. He walked into the kitchen, flicked on the lights; he then picked up the kettle, filled it and turned it on. He got his mug from the rack above and went to the fridge for the milk, poured some in his mug, picked out a tea bag and dropped it in. The three dogs were all standing looking at him. They had this routine down to a tee and he knew they were expecting him to get some biscuits out – and as always, he did. Taking three biscuits out, he threw them one at a time to each of them, which they expertly caught in their mouths. He watched them munch away for a while, and then he left the kitchen and went into the hall, picking up the mail that Maggie had placed there for him.

Turning to his right, he opened the door into his main room, switching on the lights as he went in. The dogs followed him; the log fire was smouldering nicely.

"Go and lay down," he said to the dogs.

Two went and leapt onto a large sofa, while the other lay down by the fire. He knew that they would stay like that for hours, as greyhounds were the couch potatoes of the dog world. People thought they were always on the go, but they were happy just to lie around for hours, not stirring unless they thought food or an open back door was there for them.

He laid his mail on the table beside his chair to the left of the fire, leant over, picked a couple of wood logs from the stack and placed them on the fire. He then briefly returned to the kitchen to finish making his tea, before returning to the main room and sat down. He looked up at the picture of his mum and dad, Bill and Jane Smith, standing arm in arm outside West Ham's football ground, Upton Park – Dad with his West Ham shirt on and Mum wearing a claret and blue team scarf.

* * *

His mother had often told him the story of how she had met his father.

It was in the summer and she was meeting some friends from university for a night out. The plan was to have a few drinks in a bar at London Bridge station and then go onto a nightclub. She had been sitting with her friends, drinking and chatting for half an hour or so, when she had got up to buy a round of drinks. At the bar, as she waited to be served, there was a television showing the news. Suddenly, a voice next to her made a comment about it; she turned and made a comment back. They introduced themselves, David Smith and Annabel Michaels. She told Charlie that she spent the next hour talking to his dad, who had been in there after finishing work and had popped in with a couple of mates for a drink before going home. She finally left with her friends, but gave him her parents' phone number as she was home for the summer – this was before mobile phones were the norm. He said he would call her tomorrow. She said she didn't really enjoy herself the rest of the night, instead wishing she had stayed at the pub.

His dad had left school with no exams to his name and was a

hod carrier, which was someone who carries the bricks for the bricklayer – a tough job, going up and down ladders with a stack of bricks on your shoulder all day long. In contrast, his mother had got top marks at school and was studying Chemistry at university. They were both nineteen when they met.

The next day, she said she sat near her parents' phone all day, hoping it would ring. It finally did in the middle of the afternoon. From then on, they met up three evenings a week and every weekend that summer, wandering around London and pubs in the East End were his dad lived. He took her to her first football match at West Ham – after which, she was as much a West Ham fan as anyone.

His dad had a flat on the fourth floor of a tower block, on a run-down council estate in Dagenham, and every other weekend she stayed there with him. The second month, she went to his mum and dads' for Sunday dinner. They lived two streets away in a small terraced house. She said they were so nice to her that she loved them straightaway, just as she knew she was already in love. She had said Dad was the kindest, most uncomplicated person she had ever known.

A month before she was due to go back to university, she invited Dad to her parents' house to meet them, as they had been asking who the boy she had been seeing was and wanted to meet him. Her father and mother were both chemists, with a number of chemist shops and a small business exporting pharmaceuticals to Africa and the Far East.

When his dad arrived, her parents were very nice and polite to him, chatted and asked him about his job and what he wanted to do. They had dinner and Dad left in the evening to go home.

It was about half an hour after he had left and she was sitting in the front room with her parents watching the television when her mother had said, "You're not serious about that boy, are you?"

She was a bit stunned by the question, as nothing had been said like that all day. "What do you mean?" she asked.

Her dad answered, "Well, he's not got any prospects and he's hardly the right sort of person you should be getting involved with."

She told Charlie she had then sat quiet, not saying anything because her mind was confused. Her parents had never expressed any thoughts like this to her before when she had been dating. She eventually told them that she was serious about him.

Her father told her not to be stupid, that she should concentrate on her studies, get her degree and would meet someone that was right for when she was older.

She said she had got mad, and that a lot of loud and sharp words were exchanged between them. In the end, her father had told her he would not continue paying for her university if she was going to waste her time on a loser, and her mother had told her she could not see the boy again.

She said she left the front room, went straight to her bedroom and packed some clothes in a bag. When she came downstairs, her parents were standing at the bottom.

"If you leave this house tonight, never come back," her father had said.

She said she never said another word to them and walked out.

Two hours later, she knocked on Dad's door and moved in. She never went back to university, but got a job working at the Ford Motor factory in Dagenham. Her parents didn't try to get in touch and a few years later when she had tried to reach them after Charlie had been born, she found out they had moved – so she decided to just make sure her family grew together.

He remembered his childhood fondly; there was not a lot of money, but it was a happy time. He remembered family holidays together, how they would drive down to the coast to Southend, where his dad's parents had a caravan. They always played 'see who can spot the Ferrari first' as Dad loved Formula One racing. They hardly ever saw one, but if they did, Dad would try and keep up with it so they could see what type it was. The Daytona was his dad's dream car, but they had never seen one on the road. Dad had given him a model and a framed picture of one for his sixth birthday; he still had them – the model sat on his bedside table and the picture hung on the wall. His parents had also taken him to West Ham for the football. He had nothing but happy memories of being with the two of them.

His dad died when he was seven; he was killed in an accident on a building site. Times were tough after that, but his mum tried to make things as easy as she could. His mum would drop him off at school and when school finished, he would walk to his dad's parents' house and have tea. Mum picked him up on the way home from the Ford factory. Every other weekend, they would go round there for Sunday dinner. Dad was hardly ever mentioned; Charlie knew now that it was just too painful for them to talk about him.

As he grew up, things settled down. His mum didn't go out much; once in a blue moon, she would go for a drink with some of the girls from work. He remembered that she loved watching police dramas, like *The Sweeny*, *Special Branch* and *Kojak*, with him. They would try and guess who had done the crime and laugh when they got the wrong person. He left school at sixteen and went to work for a friend of his grandparents at a greengrocer, but only to earn some money.

One evening, while sitting with his mum watching an old *Poirot* movie on the television, she had said he should join the police and catch the bad guys. He had laughed because in the area they lived, no one knew anybody who was a policeman. In fact, they went out of their way to avoid them. Still, the seed had been planted and after a year of carrying potatoes and onions around, he decided he would give it a go – not that he told any of his friends what he was thinking of doing; they would have killed him.

He told his mum though, and she helped him get the forms filled in. To his surprise, he was accepted. He went off to Hendon Police College and found that he enjoyed it, and met some great people. Coming from his background, he had only seen the police as the enemy and not to be trusted. His mother was so happy when he passed out as a full constable.

He was first posted to West End Central. What an eye-opener it was for him, but he loved the work. He always remembered his first sergeant telling him he worked to ensure people came home from work and didn't find their house burgled, and could walk home from the shops without getting robbed – bland, but true.

An inspector had then picked him to work on a team that was trying to combat pickpocketing in the West End – the dippers, as they were called, targeted tourists – and so he had spent his first summer in the police, chasing dippers in and out of tube stations, catching some and losing others. Either way, the inspector told him not to worry as they would be back – they always were.

After three years, he had taken the exam to become a detective constable, which he passed. He then went to work on the Vice Squad. As it was stationed in central London and he now knew the West End well, the inspector in charge of the team relied on him to organise the stakeouts, so all escape routes were covered. It had taught him how vital preparation was, how everyone had to know their job and what was expected of them.

After that, he found that the job came natural to him. Promotion followed; he was twenty-six and a detective sergeant.

The call had come when he was going over the papers for a case of a conman who had been fooling old people into investing money in schemes that didn't exist. His mother had had a heart attack and been taken to a hospital in Whitechapel. He had used a squad car with sirens on to get him to the hospital quickly, where he had met the doctor outside the emergency room. He remembered looking at the doctor's face and knowing that his mum had died.

The doctor said she had left work and had had a massive heart attack whilst waiting to cross the road. She was dead before the ambulance got there. He had sat for an hour with her, before going to see his grandparents. They had both sat in silence when he told them, but he saw tears running down his grandmother's face and he cried quiet tears, too.

After that, he threw himself into his job. Even though he would still pop into his grandparents' every other Sunday for dinner, the job was all he had now.

A couple of years later – he was now a detective inspector in the Drugs Squad – he had received a letter from a London solicitor requesting to speak to him. He wondered if there had been a complaint about him over an arrest, but checked with the complaints department, who found nothing. He rang the solicitors, who said they needed to meet him, as it was something that they couldn't talk over the phone about. He arranged to call in to their office the next day at eleven, as it was in Lincoln's Inn Fields and he had to be at the Old Bailey that afternoon.

He arrived at eleven and was ushered into the office of Julian Squires, of Squires, Cohen and Fitzroy solicitors. He sat down and Julian told him that an American attorney had instructed them to find Annabel Michaels, but Julian had found out that his mother had died and that he was the only next of kin.

Charlie had asked why they wanted his mother and Julian told him that her father had died and she was the beneficiary of his will. As she had died, it meant Charlie was now the beneficiary. He told Julian that he had never met his mother's parents and that his mother had not seen them since she married.

Julian had then opened an envelope and pulled two pieces of paper from it. He started to read, "It appears your grandfather died without changing the will he had made many years ago. Your grandmother had passed away five years previous, which left your mother as the sole heir. As she has died, the estate of your grandfather goes to you. Your grandfather went to America many years ago and had actually taken American citizenship; he was a chemist by trade and it would appear he was quite successful. It seems he built up a number of shops and had an export business."

He remembered Julian looking at him over the papers, "You're in the police?" he had said.

Charlie had nodded.

"Well, your grandfather's estate is worth $220 million dollars. At the current exchange rate, that's about £150 million."

* * *

He opened his eyes. The clock said quarter past midnight; he had fallen asleep in the chair. The dogs were still lying asleep and his tea remained untouched on the table. He rose from the chair, picking up the cup. The dogs' heads all came up together at his movement.

"Come on, you three, bedtime," he said.

* * *

Assistant Commissioner Walker was woken up by the sound of his phone ringing. As he picked it up, he glanced at the digital clock on the table beside his bed. It showed 1am.

The call was from one of his detective sergeants, telling him the news, which had just reached the office, of the disappearance of Ashadieeyah Khan, who was the home secretary's niece. The home secretary had called the commissioner when his brother had phoned him saying he had got no help from the local station.

"Do you think it is something we should be worried about?" the sergeant asked.

"Let's not take any chances, keep on top of any news coming in from the local force. If anything turns up, I want to know straightaway. Discreetly let the ports and airports know to keep an eye out," the assistant commissioner said.

He put the phone down and lay back, wondering if the girl had gone on the missing list again. He might have been wrong to take the watch off of her. He would get into the office early and get things moving. He lent over and reset the alarm on his clock to 5am. His wife stirred next to him.

"Is everything alright?" she asked.

"Yes, go back to sleep," he said.

* * *

Walker had arrived at Scotland Yard just before 6am. He was now sitting in his office going through reports from different branches of the anti-terrorism forces around the country, when there was a knock on the door and one of his detective sergeants came into the office.

"Just had a flash come through about the girl Ashadieeyah Khan who went missing last night. A body has been discovered on Wimbledon Common and the local police believe it's her."

"Get her file out and get hold of the officer in charge of the local force," Walker said.

The phone on Walker's desk rang and he picked it up. It was the commissioner's office. He waited a few seconds while he was put through to the office of a deputy commissioner, until a voice came on the line.

"AC Walker, I have been asked by the commissioner to speak to you about reports of the home secretary's niece being killed in Wimbledon. We don't know if it has any terrorist connections, but there could be. Have you heard any word surrounding the home secretary or his family?"

Walker thought for a moment, "No, Sir, I have not seen anything come across my desk."

"That's good, I am going to get the Serious Crime Squad to investigate it," the DC said. "That way, we can get full resources on it – the local force would probably struggle if it gets too complicated."

"Do you think that's a good idea?" Walker said. "The press might ask why this murder is getting preferential investigation."

"They might do, but we can say it is the home secretary's niece and we have to ensure all lines of enquiry are followed," the DC said. "I will be contacting them to get things moving, but wanted to check you hadn't heard anything. If you do, let the Serious Crime Squad know."

Walker put down the phone, as his detective sergeant and another officer came back into the office.

"I have the file on the girl, Sir," he placed it on the desk in front of Walker.

Walker looked up. "Sit down the two of you." They both sat down. "I have just got off the phone with the deputy commissioner, who has decided to hand the case to the Serious Crime Squad. He asked if we had any information on the girl. I told him no. We can't let our investigation leak out; she was the home secretary's niece and we can't be sure that he does not know what she's been up to. He could be involved for all we know."

"Come on, Sir, the home secretary involved in a terrorist plot?" the D.S in front of him said.

Walker looked at him, "Can you tell me he's not?"

The D.S shook his head.

"So, we have to play our cards close to our chest. Did you get the local officer in charge yet?" Walker asked.

"Yes, I said you would be calling. Her name is Myles, Chief Superintendent Caroline Myles," the D.S said.

"I want to know what the Serious Crime Squad is up to at all times," Walker replied, "but they must not know that we have an interest. Get a couple of officers over to the girl's house, use uniforms from diplomatic protection, we can put it down to saying it's to stop press intrusion on the family with the girl being related to someone important. Make sure they are told to let us know who comes and goes from the house… and I mean anyone."

"Do you want us go to the house ourselves to check the girl's room?" the D.S asked.

"No, we can't do that now, but send some boys up to the university she was staying at. Search her rooms there and bring anything they find back here. We don't want serious crimes finding anything that may interfere with our enquiry. Get on with it then. I will call the local police."

The two officers got up and left. Walker picked up the phone and called Chief Superintendent Myles. The phone was answered within three rings.

"Hello, this is Assistant Commissioner Walker. Is that Chief Superintendent Myles?"

"Yes, Sir," came the voice from the other end of the line.

"I understand you will be having the Serious Crime Squad at your station, investigating the death of the girl found on Wimbledon Common this morning. I want you to give them all the possible help you can. It's a delicate matter with the girl being the niece of the home secretary."

"Yes, Sir, I understand," Myles said.

"If you do have any problems, feel free to call me," Walker said. "I know the Serious Crime Squad can be a bit of a handful."

"Thank you, Sir, I will do that," Myles replied.

Walker put the phone down. He picked up the girl's file and began to read it to see if any new information had been added.

★★★

Charlie Smith heard the ringing, but knew it was not the alarm clock as he hadn't set it. He reached his hand out and picked up the phone.

"Hello."

"Boss, its Harry. Sorry to ring, but a girl's body has been discovered in Wimbledon. Got a call that they want us to take it."

"Why? Surely that's for the locals," Charlie asked.

"I said the same, but was told we had to take it. I've sent Manjitt and Oscar on ahead, and I will pick Hippie up on the way. Can you get Jordan? I'll let him know to be ready."

"Okay, will see you there," Charlie said.

He had wanted to fit a few things into this weekend, but as always the job came first. He rose from the bed and made his way to the bathroom. The clock said 8.15am. Half an hour later, he was on his way with the top of the Bentley down, enjoying the late November sunshine. The rain that had fallen yesterday was still sitting in puddles.

Manjitt turned the squad car into a small turning on Wimbledon Common. It was part forest on the left and grassland on the right. They came to some police tape that was blocking the road, it was tied to a road sign on one side and a tree on the other. A uniformed constable was standing behind it looking at them.

"He looks a happy soul," said Oscar.

"You looked like that once," said Manjitt.

They both laughed.

* * *

Manjitt parked the car on the grass verge behind some marked police cars. They then got out, approached the constable and showed him their warrant cards.

"Where is the body?" said Oscar.

"Follow the path over there," said the constable, pointing to his left. They ducked under the tape and made their way down the path.

The constable watched them go. *How can she be a police officer when she looks like a model?* He shook his head.

The path was not very wide, but the mud squelched under their feet. Manjitt had a pair of jeans on, which were tucked into her black leather boots that came up to her knees, and she wore a blue padded jacket.

"Can I borrow your boots?" Oscar said. "I can feel the water coming through my trainers already."

"You should spend some of your wages on shoes rather than all those records you buy," Manjitt replied.

"Ha," Oscar said, "but music is life. I have a style to keep up when I am on the dance floor."

"Mind the…"

"Shit," said Oscar.

"… Puddle," said Manjitt. She giggled to herself as she heard the repeated curses of Oscar, whose feet were now definitely wet through.

They came out into a small clearing and saw three men standing talking. As they approached, one of the men nodded in their direction and they all turned to look at them.

"Who are you?" said the man in the middle.

"This is DC Hernandez and I am DC Virdee. We are with Serious Crimes, and have been sent here by our boss."

The one in the middle turned, said something and the other two men walked off. He turned back to them, "I am Inspector West. If you want to follow me, I will show you where the body is."

"Who found it, Sir?" asked Manjitt.

"A jogger on his morning run," he said. "He doesn't normally come this way, but because of the rain his normal route was flooded. Otherwise, it might have gone undiscovered for days."

They made their way further along another muddy path, ducked under some more police tape and came to a group of forensic officers in white pullover suits, who were taking pictures of the body. She was lying on her side, with one arm stretched out by her head and the other tucked underneath her.

"Do we have a name for the girl?" asked Oscar.

"Yes, a girl was reported missing last night: Ashadieeyah Khan, aged twenty. She fits the description of the body and is wearing similar clothes. It doesn't look like a sexual assault, but we won't know for definite 'till the autopsy."

"Ashadieeyah means princess," said Manjitt. "It's a Muslim name. But why are we here? It doesn't seem to be one of our cases."

"When she was reported missing last night, our boss got a call from someone. It turns out she's the niece of the home secretary, so you can expect a lot of press on this and some pressure from above. Glad it's you lot and not us," West said. One of the forensic team approached them and spoke to Inspector West, "Two stab wounds to the front of the chest, one of them it looks like it has gone straight through the heart. It's a bit messy there, but I don't think she was killed here. The trees have covered where she's lying and kept the area reasonably dry, and I don't see much blood around the body. I could be wrong but we will take soil samples and check. There are a few marks round the neck, but I'm not sure what they are yet. The time of death was between 10pm yesterday night and 2am this morning."

He turned and went back to the body.

"Who's he?" asked Manjitt.

"Doctor Taylor, Head of Forensics. Who's this coming now?" said Inspector West.

Oscar and Manjitt turned to see Harry and Danny walking towards them.

"Hello people," said Harry. "What have we got?"

"Inspector West, this is Chief Inspector Davies," said Oscar.

"Hello, Sir," said West. "We have a girl's body: two stab wounds, killed between 10 and 2."

"Have you made a search of the area yet for the weapon?" asked Harry.

"Not yet, Sir, I am waiting for more uniforms to turn up. There's only a couple of DCs, myself and two uniforms who I have on duty at the tapes."

Manjitt, Oscar and Danny looked at each other and smiled, anticipating Harry's reaction.

"Not enough uniforms here?" said Harry, raising his voice so that even the forensic team looked up. "You get me more uniforms here in half an hour, Inspector, or you and your DCs will be crawling through the mud looking for the weapon yourself. Go on, move it. If you get any trouble from anyone about resources, send them in my direction. I want forty officers here and a thorough search of the area – and I mean, thorough. I don't want to come back and ask you why you missed somewhere. Understand?"

Inspector West turned and hurried off.

Danny was the first to speak, "Why do you always do that? The poor inspector seems a nice bloke."

Harry turned to him, "He will go out of his way now to make sure that it gets done right, and I will make sure I tell him what a good job he's done and let him know I will tell his boss what a good copper he is. So, everyone's happy in the end. It's about time your hair was cut; it's longer than it's ever been."

"My mum said I should keep it long to keep the cold out my ears," Danny replied.

"Right, let's have a look around a bit for ourselves," said Harry.

The constable behind the police tape saw a metallic silver-blue Bentley convertible with the top down coming towards him, stopping just before it touched the tape. He looked at the two men sitting inside: a large black man in a brown leather jacket and the driver, a shaven-haired white man wearing a white mac. They sat there looking at him, but not saying anything. He thought they might be drug dealers or might be mixed up with the murder – it might be an idea to give them a search.

"Sorry, you can't come through this way," he said. He ducked under the tape and approached the driver who was still staring at him. "There's been an incident and the area's closed off to the public. Can I ask you what you're doing driving down here?"

He saw the dark-skinned man reach inside his jacket and for one horrid moment thought he was getting a weapon out, but he saw he had a wallet in his hand. "I'm Detective Sergeant Rhodes and this is Chief Superintendent Smith."

The constable was at the side of the car now and could see the warrant card, "Oh, sorry, Sir."

The chief superintendent spoke to him, "Where is the scene of crime?"

"It's down the path over there, Sir – 100 yards or so," said the constable.

"Is there another way in and somewhere better to park?" asked the chief superintendent. "If I put this on that grass verge, it will sink."

"Yes, Sir, if you follow this road round for a couple of hundred yards, you will see a turning on the left. If you take that, it leads to a car park. The forensics have their vans parked up there."

"Thank you, constable; can you lift that tape for us?"

The officer lifted the tape and the Bentley passed by. He watched it go, shaking his head. *Surely it's not possible to drive a car like that on police pay? They have to be crooked or something.*

* * *

"I love arriving at jobs with you, boss. I bet he had us down for drug dealers or something when we pulled up," Jordan laughed.

"Well, you at least," said Charlie.

He followed the directions of the constable and came to the small car park. He parked the car next to one of the forensic team's vans, pressed a button on the centre console and the roof started to silently rise. It came over them and down onto the front windscreen; there was a slight click and all the windows went up automatically – it was now locked in place.

"Come on," said Charlie, "let's see what we have."

They got out of the car and walked to the back. Charlie touched the lock and the boot started to open. He was wearing a grey Pierre Cardin suit under the white Bugatti trench coat. When the boot was fully open, he reached in and pulled a large old style wicker picnic hamper forward.

"You could house a small family in that boot, boss," said Jordan.

"I don't do squatters," Charlie said.

He sat on the edge of the boot and opened the hamper. Inside were a pair of black Barbour wellington boots, a large torch, police issue overalls, a crow bar and police baseball cap. Charlie took the wellington boots out and placed them on the ground. He lifted his foot up and started to undo the laces of his handmade made-to-measure Lobb shoes.

"Nice ones and twos, boss," Jordan said. "I won't ask how much they cost, as I don't want to be upset for the rest of the week."

Charlie looked up at him, smiled and said, "I didn't know you came from the East End like me, Jordan, with your cockney slang. I put myself out twice a year to go and have my feet measured. I remember having to rely on my mum going to jumble sales to get me shoes when I was young, so I decided I would enjoy the luxury of the best there is when I could afford it – and now I can, so I make no apologies to anyone."

He took his shoes off and placed them in the hamper, pulled on the wellingtons and looked at Jordan, "And talking of shoes, why have you got your laces all undone and hanging loose? How are you going to chase anyone like that?"

Jordan glanced down at his khaki combat boots. "It's style, boss – not how you would define it, but I am not of the Victorian era like you. If I have to chase someone, I will ask them to wait while I do the laces up," he said.

Charlie smiled, stood up, touched the boot of the car slightly and it started to close, locking with a reassuring clunk. Three police vans came into the car park; they watched as they stopped, the front and back doors opened and police officers tumbled out. These new arrivals were met by, what they assumed to be, three plain-clothes officers who proceeded to give them orders.

"Come on, let's find the others," Charlie said.

They walked past the forensic vans on their left and passed through a gap in a small fence that circled the car park onto a small path between trees. As they came to a clearing, they saw the other members of the team standing in a group. They made their way towards them; the team saw them coming and turned to greet them.

"Good morning people, what have we got?" asked Charlie.

Manjitt proceeded to fill him in on all they knew. Charlie went with Harry to look at the body, had a brief word with Doctor Taylor, and then came back to the team.

"Right," Charlie said. "Harry, you take Oscar with you, go to the local nick and get an incident room set up. Danny, I want you to scout the local roads for CCTV cameras, shops or private houses with cameras pointing to the roads – get in touch with the local council and see if they have any in the area that might help us. If she wasn't killed here, she must have been brought here in a car or van, so work your way back from the car park entrance. You know the time she was killed between, so the later it gets, the less cars will be about. Do we have an address for the girl?"

"Yes," said Manjitt.

"Okay, Danny, work from here back towards the girl's address. Take various routes – you never know, something might show up. Manjitt, give him your car. Jordan and Manjitt, you're coming with me. We'll go to the girl's address and interview the family. Two other things: Harry, take that nice Inspector West you told me about with you to the local nick. He will help smooth things out and I know what a charmer you are with people – we don't want the locals upset before we even start… and, Oscar, don't walk into the nick with those on."

He pointed down; all the team looked to where the boss was pointing and saw two muddy blobs where there should be shoes. They all laughed.

"It's my ethnic jungle look," Oscar said.

"Well, leave the jungle here and don't walk it all over the local nick," Charlie said. Harry and Oscar went off to get Inspector West, while Danny took the keys to the squad car of Manjitt and disappeared back up the path.

"Come on, you two, let's go and visit the parents."

★★★

It took about fifteen minutes to reach the girl's house, which was quite large, 1930's style, situated in a tree-lined road not too far from Wimbledon tennis club.

"Wouldn't get much change out of a million if you wanted one of these houses," Jordan said. "A very nice area."

"Well, bear that in mind. Don't rule out a kidnapping that might have gone wrong," said Charlie. He drove onto the drive and parked next to a black Mercedes. "Remember, she's apparently the niece of the home secretary, so let's go easy to start with until we have better idea of what's gone on. I will do most of the questioning, but Manjitt you speak to the wife."

They saw two uniformed policemen standing by the front door looking in their direction, so they got out of the car and went up to the door.

"Can I help you?" said one of the officers.

Jordan showed them his warrant card, told them they were investigating the murder and they both moved back into the shadows. Manjitt pressed the bell. Within a second, the door was opened by a man who looked to be in his late forties. He wore a dark suit that was buttoned up.

"Can I help you?" he said.

"I am Chief Superintendent Smith and these are my two colleagues. We have come to speak to Mr Khan."

The man ushered them into a large hallway with what appeared to be a marble floor, a chandelier hung above it in the centre, with a wide stairway going up to their right.

"Will you take your shoes off, please?" he asked. They all proceeded to remove their shoes and place them by the door. "Follow me," said the man. He took them past the bottom of the stairs to a set of double doors on the left, which he knocked on and then opened.

"The police are here, Sir," he said, as he stood aside to let them enter the room. As they did, he went out and closed the doors behind them.

It was a large room with three big sofas arranged in a sort of semicircle around an unused fireplace. The carpet under their feet was deep red and looked expensive, while all the walls were painted white. A number of tables dotted the room, holding pictures and ornaments, and at the far end was another set of double doors that were closed. There were five men in the room; two stood by the fireplace and the others were seated on the sofas.

"Mr Khan," Charlie said.

One of the men who had been seated rose, "I am Safwan Khan."

He looked to be in his middle forties and was wearing a grey two-piece suit with a blue shirt.

"Hello, Mr Khan, I am Chief Superintendent Smith. These are my colleagues, Detective Sergeant Rhodes and Detective Constable Virdee. We are sorry to have to come here now, Sir, but we need to ask you some questions about your daughter Ashadieeyah."

"I understand. I will do anything I can to help," Mr Khan replied. "It's just a great shock; her mother is distraught. She was a very good girl, never a problem."

"I understand, Sir. We won't spend too much time with you now, as we don't want to intrude. It's just to get an understanding of when she went out, what she said, how she seemed and who was in the house. We can come back tomorrow and take formal statements then," said Charlie. "Is there anywhere we could sit with you alone and talk?"

"We can talk in here," Mr Khan said.

He turned to the other four men in the room and told them to go and wait in the study. The four men left the room, closing the doors behind them.

Mr Khan sat down on one of the sofas. Charlie sat opposite him, and Jordan and Manjitt sat to one side. Jordan had a notebook open, ready to take notes.

"Can my officer here," Charlie pointed to Manjitt, "speak to your wife, Sir?"

"She is very upset and has hardly stopped crying since we were informed. I don't know if she will be able to talk about things and I have had to call a doctor out to see her. Ashadieeyah was her life," Mr Khan said.

"Okay, Sir, perhaps if my officer comes back tomorrow and speaks to her?"

"Thank you, Chief Superintendent, for being so understanding."

"Right, Sir, we just want to get an idea of what she did yesterday and how she was."

"Well, she only came home yesterday morning," Mr Khan started, "about eleven, from university, Oxford. She was studying law; her mother was so happy. It is my son's birthday today and we had planned a family party for him. Ashadieeyah was going to help her mother with the food and arrangements. She spent the day with her mother and aunts, just catching up. We all had tea together, and at about five, she said she was going to see some old schoolfriends and would be back in a couple of hours."

"Did she say who the friends were?" asked Charlie.

"No, but she went to the local grammar school, so I assume they are in the area. Anyway, she didn't take a coat and it was cold out, so I imagine they didn't live too far away."

"And she didn't call again to say she would be late getting back or anything?"

"No, we never heard from her. At about nine, her mother was getting worried and phoned some of the family to see if she had called in to see them. I phoned the police at ten, but they said she was twenty and might have just met friends and I should not worry. I called them at midnight, but got the same reply – it was then I phoned my brother, the home secretary. A policeman came round about twelve thirty to take a description and said local officers would be on the lookout for her."

"Would she have gone to a club or pub with her friends?" asked Charlie.

"No, she never went to pubs or clubs. We are Muslim, Chief Superintendent, we don't drink alcohol."

"Was she happy at university?"

"She told us all about it at tea; her classes were going very well and she had made some good friends."

"Thank you, Sir. We will leave you now, but will call in tomorrow to take formal statements."

"Thank you, Chief Superintendent."

Mr Khan rose and put his hand out to shake Charlie's. He turned and pushed a button over the fire, and the double doors were opened within seconds.

"Raju will see you out," he said.

* * *

The chief superintendent, Jordan and Manjitt arrived at the local police station, the chief stopping the Bentley in front of the closed gates that led to the police car park.

"Jordan, jump out, go to the front desk and get the gates open," said the chief. "Then, find out where Harry has got us offices in the station."

Jordan got out and went along the front of the two-storey building and up the front steps. A minute later, the gates slid open.

Charlie parked the car in a space close to the back door. Once out of the car, Manjitt pressed the button to the side of the front door and it buzzed open. They saw Jordan standing at the end of a short corridor holding a door open. They walked to him, and as they passed through the open door, they came into a large custody suite. Facing them was a counter that was about five feet in height and seated behind it was a sergeant, with a woman police constable at his side, both looking in their direction.

Jordan said, "This way, boss, Harry has got us some offices on the second floor."

Charlie turned to his right with Manjitt close behind. He stopped for a second as he passed the counter.

"Hello sergeant," he said. "Hope we won't get in your way too much. Not sure if we will be hauling anybody in very soon, so hopefully we won't take up too many of your cells. If any of my squad's cars are in the way, let me know."

"Okay, Sir," said the sergeant, "but if there's anything you need, let me know."

"Thank you, sergeant, I will bear that in mind," Charlie said.

They followed Jordan down another corridor.

The woman police constable turned to the sergeant and asked, "Who are they, sarge?"

"They're the Serious Crime Squad," the sergeant said. "That was Chief Superintendent Smith – heard of him a few times, seems a good copper by all accounts, but have you ever heard of a copper who drives a brand new Bentley? Be careful how you mix with them."

"Okay, Sarge."

★ ★ ★

They arrived at the second floor and Jordan led them to the left, where they saw Harry standing behind two seated police constables through an open door. Charlie entered the office.

"Harry, how are things going?" he said.

Harry turned. "Okay, boss, these two…" he said, pointing at the seated constables, "are just setting our computers up for us. Pelé and Inspector West are getting us some filing cabinets, couple more tables, chairs and a whiteboard, as well as some phones."

"Have you heard from Danny yet? About any progress he's making with the CCTV?" asked Charlie.

"Nothing yet, boss," Harry said.

"Okay," said Charlie, "I'm going to go find the station commander, introduce myself and make excuses for you lot in advance of any complaints. I think I will ask if we can second Inspector West onto the team while we are here – a bit of local knowledge never goes amiss." He turned to Manjitt and Jordan, "In the meantime, Manjitt, see if you can get hold of the name of that grammar school Ashadieeyah went to, then try and get in touch with the headteacher. I want a list of classmates – those that can be identified as close friends, get addresses. Don't take the fact that it's the weekend as an excuse. I want them to come and open the school up today if they have to.

"Jordan, get the name of the college she was at, get hold of her tutor and have a quick word about her, get some background. We can look into it more later if we need to. Harry, make sure we get a kettle and cups up here – we can't work without tea."

He turned to the seated police constables and asked, "Where is your station commander's office?"

"On the first floor, Sir," said the one closest to Charlie. "When you get to the first floor, turn right and it's the third door along on the left."

"Thank you," said Charlie, and he turned and left them to get on with things. He made his way down the stairs and found the door, knocked and heard 'Come in'. Walking through the door, he found himself in a large office; it had a window all the way along one side, while the other side was covered in charts. In front of him was a large desk and seated behind it was a woman.

She stood to greet him, "I am Chief Superintendent Myles."

Charlie stretched out his hand. "Chief Superintendent Smith, Charlie Smith. Nice to meet you."

"Take a seat," she said.

She was about 5 feet 7, about forty to forty-five Charlie thought, her hair was short and blonde, and she was dressed in a dark blue two-piece suit.

Charlie pulled a chair from underneath the window and placed it slightly to one side so as not to be directly opposite.

"I just came to say thank you for giving us the office space and the help in getting things set up," said Charlie.

"That's okay; I actually got a phone call from an assistant commissioner from Scotland Yard telling me that I had to give you all that you needed."

It was said like she was not too happy about things.

"Well, I don't know anything about that," said Charlie, "as I have not spoken to anyone from the yard. What was the assistant commissioner's name?"

"Walker," she said.

"Can't say I've heard that name," said Charlie, "but then again, I don't get invited to many of the same parties as the big wigs at the yard. Maybe it's to do with the murdered girl being the home secretary's niece."

"Oh well, I will take it as someone just being a bit officious. Is there any progress yet or is it a bit too soon?" she said.

"Just getting some background about the girl and running some checks to see if we have any CCTV. We are waiting for the autopsy report, which might also give us something," said Charlie. "I will need some of your officers to do door-to-door in the area of her home tomorrow if that's okay and is it possible to let us have Inspector West to work alongside us? He will be a good point of contact for any of your people we are using and we could do with his local knowledge."

"I am sure that will be fine," she said, "but I am a little constrained by my budget. I have been under pressure to cut back on overtime and since the last cutbacks, I have lost four officers – so we are pretty thin on weekends and evenings. That's what I was doing this morning…" She pointed to two stacks of files on her desk. "Trying to juggle the budget around… checking that the priority crime targets are not falling behind."

"I think I can help there," said Charlie. "Any of your people I use, you can put them as seconded to my squad so that it doesn't affect your budget. If I have no need of them at any point but might need them at short notice, you can take them away to use till I need them back – you'll get a few of your outstanding jobs cleared up, but they will still show up as with me."

"I think we have a good working relationship," she said, smiling.

"There is one other thing," Charlie said, "my team can be a bit unconventional at times in attitude and appearance, but they're all good coppers."

"I will bear that in mind and if you need any feathers smoothed over, just let me know," she stood up as she spoke.

"Thank you," Charlie said as he stood.

She put her hand forward "… by the way, it's Caroline."

"Thank you, Caroline. Oh, and did you put two officers on guard outside the Khan's house?"

"No."

* * *

Charlie went back upstairs. Things were looking a bit more organised now the computers were on: Jordan was seated at one looking at something on the screen with a phone in his hand talking, while Manjitt was perched on the edge of a desk on another phone taking notes onto a pad. He went into the next office where he found the others.

"Well done, Harry. Looks like we're up and running. Is that my desk?" He pointed to the one by the window.

"I know how you like a view, boss, and you can see all the way over to the railway lines and the industrial park," said Harry.

"You see, Inspector West, that's how you can guarantee promotion," Charlie said.

"And don't forget the boss's tea, no sugar – though I've been bringing it for years and it's not done me any good," Oscar said.

"Well, keep at it and one day I will recognise your commitment to the cause," replied Charlie. "Right, Harry, get everyone in here. I want to have a quick word about what we are going to do. Inspector West, you stay, too. I have spoken to Chief Superintendent Myles and she's agreed you can be seconded to us while we are here."

"Thank you, sir," said West.

"You'll regret saying that!" said Oscar, laughing.

Harry quickly got Jordan and Manjitt in.

"Right," said the chief, "Inspector, I want you to organise a door-to-door questioning of the neighbours."

"Sir," West said, "we might have trouble getting enough officers for that."

"Just speak to Superintendent Myles; she will give you all the resources you need. Here's a picture of the girl." He passed the picture to Inspector West. "Get some handouts made for them to take round and make sure that photograph comes back here – give it to Harry when you're done. Manjitt, how are you doing with the school?"

"I got hold of the headmistress and have arranged to meet her in an hour at the school to go through her school records," Manjitt said.

"Good," said Charlie, "but give Oscar all those details as he can meet her. Oscar, find out who her close friends were, their addresses if the headmistress has them and what she was like at school. Did she ever have any problems, etc?"

Okay, boss," said Oscar.

"Manjitt, I want you to find out about the family. What does Mr Khan do? His business? Have they lived in that house long? Where did they live before? You know the stuff and tomorrow you go back to the house, take the statements and make sure you get to speak to Mrs Khan. I want a doctor's certificate if you can't speak to her, and make a note of who else is there. Jordan, did you get anything on the university?"

"Yes, boss," said Jordan, "I managed to get someone in the university office, but as it's Saturday, there's not many people about. However, I have a phone number for her tutor, so have left a message on his answer phone to ring me. Also, Ashadieeyah was living in the student's hall of residence, which I also got the address of."

"Good start," Charlie said, "but I think you should take a trip up there. We can't wait till everyone's back on Monday before we get any answers. You take one of the cars, drive up there this afternoon, speak to everybody you can, get a look in her room and have a good root around. If you have to stay up there for the night call Harry, he has my credit card, but its bed and breakfast only and any booze is on your bill."

"Lovely," Jordan said. "I will check out a nice hotel before I leave."

"Okay, get to it," said Charlie. They all left the office, bar Harry, "Well, Harry, what do you think?"

"I don't think it's a kidnapping gone wrong, because even if she was killed, they would still demand a ransom and hide the body. It might be a one-off – someone she just met or unfortunately bumped into walking about, though the doctor thought she was killed elsewhere and the body dumped there. You can't rule out the family yet or any close relatives or friends. The body was not well hidden; it was just off the path, so either they were disturbed dumping the body or they didn't care. I will check for any other local cases like this, just to make sure we have not got a madman on the loose."

"Yes, I agree, you can chase down Doctor Taylor for the autopsy report and get hold of Danny. We need to know if we have anything on the CCTV; I want to know if we have been lucky. There are a couple of other things you can check up discreetly for me, too, Harry," Charlie said. "Find out who arranged for the two police officers to guard the front of the Khan's house, as they're not from this station, and find out what Assistant Commissioner Walker does at the yard."

"Shall I give you a call about the yard as soon as I get anything?" said Harry.

"No, just let me know when I come back to the office if you hear anything. I am off out, so will see you later. Make sure the desk has our numbers in case we are needed."

⋆ ⋆ ⋆

After Walker had finished reading the file on the dead girl, he called one of his officers to come to the office. When the officer arrived, Walker said, "I want you to do some delicate work for me in the coming days and I need someone I can rely on."

The officer nodded, "What is it you want me to do, Sir?"

"Firstly, our investigation concerning the home secretary's niece could be compromised by the Serious Crimes Squad, and we don't want them treading on our toes. I feel we have a real chance of catching some highly connected terrorists. We don't want them tipped off that a bunch of idiots from Serious Crimes are onto them. I want you to find out more about the officer in charge of the operation; I have heard stories about him that make me suspicious. I want to know what his background is – you know the stuff to check. If he seems okay, we might consider having a word."

"Do you want just him checked out or all his team?" the officer asked

"No, just him and I want it done quickly. Have we heard from the boys who have gone up to the university, yet?" Walker asked.

"Nothing yet," the officer said as he looked at his watch, "but I think they should be there by now, so we might hear from them soon."

"Get on with running that check for me," Walker said, "and let me know straightaway if you hear anything from Oxford."

The officer got up and left. Walker's phone rang; it was the deputy commissioner. He told Walker that the Yard had been getting calls from the press regarding the murdered girl, asking about her association with the home secretary. He had spoken to the Home Office and it had been decided that a press officer should be attached to the team investigating the murder.

Walker thought for a moment, before telling the deputy commissioner they had a good press officer they could spare who understood how important it was to be discreet when the names of highly-placed politicians might come up. The deputy commissioner was happy to go along with Walker's recommendation. He told Walker to tell the press officer to get in touch with his office and he would pass him onto the Serious Crime Squad.

After speaking to the deputy commissioner, Walker checked in his phone for the number of the press officer they had used on a couple of cases. He then placed a call to Christopher Wade and asked him to come up to his office in ten minutes. He knew Wade was ambitious to get to the top of the Yard press office and would do as he asked if he thought it would further his career.

When Wade arrived, Walker explained that he would be working on the case of a murdered girl who was the home secretary's niece, and that he would have to go over to Wimbledon.

"It could be delicate, though, as the girl is known to us. We don't want the Serious Crime Squad knowing about that, as it could have a serious effect on the big investigation we are running ourselves. No news of it must leak out, so I want you to keep me informed of anything you feel the serious crime boys find that may help or hinder our investigation."

"I understand, Sir," Wade said.

"This is the number of the deputy commissioner." Walker handed him the piece of paper he had written it on. "Call that number, say who you are, that you have spoken to me and have been told you are to help with the press on the girl's murder. He will arrange for you to go over there."

Wade stood up, "I will be in touch if I see or hear anything that you need to know."

"I need to know everything," Walker said, "and I will call you if I have anything special that needs doing while you're there."

★★★

Danny had spent all morning walking up one side of a road, then back down the other, making notes on which houses or shops had CCTV cameras that were pointed towards the road – he had quite a few on his list. He had also rung the local council, who had told him they had cameras on the high street and a few of the surrounding roads. They had agreed to make copies from all their cameras that were working from 5pm to 4am, as it might allow them to identify any car that appeared to be driving aimlessly in the area because it would pop up on more than one camera. Danny arrived back at the station, showed his warrant card at the front desk and was told the squad's office was on the second floor.

He was buzzed in and was just climbing the first flight of stairs when a voice said, "Who are you?"

Looking up, he saw a woman coming down the stairs towards him.

"I'm Detective Constable Kane with the Serious Crime Squad."

The woman looked him up and down. "Ah," she said, "I am Chief Superintendent Myles, have you been working undercover or something?"

"No, Ma'am," Danny said, "I have been out checking on CCTV coverage in the streets around the murder scene."

"Okay, carry on."

Caroline Myles shook her head and watched as the officer passed her on his way up the stairs. He looked like he had been sleeping rough in a squat or something, and his hair was halfway down his back and didn't look like it was washed that often. Charlie had told her they were a strange bunch and it looked true.

Danny carried on up the stairs and coming to the second floor, he found the offices. Manjitt was sitting in one on a computer; he went into the other one where Harry was.

"I thought you had deserted us," Harry said as Danny came into the office.

"I have ruined a good pair of shoes with all the walking I've done," Danny replied.

Harry raised his eyebrows as he looked down at the shoes Danny was wearing. They looked older than the ones he had on and his were five-years-old already.

"Okay, forget the shoes," Harry said. "How did you get on?"

"Not too bad," Danny said, "the council have good coverage in the high road and the surrounding areas, so they are going to get us copies and send them over. I made a list of all the shops and houses that have cameras pointing out towards the street."

"Okay, well done. Go and find Inspector West, claim a couple of officers off him, take them out with you and get all the film you can," Harry said. "Then get back here and start going through it; see if the girl appears and anyone else, or whether a vehicle keeps popping up when they shouldn't – especially near the murder scene."

"I take it from that," Danny said, "that you have me a bed made up somewhere close by."

"On your bike," Harry said.

Danny shot out the office door, closely followed by Harry's pen.

In the meantime, Manjitt had been looking on the Internet for any information on Mr Khan. She had found out through looking on various websites that he was managing director and majority shareholder of a number of companies, with the largest being a stationary business that had had a turnover of £30 million last year.

There was also one other big earner, a car parts importer business, which had had a turnover of £14 million in its last accounts. He was also a trustee on a couple of charities. Manjitt had found some photographs of him with his brother, the home secretary, at dinners and events. She made notes, but there didn't seem to be anything that looked out of place. She carried on trawling through and printing pages she thought might be of interest to the rest of the team.

The phone on Harry's desk rang; it was Doctor Taylor from forensics. He told Harry he was phoning to give him an overview from the autopsy on Miss Khan. She had two stab wounds to the chest, one that penetrated her heart and would have killed her straightaway. The marks around her neck showed that she had been held from behind, whether at the time of the stabbing or before, Doctor Taylor couldn't say. She had not been killed where the body was found; as there would have been a lot of blood where she had been killed because of the stabbing to the heart and the area around the body did not show enough blood in the soil.

He told Harry he would send over a full written report in a day. Harry asked if any possessions had been found with the body. The doctor told him there had been nothing at all. Harry thanked Doctor Taylor, putting the phone down just as Oscar walked into the office.

"Well," Harry said, "how did you get on?"

"Her headmistress said she was a good student, got very good exam results, and she gave me the names of the girls she was close with at school."

Oscar said, "I managed to call round and see them, but none had seen her since she went to university. One of the girls had emigrated to Australia, so a bit of a dead end there."

Harry's phone rang again. He picked it up and had a

conversation for five minutes. When he put it down, he looked at Oscar, "Well, the press are onto the home secretary angle… that was the Yard, they are going to send a press officer over to handle all of it."

"I just know the boss is going to love that," Oscar said, smiling.

"Well, I will let him know," Harry said. "In the meantime, the girl's phone wasn't found on her body, so just check with the family that she hadn't left it at home. If she didn't, find out what network she was on and get a list of all the calls she made in the last few days."

Oscar left Harry and went next door where Manjitt was still on the computer. "How are things going?" he asked.

Manjitt looked around. "Hello Pelé, quite an interesting family – got a lot to read through. How did you get on at the school?"

"No, nothing there," Oscar said. "I am going to try and track down her phone, but I am going to make some tea first. Do you want one?"

"Yes, love one," Manjitt said.

Oscar walked over to where a kettle stood on a table in the corner. "Oh, and the Yard are sending over a press officer," he said.

Manjitt looked up, "Does the boss know?"

"Not yet," Oscar said.

Manjitt started to laugh.

* * *

Charlie had driven back to the murder site and was standing watching twenty or more officers combing through the undergrowth in a search for clues. He called over one of the detective constables who had been left to supervise the search. He told Charlie that nothing had been found and because of all the rain, it was taking longer than they thought it would. Charlie told him that if anything turned up, he should contact the station straightaway.

Charlie walked back to his car and stood for a moment. This place was ten to fifteen minutes from the house, and wasn't a well used part of the common. He hadn't seen many people wandering around, so someone most know the area and had been here before. They must have brought the body here in the knowledge that it would be quiet, but this gave him a problem. If she was killed somewhere else and the doctor said there would have been a lot of blood, he was going to have to check the family home out. *Ah well*, he thought, that *should be interesting*.

He climbed into the car and set off back to the station.

***

Jordan turned into Broad Street and found a parking spot in one of the bays that ran down the centre of the road. He got out of the car and crossed to stand in front of Baliol College were Ashadieeyah had been studying law. He passed through the gates and stopped at the security window, showed his warrant card, asked where the students' residence was located and was given directions by security.

Leaving the college, he walked through Oxford's streets and past the old buildings. He wondered if any of the people he went to school with had made it to university. *Not much chance*, he thought. In fact, a number of them, to his knowledge, had ended up in prison. He didn't think many of the others would have had a chance of getting here, unless it was on a visit for the day to see the sites. Then again, they would rather go off to Spain for a break.

He found himself outside a large building with a glass front, which seemed quite modern-looking set amongst the old colleges. He went through the doors and up to the desk, where a young woman was sitting and reading a book.

"Excuse me," he said, "I wonder if you can help me." He showed her his warrant card. "I need to see Ashadieeyah Khan's room and speak to some of her friends."

She put down the book, asked him to wait a moment, picked the phone up and had a brief conversation with someone. She replaced the phone and asked him to please wait over there, pointing to a long orange sofa that sat under the overhang of the stairs. He sat down, noticing the constant comings and goings of students through the doors. He saw a man approach the girl behind the desk. She looked up, pointed in his direction, and the man turned and came towards him. He was dressed in jeans and a shirt, and looked about forty Jordan thought. As he reached Jordan, he held out his hand.

"Hello," he said, "I'm David Silver, Head of the Student Residence."

Jordan stood up. "Detective Sergeant Rhodes. I am investigating the death of one of your students, Ashadieeyah Khan." He showed his warrant card to Mr Silver. "I would like to see her room and, if possible, you might be able to track down some of her friends for me. I have their names and need to speak to them."

"Well, I am not sure they will be in," Mr Silver said. "Students are always coming and going at the weekend, but if you give me their names, I will get the room numbers for them." Jordan handed him the list. "It was a terrible thing that happened to the girl. I heard it on the local radio; they said she had been murdered."

"Well, it's early in the investigation so we don't know yet," Jordan said.

"Well, if you wait here," Mr Silver replied, "I will go and get the room numbers of these students and the key to Miss Khan's room."

Jordan sat down again. *So, the press are onto the story*, he thought. *Hope they don't start lots of lurid speculation in the papers, which would mean lots of people ringing in with leads that led nowhere and tied up your time. I bet Harry and the boss will love having the press boys hanging around.*

He sat watching the world go by for ten minutes, and then saw Mr Silver returning. Jordan stood up.

"I have the room key," Mr Silver said, "and the room numbers of her friends you asked me for. If you would come with me, I will take you up."

Jordan followed him through double doors into a corridor. They stopped about halfway down by a lift; Mr Silver pressed the button and they waited.

"Do you have much to do with the students?" asked Jordan.

"No, not too much, unless there's a problem with their accommodation or there has been a complaint about noise," replied Mr Silver.

The lift arrived and they both got in. Mr Silver pressed the number three button, the doors closed and they went up.

"So, have you had any problems with any of the names on the list I gave you?" asked Jordan.

"None that I can recall," Mr Silver said.

The lift doors opened and Jordan followed Mr Silver out. They turned right, went through some doors and stopped outside number sixty-seven. Mr Silver opened the door and they entered. It wasn't a large room, but was comfortable, with a bed in one corner, neatly made with a small bedside table next to it. A small lamp sat on the table, a larger table was over by the window with a couple of books on it, two chairs were tucked under the table, a wardrobe and a set of drawers with a mirror on top were along the wall opposite the bed – it was all neat and tidy.

Jordan went to the wardrobe and opened it, looked at the clothes hung neatly on hangers and the four pairs of shoes at the bottom. He picked them up one at a time and felt inside – nothing. He patted the clothes down that were hanging up and checked any pockets – clean.

"She seemed a very tidy girl," Jordan said.

"Yes, this is one of the better rooms. Some of them look like they have not been cleaned for years, with rubbish thrown everywhere. We have to issue warnings," Mr Silver replied.

Jordan nodded. He started to look through the drawers next, taking them fully out one at a time, checking inside amongst the clothes and then underneath in case anything was stuck there. He went through all three drawers and had a look in the inside of the structure, before he replaced them back into place. Going to the bedside table, he opened the small draw and pulled it fully out. There were some pens, a small radio and pictures. He took the pictures out and placed them on the bed; he checked the inside of the bedside table, found nothing and replaced the drawer. He knelt down on the floor and lifted the blankets, but there was nothing except a cable. When he stretched the cable out, it was the lead to a laptop computer. Standing up and walking to the table by the window, he noticed the two books on it were on English law.

Scanning the room once again, he asked, "Where are the bathrooms?"

"There are two for each sex on every landing, at each end of the building," Mr Silver replied.

"I don't see any of her classwork here," said Jordan, "and there's a lead for a laptop, but no computer. Would she have left them anywhere else?"

"I don't know," Mr Silver said. "It's not really my side of things, but it is a very tidy room – don't see many like this."

"Okay, thanks," said Jordan. "Can you make sure no one else enters this room? I will be sending some forensics officers to have a look around." He picked up the pictures off the bed and put them in his pocket.

"Okay," Mr Silver said, "I will put a note in the log. You can tell your people to ask for me and I will help them all I can."

"Thanks," said Jordan, "have you got my list of names?"

Mr Silver handed him the list. "I wrote their room numbers beside them."

They left the room and Mr Silver locked the door.

"Thank you for your help," said Jordan, "and here's my card in case you come across anything of hers or something turns up."

They shook hands and Mr Silver turned and went back towards the lift.

Jordan looked at the names on the list and noted the number seventy-five beside the name Michelle Riley. *That must be on this floor,* he thought. He checked which way the door numbers went and made his way along the corridor. When he came to seventy-five, he heard voices coming from inside. *Might be in luck*, he thought.

He knocked on the door. Within a couple of seconds, a young girl with very frizzy red hair opened the door.

"Yes, can I help you?" she said.

"I am looking for Michelle Riley."

"Michelle!" the young girl called out, looking back over her shoulder. "There's a man here that wants you."

Another girl appeared. She was about the same height as the first, but with dark hair that hung straight down past her shoulders.

"I'm Michelle," she said. "What do you want?"

"I am Detective Sergeant Rhodes, and I would like to speak to you about Ashadieeyah Khan." He showed her his warrant card.

"Why? What's happened?" she asked.

"Well, if I can come in and speak to you," Jordan said, "I will explain."

"Okay, come in."

The two girls stood back from the door and Jordan entered. The room was much like Ashadieeyah Khans, but this was a lived-in room: clothes were slung on chairs and there was a pile beside the bed. A young man was sitting on the bed with a newspaper.

"Excuse the mess," Michelle said, "it's not washing day till Tuesday."

"That's okay," Jordan said, "but I would like to talk about Ashadieeyah."

"Why? What's she done?" said the young man on the bed. "Can't think that Ash would get into trouble with the police, not with her uncle being the home secretary."

Jordan looked over at the young man. "Sorry, Sir, I didn't get your name."

"Chris Levisohn."

He was on the list. Jordan turned to the redheaded girl, "And you are, Miss?"

"Francis Debuison." A third name from the list.

"Well, if you would all like to sit down. Now, I know you're all friends with Ashadieeyah..." Jordan said.

Francis went and sat on the bed beside Chris, while Michelle took a chair at the end of the bed.

"So, come on, what's she been up to?" Francis asked.

"Well, I have bad news. Her body was found on Wimbledon Common. She's been killed," Jordan said.

There was silence in the room, and then a sob broke from Michelle. Francis jumped up and they hugged each other, both breaking down in tears. Jordan waited a minute until they had both settled down a bit.

The young man, Chris, was the first to speak. "What happened? We all saw her on Friday. She was going home for her brother's birthday and was coming back Sunday evening."

"How was she when she left?" Jordan asked.

Michelle, with tears still running down her face, spoke, "She was fine. Francis and I saw her before she left. She told us we could get together when she got back on Sunday and she'd tell us all about her weekend. How did it happen?"

"Well, it's early in the investigation, but it would seem she was murdered. Have you not been listening to the radio?" Jordan said.

"No. I don't have one in here. I broke it, knocked it off the table and haven't bothered to get one since," said Michelle. "Why would anyone hurt Ash? She was just so nice." She started to sob again.

"You call her Ash?" Jordan said.

"Yes, we all had trouble at first with her name, so she became Ash to us," said Francis.

"How had she been lately? Did she seem upset or worried about anything?" Jordan asked.

"Not as far as I know," Chris said.

The two girls nodded in assent.

"I have a couple of her other friends I would like to speak to." Jordan looked at the list, "Leanne Trumain and Karl Bauer."

"Well, Leanne went home for the weekend to her parents, and Karl went back to Germany a couple of weeks ago as his father was taken ill," said Francis.

"How did she get on with those two?" asked Jordan.

"Great, we all got on well together," replied Francis. "We are all studying law and just sort of got together. We don't have wild parties or anything, but we all seem to like the same things."

"I understand you all went on a walking holiday together in the summer," Jordan asked.

"We were supposed to," said Chris, "but odd things popped up and one by one we dropped out. In the end, only Ash and Karl went. They had two weeks in the Lake District; Karl loves his walking and Ash had always wanted to go up and see the lakes."

"Were they romantically involved?" asked Jordan.

"I very much doubt it – Karl is gay," said Michelle.

"Where did they stay whilst they were up in the lakes? Do you know the names of any the hotels they used?" Jordan asked.

"They didn't use hotels," Michelle said, "they were camping. Karl went out and bought Ash a little tent as he already had his. They had a great time; Ash said it was lovely and that we had all missed a wonderful time."

"Well, thank you for taking the time to help me," Jordan said. "I've been to her room and I didn't see any of her coursework or her laptop. Would she have left it anywhere or taken it home with her?"

"She didn't take anything home with her – all she had was her purse. She said she had enough clothes at home," Francis replied.

Jordan stood up. "I will leave you my card in case you think of anything that may help," he passed the card to Chris, "and when Leanne and Karl get back, could you get them to call me?" They all nodded.

Jordan let himself out and made his way back along the corridor to the lifts. *It was strange how her papers and laptop were missing.* The doors of the lift opened and he got in and pressed the ground floor button. When the lift doors opened, he got out, went along the corridor through the double doors and into the main hallway where he had sat. He had just got to the main doors when he heard someone call his name. He turned to see Mr Silver coming towards him.

"I am glad I caught you, Detective," Silver said.

"Have you remembered anything?" asked Jordan.

"No, it's just that when I went to make a note in the log about no one going into room sixty-seven unless I say it's okay, there was already an entry saying that two policeman had called to check the room out earlier."

"What time was the entry in your log?" asked Jordan.

"Ten thirty. Someone must have forgotten to let you know they were checking it out," Silver said.

"Yes," said Jordan, "thank you and don't forget that if anything turns up, let me know. I will make sure the forensic team ask for you. If anyone else turns up, including other policeman, let me know before you allow anyone to go in that room."

***

Walker's detective sergeant came into the office and told him the boys were back from Oxford.

"Get them in here," Walker said.

The D.S went to the office door and called the other two officers in. Once they were in his office, they laid a laptop case on Walker's desk.

"The room was pretty clean. We had a good look around, but there was nothing except the laptop," one of them said.

"I want that checked out to see what's on it. We might find some names to help us. There was nothing else in the room?" Walker asked.

"No, Sir, very clean," the officer replied.

"Alright, get on with looking at the laptop."

The two officers left the office.

"Let's hope we get something off that laptop, otherwise our trail is going cold," Walker said.

"I ran some checks on the senior officer in charge of investigating the girl's murder like you asked, Sir," the D.S said.

"What did you find out?" Walker asked.

The D.S looked at his report. "His name is Chief Superintendent Charlie Smith; he has spent time in various branches, always had good reports on his work, though there are a few questions about his standard of living."

"What do you mean his standard of living?" Walker asked.

"It seems he likes fast and expensive cars, and wears very expensive clothes," the D.S said.

"Everybody has a hobby. Is he married?" Walker asked.

"No, not married and his hobby means driving a brand new Bentley, owning a classic Ferrari and other cars. Apparently, he also has a large house in Essex," the D.S said.

Walker sat for a moment, thinking. "Do you think he could be on the take from someone?" he asked.

"He would have to be taking a lot from what he has on this list; he must have been at it since he joined the police force," the D.S replied.

"Has there been any investigation into his income by police complaints or anyone else?" Walker asked.

"No, nothing, he seems to keep a low profile and doesn't put in too many appearances at the Yard. All the senior officers who have worked with him found he was efficient and did a good job, but they did not know him on a personal level," the D.S replied.

"I don't think he sounds like someone we can place our trust in. I think we might need to know more about him," Walker said. "I want you to go and give his house the once-over, see if you can find something that tells us what he's up to. We might find some papers on this case, too. If we get anything dodgy, we can pass it on to complaints and we will be rid of him and can get on with things. Be careful how you go in, I don't want any neighbours calling the local police about suspicious men."

"No problems, I will do it this afternoon. I will take one of the boys with me – we can be the gasmen checking for a leak or something if neighbours ask," the D.S said.

"Okay, get on with it," Walker said.

★★★

Harry had taken a call from Jordan and told him to get back to the station as quickly as he could. He had placed a call to the Oxford Constabulary HQ and a phone call to the home of Mr Khan. He had only just put the phone down when Manjitt came into the office with a pile of papers.

"I have printed off all the information I found out about Mr Khan, and have made a few copies for everyone to read," she said as she handed Harry a stapled set of papers. "There's a set for the boss, too."

"Okay," Harry said, "Jordan will be back in a while, so get hold of Pelé and Hippie and tell them to get back here. We need to sit down and go over a few things."

Manjitt left the office to find the others. Harry began going through the papers Manjitt had given him. He had just finished reading it, when there was a knock on the door. Harry looked up to see a constable.

"Sorry to interrupt you, Sir, but the report from forensics has arrived."

"Thank you," said Harry, taking the report from the constable. He opened it and began reading.

* * *

Charlie got back to the station and went upstairs to the office. He found Harry sitting at his desk, the top of it covered in papers. He closed the door and sat down. "Well, Harry, what's happening? This one seems strange to me."

Harry stood up, picked up some of the papers and took them over to Charlie. "This will make things even stranger. Boss, I did some ringing around and those two coppers outside of Mr Khan's were from the Diplomatic Protection Group and Assistant Commissioner Walker is with the Anti-Terrorism Squad."

Charlie looked up.

"It gets even stranger," said Harry, and he told Charlie about Jordan's visit to Oxford. "I phoned Oxford Police HQ and they never sent any officers to the students' residence. I spoke to Mr Khan about his daughter's laptop and he checked – it's not in the house. I've got all the team coming up soon for a sit down. Do you want Inspector West in the meeting?"

Charlie nodded.

"What do we tell them?" said Harry.

"We go over it all, don't leave anything out," said Charlie. "Let's get some tea in here, Harry. I think better with a cuppa."

* * *

All the team were assembled in the office.

"Right," Charlie said, "before Harry goes over where we are with the case, how's the house to house going?"

"We have done a lot of the streets around the girl's house and have got nothing," said Inspector West.

"Okay, keep at it. Did we find anything at the murder scene?" Charlie asked.

"No, Sir, nothing," West replied.

"What about the CCTV?" Charlie asked.

"I have got quite a lot to go through," Danny said, "but Inspector West has given me a couple of bright officers to help me, so we should start to whittle it down tomorrow. Fingers crossed something might come up."

"Okay, what about the autopsy report?" Charlie asked.

"It's as the doctor said: two stab wounds to the chest and it was the one through the heart that killed her," Harry said. "The marks around her neck are from someone strangling her from behind and the stab wounds have come from someone to her right, because the knife entered at an angle and not from directly in front. The weapon was a thin blade about 6 inches long, and she wasn't killed where her body was found."

Charlie nodded. "Right, Harry will now go over everything, so listen carefully. If he forgets anything, jump in. Right, Harry, from the beginning."

For the next forty minutes, Harry went over all the information they had gathered. When he had finished, the team sat there for a minute not saying anything.

Jordan spoke first, "There is something not right about this, boss. Is it just a murder?"

"That's what we get paid to find out," Charlie said. "Now, I know we keep our own counsel, but let's make doubly sure we only speak to each other about this and don't leave any papers laying around now we are stuck in these offices and not at the Yard. Harry, I want you to get the locks on both doors changed. Let's be paranoid: only get seven keys made up; give one to each of us; anyone leaving the office, even to go to the toilet, locks the door, understand?"

They all nodded.

Charlie looked at Inspector West, "Inspector, I know this might put you in a delicate position with your superiors here at the station, but any questions you get from anyone outside this team about the case; either say you don't know or refer them to Harry and keep a note of who asks you." The inspector nodded. "If not, we will have to kill you."

Inspector West laughed, but noticed the team were all looking at him.

"He thinks we are joking," Manjitt said.

No one said anything for a minute, until Danny said, "It's okay, we are joking. Welcome aboard."

The team laughed and Inspector West had a relieved look on his face.

"Now, there are a few things to do," Charlie said. "Manjitt that was good background you got on Mr Khan's family. Apart from the home secretary, I want his other brother and his two sisters checked out. Oscar, take Manjitt's report and go through it, then do some traces on the others, but be discreet."

Oscar nodded.

"Manjitt, you are going to take the formal statements from the family tomorrow. Harry and I have to do a search of the house, as Ashadieeyah wasn't killed where she was found. Once you have taken the statements, I want you to broach the subject with Mr Khan, but play it by ear. Don't insist, instead try and persuade him that we will do it quietly so as not to embarrass the family. Nevertheless, we have to do it."

"Okay, boss," Manjitt said.

Charlie continued, "Danny, I want you to follow Manjitt in another car, but park outside and stay there till Harry calls you back. I want to know who turns up after Manjitt leaves. Take a camera; I want pictures of anyone – and I mean, anyone – including the paperboy if they have one."

"Harry, can I have a flask to take with me?" Danny said.

"Jordan, I want you to go back to Oxford," Charlie said. "Go see your Mr Silver. They must have some CCTV coverage of the building and entrance hall, so go through it and see if our two mysterious officers turn up. Get pictures if you can; if not, bring the CCTV back with you. Also, tie up the other two friends you didn't see. Get phone numbers for the girl and the boy who went back to Germany. If you can't get a number for him, get his address.

"Inspector, I want you to take over checking all the CCTV Danny brought in. You know what we are looking for – anything that looks out of place or is in the wrong place. I don't know where this investigation is leading us, because I get the feeling someone is running a parallel operation that we don't know anything about, but we are investigating the murder of a young girl and we will get to the bottom of it for her and her family. Let's not get distracted from that. To make matters worse, we have a press officer coming to hold our hands, but remember that the only one who gives him information is Harry, but – and listen up, Inspector – I want to know what he's asking any of you about."

Charlie looked around the team, "Any questions?"

"Can we all go and get a drink?" Harry asked.

"Well, seeing as we are not in East London," Charlie said. "It's down to the Inspector to recommend somewhere on his patch."

"Make it expensive – the boss is paying," said Oscar.

"Okay, meet you downstairs in ten minutes," Charlie said.

The team all exited the office, leaving Harry and Charlie alone.

"Well, Harry, what do you think?"

"It doesn't hang right, that's for sure, and are we all right with this inspector?" Harry asked.

"I think he looks a good honest copper," said Charlie. "We will know soon enough. His boss will be onto him about the case and when I speak to her, she is either going to ask me why her inspector can't talk to her about the case or she won't, in which case we will know whether to trust him."

"What about the press officer you want me to spoon-feed?" Harry said, smiling.

"Yes, let's see what he knows by himself," Charlie said, "and what he wants to know from us that has nothing to do with talking to the press."

"You think our friendly press officer might be reporting back to someone?" Harry asked.

"Well, I get someone from the Anti-Terrorism Squad ringing here asking the senior officer to give us all the help we need," Charlie said, "then we get a press officer who we haven't requested. Harry, this could be a lot trickier than we first thought. Tomorrow, I am going to pop into Scotland Yard for a chat. Make sure everyone is out and on the ball. Now, let's go and eat."

★★★

The health secretary was sat with the chief whip. She was a bit surprised by what she had just heard him tell her, as she had not been at the earlier meeting.

"Are you saying that the prime minister is going to announce he's stepping down tomorrow?" The chief whip nodded. "And that a number of senior figures and other MPs have told you they would back me if I was to choose to run for the leadership?"

"Yes, quite a few have expressed that opinion," the chief whip said.

"But surely one of the senior figures like the foreign secretary will get the party's backing?" she said.

"He would be the obvious choice, but there have been rumours about his health. I don't think the party would like to be in the situation where they had to go through another election for leader if he was taken ill too."

"I am not sure," the health minister said. "There are still some important members of the current cabinet who would be better placed than me to become leader."

"That's a real shame," the chief whip said. "From what I have been hearing, you are well liked and have a lot of backers. They feel the party has drifted away from its roots and you would be the right person to fight for its core principles."

The health secretary sat quietly. It was a complete shock; first hearing the news about the prime minister, and now sitting in the chief whip's office, being told people wanted her to be the next leader of the party and prime minister. She thought the chief whip had called her in because she had done something wrong.

The chief whip now interrupted these thoughts. "You need to decide now. The others are old hands at the party game and will be organising support already," he said.

She looked at the chief whip, "But I don't even know anyone I could get to start a campaign for the leadership on my behalf."

The chief whip passed her a piece of paper. "The names on this paper are enthusiastic for you to run and have already expressed their willingness to organise a campaign for you. Of course, I will be speaking discreetly to some of the older and more influential MPs and members of the party on your behalf. Although I cannot be seen to be taking sides, I am sure if you were to win, you would see fit to put people you can trust in the right government jobs." The chief whip looked at her steadily, "After all, we know how tough it can be for a new prime minister and it's always wise to have friends close."

The health secretary looked at the three names on the list. She recognised two of them as older MPs, while the third was a new MP – the latter was surely just making a name for himself. Could she do it? Was she ready? If she didn't do it, would the opportunity come round again?

"Well, what is your answer?" the chief whip asked.

The health secretary looked up. "Yes, I will run," she said.

"That's good," the chief whip said. "Now, you will have to make sure you get everything in place and contact those MPs on the list. I will let you know if I hear anything about the other people standing, but I cannot come out publicly and back you. However, I will give you any advice I can on situations as they arise. The prime minister will make his announcement to the full cabinet tomorrow; followed by a press conference, so you might want to have a quiet word with any journalists you know who could be useful to you in the leadership race."

"Should I speak to any MPs myself?"

"No, don't say anything to anyone," the chief whip said. "Leave that to the names on the list. After the prime minister's announcement, you can throw your name into the ring as a candidate."

The health secretary stood, "I will get in contact with them now."

"Good luck," said the chief whip. "Remember, I must not be seen to be backing you."

When she had left the office, the chief whip placed a couple of calls to well-respected party members who were not MPs but held influence through their financial backing. He then called the party chairman to discuss the leadership race.

⋆⋆⋆

The chief whip sat in the small flat he owned, which was about a ten-minute walk from parliament. Sat opposite was a journalist, who he had known him from school and had on occasions, fed stories about MPs or government policy when he needed to move something in the direction that suited him. The journalist had also tipped him off if he heard a story about an MP who had been doing something he shouldn't have.

At the flat, they had been making general small talk about the current goings-on in the government.

"Would you like another brandy?" the chief whip asked.

"No, not for me. When I leave here, I'm going back to the paper to do some work," the journalist replied.

"How do you think the government is doing at present?" the chief whip asked.

"As a whole, not too badly, although the home secretary's new anti-terrorism bill has caused some problems. However, it looks like it should pass into law with the prime minister standing fully with him and if the party stay united behind it," he said.

"You're probably right," the chief whip replied. "We were only discussing that in the office today. If it was a different prime minister, would it get through?"

The journalist looked across at the chief whip. He had known him many years and knew you had to look behind what he actually said to find the real meaning. "The home secretary has the full backing of the prime minister, so he couldn't not back him on this bill now – not after it's taken so long to get it to the final vote. It would look too bad for him, the home secretary and the party. It would be a disaster."

"Yes, you're right, that's what we all thought," the chief whip said. "It has been a battle to get it this far."

The journalist realised that the chief whip only ever invited him to his flat if he wanted him to know something without people seeing them together, but he never actually told him straight out what it was. In that way, he could stand in front of cameras and say, in all honesty, the story had not come from him.

"I can't see the prime minister pulling the plug on it now and the home secretary would be forced to resign. He has staked his reputation on getting it into law," he said.

"That's very true, the home secretary would be left with no alternative," the chief whip replied, "but a lot in the party never wanted this legislation and we know not everyone in the police service were in favour of it. Even so, with the prime minister's backing, it should get through. It was just that in the office they were speculating if it were a different prime minister, would we have gone down this road? You know how people speculate."

He is either telling me that there has been a row between the prime minister and the home secretary, or someone else high in the party has raised serious objections about it and has threatened to resign, the journalist thought.

"There is no chance of a change at the last minute," the journalist said, "not unless someone has threatened to resign over it and are high up in government, which could lead to a split. Perhaps it would get defeated in the house or the prime minister is thinking of changing the make up of the cabinet in a reshuffle – but I haven't heard anything about that. It would be madness to do that now."

"No, there is nothing like that going on," the chief whip replied. "There have been no threats of resignation or rows at the top – you do let your mind go off in fanciful directions. As I said, it was just idle chat amongst staff. By the way, how is your mother's health now? Is she better?"

The chief whip knew all about the journalist's mother as he had spoken to a mutual friend only a few days ago.

"Yes, she is on the mend," he said. "However, she'll have to rest up for a good while. It takes some time at her age to get over things. She has had to give up helping my father in the shop they have, so I think he'll sell up now as it's too much for him on his own."

"Yes, that's true," the chief whip said. "Any serious illness at any age does take time to get over, but the older you are, the longer it takes and it's a shame about her having to give up work. It can happen to anyone from any walk of life."

The journalist began to think that the chief whip had simply invited him here for a catch up, but he could have met him at parliament without any problem.

"You're not ill, are you?" asked the journalist.

The chief whip laughed, "No, not me. I have a long time ahead."

The journalist took a moment before he realised what the chief whip had said. 'No not me', he was telling him something. "That's good, I would hate having to find someone else instead of you, who knew as much about politics and all that was going on," he said.

"I aim to be around for many years," the chief whip replied. "Maybe I won't always be chief whip; it could be another government post. Who knows, it could even be under a different prime minister, you never know."

The journalist caught the stress placed on certain words. *Surely he's not saying the prime minister is on the way out?* He thought about this for a moment, "I would hope we could still have our chats," the journalist said, "but I expect you will be chief whip for many years to come. The prime minister doesn't look like he will lose his majority in parliament and there is no need for a general election for a couple of years."

"I expect you're probably right," the chief whip said, "but your mother was suddenly taken ill without any warning… she had to give up her work and have her operation straightaway, so you can never be sure."

Who was the chief whip talking about being so ill they would have to step down straightaway? The chief whip would never come out and tell him openly, so he would have to try another tack. It was not going to be subtle, but he had no other way of getting it out of the chief whip.

He smiled as he asked, "Is the foreign secretary going to run the London marathon again next year? He got himself some good publicity and raised quite a lot of money for charity."

The chief whip took a drink of his brandy. Looking over the glass, he answered, "Oh yes, he has another marathon in him. I think he has asked the home secretary to do it with him next year."

So, it's not those two. The journalist looked at the chief whip and asked, "It would be good if the prime minister joined them – that would look great in the eyes of the public."

The chief whip sat back in his chair, drunk the last of his brandy and said, "I don't think the prime minister would be up for running a marathon next year." The chief whip put his glass down and continued, "I don't think he has the time."

He stood up. The journalist also rose from his chair; *did I just hear the chief whip tell me the prime minister is on the way out?*

The chief whip held out his hand. "Thanks for coming," he said, "and give my regards to your mother when you see her. I wish her a speedy recovery. You will let me know if you hear anything you think I should know?"

The journalist nodded and shook hands, and the chief whip showed him out.

Once outside, the journalist walked to his car. *Did I just get a story on the prime minister standing down?* He stood by his car. It was raining, but he made no move to get in. He ran over in his head what had been said, until finally he opened the car door and got in. Reaching for this phone, he dialled the number of his editor at the paper.

In the flat, the chief whip sat back down in his chair now the journalist had gone. He felt he had got the story over by the end of the conversation. It could never be traced back to him. He expected to be contacted later that night by other journalists who would start hearing rumours. He would deny the prime minister was stepping down and would phone the Prime Minister to let him know it seemed as though someone had let the cat out the bag early.

⋆⋆⋆

It was a bright, sunny morning and Charlie was walking along the pathway away from the house. The dogs were running around and chasing each other in front of him. It was cold and the sun didn't quite seem strong enough to break through the clouds, but at least it wasn't raining.

He had got in last night and felt tired, so had gone to bed early and slept surprisingly well. He now followed the dogs through a small gap in the hedge, which ran along the bottom of the path. It opened up into a large field where the grass was about a foot high. The dogs began to leap through it. Charlie followed; he loved wandering on a Sunday morning with the dogs. They usually walked for an hour, getting right to the end of his property, which finished at a small rise. The view was fantastic and in the summer you were able to look down across the Essex countryside stretching away in front of you.

He decided he would circle back and call in at Mike and Maggie's. Mike always got up early and would have been to the shops, so Charlie could pick his newspapers from them. He had been out with the dogs for about forty minutes when he arrived at the cottage, gave a knock on the door and Mike opened it.

"Morning, Charlie," he said, the aroma of freshly cooked bacon coming through the door. Mike handed Charlie an armful of papers and continued, "Maggie says your name's in a couple of these, about the investigation you're working on."

"Well, let's hope it doesn't appear too often," Charlie replied. "Thanks for the papers, Mike, I will be putting in some strange hours on this one, so might not be home the odd night."

"That's okay, Charlie, just ring as normal. I will fetch the dogs down here to stay with us. Oh, by the way, two blokes turned up at the front yesterday. They said they were from the gas supplier and needed to come in to check a suspected leak, because there was a drop in pressure in the area. I told them they couldn't and would have to make an appointment like you said we should if anyone turns up out of the blue. There was a bit of a row; they told me I was breaking the law not letting them in as it could be dangerous."

"You did the right thing, Mike. What time was it?" Charlie said. "What did they do?"

"About three. They moaned for a bit and said they would get the police back with them if they had to, but they went away and haven't been back."

"If they come back, let them in," Charlie said, "but ring Harry and let him know. Take them up to the house once they're in, leave them on their own for a while, and say you have to see to the dogs or something, then go and switch the security cameras on from inside the house."

"The switch in the dog lead box?" asked Mike.

"That's the one," said Charlie. "Then, go back in and stand with them. Don't worry if one says he has to go and check something in another room; just let them get on with it."

"Will do, Charlie," Mike said.

"I will be off about midday," Charlie said. "See you later."

"Bye, Charlie."

Charlie turned, called the dogs and walked up the driveway towards the house. *Might just be some chancers looking to rob the house*, he thought. *Still, he would have a look at the security cameras from the front gate for yesterday*.

He got to the house and went round the back. The dogs went straight to their water bowls, and Charlie took a large bag of food from the shelf and poured some into each of their bowls. He went to the dog lead box, opened it and checked that everything was working. It had been Julian's idea to have the system installed and to have small state-of-the-art cameras placed all over the house.

He had a separate system for the outside cameras, so if one was tampered, the other would still work. The outside ones were constantly on, but you had to switch the inside ones on from the dog lead box, put in by a Swiss company that Julian said his business used. The pictures from such small cameras were crystal clear.

He left the dogs happily munching away and walked through to the kitchen, putting the newspapers down on the table as he switched the kettle on. Whilst he was waiting for it to boil, he went into the front room, got the television remote and switched the TV on. Pressing channel 7 on the remote, the screen went snowy. He lent down and reached under the bottom of the chair and pulled out a smaller version of the television remote, pressed the green button and the television screen went blue. A question then appeared, asking for the date – he tapped in the date for yesterday. A second question, asking for the camera number – he tapped in one. A third question, asking for the time – he tapped in 14.45.

The screen then came up with a clear picture of the front gates. He pressed hold and went back to the kitchen, finished making his tea, got a biscuit out for each of the dogs who were all standing looking at him expectantly and threw them one each. "Now, settle down you lot," he said, picked up the papers and walked back through to the front room. Placing the tea on the table next to his chair and the papers on the floor beside him, he lifted the remote and pressed play.

It wasn't until 14.54 on the screen when he saw a small van pull up at the gates. The driver got out and pressed the bell on the wall at the front gate. A minute later, Mike appeared and had a conversation with the driver that lasted two minutes. The driver then went back to the van and had a word with the passenger, who eventually got out. They both came back to talk to Mike, before going back to the van. The time showed two minutes past three when they drove off.

The good thing about this system was its versatility. He pressed rewind, stopped on the two men, pressed a couple of the buttons and was able to zoom in on their faces. He pressed print on the remote and heard the colour printer in the far corner of the room purr, then start to print. He did the same for the number plate on the van. He would pick up the prints and take them with him when he left. For now, though, he sat back, picked up his tea and one of the papers. *Better read about how the investigation is going according to the papers.*

★★★

He had decided to take the Ferrari Daytona out today, as he had not driven it for a few weeks. He loved the sleek lines of the car and understood why his dad always said it was the best looking car ever made. The traffic was not too bad and he made good time into central London, arriving at Scotland Yard at 1.30pm. He pulled into the entrance to the car park and stopped in front of the barrier, where an armed police officer approached the car. Charlie wound down the window.

"Can I help you, Sir," the officer said, leaning down to speak. Charlie got his warrant card out and showed it to the officer. "Thank you, Sir."

The officer took his warrant card and passed it through the window of the security hut. After thirty seconds, it was handed back and the officer walked back to Charlie's car to return it.

"That's a great car; don't see many of them on the road."

He waved his hand to the guard in the reinforced security box and the barrier rose. Charlie pulled in and stopped in front of another barrier, while the first came down behind him. Once that was fully closed, the next one opened and he drove down the incline and under the building into the parking bays. He manged to find a parking space away from most of the other parked cars, as he did not want anyone opening their door and banging it into his and scratching the paintwork.

Satisfied, he locked the car and walked across the car park towards the lifts. *There were quite a few cars parked here for a Sunday*, he thought. He pressed for the lift but did not have long to wait before the doors opened. With the doors closing behind him, he pressed for the seventh floor.

★★★

Manjitt and Danny arrived at the station at the same time.

"People are going to start talking about us if we arrive at work together," Danny said.

"Well, my reputation will be mud," said Manjitt, "but I dare say they would wonder how a long-haired dwarf like you could pull such a beautiful woman."

"It's lucky I don't have an ego," Danny said, smiling.

They made their way up to the offices, where they found Harry.

"Morning, Harry," they both said.

Harry looked up, "Nice of you to drop in. Sit down. Let's go over what you're doing and what you're not going to do."

They both pulled up chairs and sat opposite Harry.

"Right, hippie boy," Harry said, "you first. As you're easy, you are going to take pictures of everyone who goes in or out of the house. You are not going to get caught taking pictures of anyone going in or out – simple."

Harry handed him a camera and a number of lenses. "I've got a van from Inspector West, which they usually use for surveillance." Harry gave him the keys. "Make sure you go to the toilet before you leave."

"Do I get a flask for tea?" Danny said.

Harry bent down and produced a tea flask, which he placed on the table. "Don't break it," Harry said.

"Do I have to sign for it?" Danny asked. Harry gave him a look. "I take that as a no," Danny said.

Harry turned to Manjitt. "Now, the boss laid out your job yesterday. Get the statements from the family and get a look at Ashadieeyah's room. As Jordan said, her room at university is immaculate – is it as neat at home? Then you have to explain to Mr Khan that we need to search the house to eliminate the family from our enquiries. Mention that we can do it discreetly and without fuss, but we will have to do it. You're not going to take no for an answer. I know you can be discreet, which is why the boss gave you this job, but at the end of the day, we are going into that house to search it. Now, we know he's the brother of the home secretary, but all we care about is the murdered girl. If we can eliminate the family and their home from the investigation, it would be a big plus."

"What if he still objects to us searching the house?" Manjitt asked.

"Phone me straightaway," Harry said. "I have already spoken to a magistrate about a search warrant if it's needed. I will bring it along with Inspector West and a few of his boys in no time at all, but let's hope it doesn't come to that. Okay, on your way."

Manjitt and Danny got up and left. Harry got on the phone to Ashadieeyah Khan's mobile phone company. He wanted a list of all the incoming and outgoing calls she had made in the last two weeks.

★★★

Jordan had rung Mr Silver yesterday about the CCTV coverage and was told that they did have it in the lobby area and on the street outside, and that he could come and look at it. He left early Sunday morning to get to Oxford and had parked up in nearly the same spot as before. He waited till 10am to call Mr Silver, who said he was at home but would meet him at the students' residence in half an hour.

It was a pleasant walk to the residence. There were lots of people about for a Sunday. Many looked like they had come into Oxford for the day, as they had cameras with them or were admiring the buildings. He found he quite liked Oxford.

Jordan got to the students' residence and pushed open the doors. He saw Mr Silver standing by the table, but a different girl was sitting behind it now. Mr Silver spotted him.

"Hello, Detective," he said as he held out his hand.

Jordan shook it. "Hello, Sir, can we see the CCTV footage from yesterday?" he asked.

"Follow me, Detective. I will take you to our office," Mr Silver said. "The students are all talking about the poor girl who was killed."

Jordan followed him through some doors to the right of the front desk, which led into a large office space. There were only a couple of people in it working at their desks.

"There is only skeleton office staff on over the weekend," Mr Silver said.

They walked the length of the office to the back, where Mr Silver opened the door. "This is our security room."

There were six televisions showing different parts of the building, with a security guard sitting at the desk watching them. He had a keyboard and two telephones in front of him, while a cup of coffee and a paperback book were close at hand.

"This is Martin, one of our security guards," Mr Silver said. "He will get the video of yesterday up for you. What time do you want?"

"Well, you said an entry was made into your log at 10.30," Jordan replied, "so let's try from 9.30 onwards. Can we have the entrance hall camera first? If we need to look at the others after, we can."

The security guard tapped a few numbers into the keyboard in front of him. One of the television screens went blank for a second, and then a picture came up with yesterday's date and the time 9.30. The security guard started the CCTV footage, and all three began to watch the procession of people coming and going.

* * *

Harry was just going through the autopsy report again and noticed a few things that might need chasing up. The mobile phone company had promised to get the list of calls from Ashadieeyah's phone to them as soon as possible.

"Excuse me, Sir." Harry looked up and saw Inspector West standing at the door. "The desk rang; there's a locksmith downstairs for you."

Harry nodded, picked up the phone and spoke to the front desk. After a brief chat, he replaced the receiver. "He's going to fit the locks on the doors now," Harry said. "Is there something else?"

"Yes, Sir."

"Wait a minute," Harry said. "You can call me, Harry. I am only 'sir' if you have done something wrong or I'm shouting at you. Now, what have you got?"

The inspector nodded, "We have been going through the local CCTV we have – Danny had logged it all by which part of the area it was located. There was nothing within a few streets of the murder scene, so we worked back from the cameras closest to the murder site. We have a black BMW going in that direction at 23.40 and at 23.50, it is coming back from that direction. It's not clear enough to give us a registration number. We have only two other cars that appear in the area at that time, but they don't reappear, so I assume they might be residents in the area who were driving home. We see the BMW again on another camera at just after midnight heading towards the A3."

"Well done," said Harry, "get the best pictures you can of the car. I want those other two cars eliminated from the enquiry, so get their descriptions and makes if you can, get a couple of your officers to crosscheck ownership against local people in the roads near to where they were driving, then send someone down to knock those people up and find out if they were driving home that night."

"Will do, Harry," said the Inspector. "I have also asked motorway traffic control if they can check their cameras, as I know they have some that cover the A3 and the M25. I gave them the time span, and I know it's a long shot because a black BMW is not a rare car, but at that time of night, there might not be too many in the area."

"Good idea, keep chasing it," Harry said. "Tell them you will send someone down to look for us if they can't do it quickly."

Inspector West left the office feeling he had contributed to the inquiry.

The boss might be right about West, Harry thought. *Could be a good one.*

The locksmith appeared at the door. "I am here to change some locks," he said.

"Have you got your identity card?" Harry asked.

The man came forward and passed his card with his name and picture on it and the company name underneath to Harry.

"One minute," Harry said.

Harry logged onto the local business website, looked up locksmiths and found the company. "What's your boss's name and phone number?"

The man told Harry, who wrote it down, then checked the phone number on the police database and the name came up.

"Okay, the office next door and this one and I want seven keys made up."

The locksmith got down to his job.

★★★

Jordan phoned Harry when he had got back to his car. He had a copy of the CCTV in his pocket, which showed two men entering the building at 9.55. It was not the best picture, but you could get a reasonable description of them from it. They had met Mr Silver's colleague and disappeared in the direction of the lifts. They reappeared at 10.15 carrying a black laptop. There was nothing on the outside cameras that might have given them the type of car they had been driving. He had arranged for Mr Silver to get his colleague to phone him, so he could get a statement and as good a description of the men that he could remember. He had also got the phone number of Leanne Trumain and contact details of Karl Bauer. He would chase them up as soon as he got back to the office.

★★★

Charlie got out on the seventh floor at Scotland Yard and turned to his right. He was happy he did not have to come in here every day – too much politics for him, surrounded by fast-tracked graduates who would try telling you how things should be done now.

He came to a door near the end of the corridor. The sign on it read Assistant Commissioner Crick. Charlie knocked on the door and heard 'Come in'. He pushed open the door and went into a well-decorated room with a deep blue carpet. At an angle to his left was a large desk, and the man behind it now looked up. He was dressed in the uniform of assistant commissioner, though his hat sat on the desk half covering some folders.

"Charlie," he said, "good to see you. I was only thinking it's about time we got together to go over how the new case is going."

"Hello, Sir," Charlie said, "that's why I popped in – to keep you up to speed on the progress."

"Fine, take a seat, Charlie," AC Crick said.

Charlie sat in a nice leather chair opposite his boss, whose silver grey hair was starting to thin. He seemed to have a permanent tan, and it was up for speculation whether it was the sunbeds or a spray tan.

"I have got you a press officer coming down on Monday," Crick said. "I want you to get a press conference arranged for Monday afternoon. We have to give the press something, as they are banging on the doors about wanting a story. This is a delicate inquiry with the girl being the niece of the home secretary, so go lightly Charlie."

"I will do all I can not to tread on anyone's toes," Charlie said, "but I don't want anyone treading on mine either."

"What do you mean?" Crick asked.

"Well, the local nick had a call from Assistant Commissioner Walker on the morning the girl's body was found," Charlie said. "I understand he's with the Anti-Terrorism Squad, asking that the locals should give us all the help we need. What's he got to do with this case? I have two men turning up in Oxford saying they're police officers, searching the girl's room and, we suspect, taking her laptop away. Now, if there's something more about this case that I should know, I want to be told."

"I know, Walker. Yes, he is with the Anti-Terrorism Squad. I will speak to him, but perhaps he heard from the home secretary's office and just thought it would be helpful to ring the local nick and smooth things for you," Crick said. "Do we have much progress yet?"

"It's a very foggy picture at the moment, but we're going to have to search the house. I know that could be delicate, with the father's connections, but it has to be done."

"Well, go easy, Charlie. I will follow up on Assistant Commissioner Walker to see what he's got to say. I'll let you know when I find out."

"Okay, Sir, I will be in touch if anything happens." Charlie stood.

"Remember, Charlie, delicate on this one," said Crick.

Charlie left the office.

* * *

Danny had set out just before Manjitt and was parked about 60 yards from the house on the other side of the road, giving him a clear view of anyone who came and went. The van had what looked like blacked-out rear windows, but had a 4-inch square left out in the top right-hand side. Danny had placed the small stool he had brought with him in a nice position, so he could sit comfortably. The flask of tea was at his feet and he had stopped off and got some sandwiches. He noticed to one side of the house's drive that some members of the press and paparazzi had taken up places hoping to get a story.

Danny took a couple of pictures of the two cars on the drive – a black Mercedes and a silver Lexus – making sure he got their registration numbers. He then snapped a few of the two police officers standing either side of the front door. He saw Manjitt arrive and snapped a few pictures of her, too. He wasn't going to get caught out by Harry saying he had missed something.

Manjitt arrived at the house, noticing the half a dozen reporters standing to one side of the drive. She parked her car next to the black Mercedes, which she remembered being there when they had first called at the house. Approaching the door with her small satchel over her shoulder and flashing her warrant card at the two officers, she rang the bell. The door was opened by the man she remembered as Raju.

"I am here to see Mr Khan," she said, showing him her warrant card.

"Please come in. Will you remove your shoes and follow me?" he said.

Raju shut the door, while Manjitt slipped her shoes off. Raju led her to the same room as they had met Mr Khan last time, lightly knocked on the door, opened it and said, "There is a police officer here to see you, Sir."

He stood aside and she found Mr Khan and one other man in the room. Both were seated, though they stood when Manjitt entered. Raju quietly closed the door behind him.

"Hello, Mr Khan, I'm Detective Constable Virdee. I have come to take your formal statements."

"Yes, of course," Mr Khan said. "This is my brother, Khurram."

"Hello, Sir," Manjitt said. "Mr Khan, is your wife able to give her statement today?"

"Yes, she is a little better. My sisters, my brother's wife and some other family are with her," Mr Khan said, "but I am sure she will be able to tell you what she knows."

"Thank you, Sir, if I can start with you," Manjitt said.

"Would you like to take a seat, officer? Is it alright if my brother stays?" Mr Khan asked.

"Of course, Sir." Manjitt sat down in one of the armchairs.

Mr Khan sat opposite, "Would you like some tea, Officer?"

"No thank you, Sir," she replied.

"Khurram, ring for Raju. Get him to bring some tea for us," Mr Khan said.

Khurram pressed the bell by the fireplace; Raju appeared at the door and was told to fetch tea.

"I will have to take a statement from Raju, too," Manjitt said, "and is your son at home? I would like to speak to him also."

"Yes, he is in his room. He is very upset; Ashadieeyah and he were very close. I will tell Raju to speak to you," Mr Khan replied.

Manjitt pulled out some official statement papers, "Right, Sir, if we can begin…"

At that moment, Raju brought in a tray. Khurram told him to put it on the table and leave, which he did without a word.

"Are you sure you wouldn't like some tea, Officer?" Khurram asked.

"No thank you, Sir," Manjitt replied, and waited while he poured the tea. He handed a cup to Mr Khan and stood with his cup in hand slightly behind his brother.

Manjitt started to question Mr Khan, going over the whole of Friday with him and getting as much detail as he could remember.

"Well, I think that is everything, Sir," Manjitt said. "There's nothing else you can recall?"

"No, Officer, I think you have got everything I remember from the day," he said.

"One last thing, Sir, did you see your daughter use her mobile phone while she was at home?" Manjitt asked.

"No, I can't remember her using it," he said.

"Well, Sir," Manjitt said, "if I can just ask you to sign the bottom of each page."

She handed the pages of the statement to Mr Khan, who took a pen from the inside of his jacket and signed the bottom of each page. Handing them back to Manjitt, she put them in a folder and then into her satchel, "Now, Sir, if I can just speak to your wife?"

"Of course," Mr Khan said. They both stood up.

There was a knock at the door and Raju came in. "It's your brother, Sir," Raju said.

Manjitt turned to see the home secretary come in, followed by another man.

"Safwan, how are you?" the home secretary said, coming forward to embrace his brother.

"Mahbeer, it's so good to see you," Mr Khan said.

The home secretary turned to his other brother. "Khurram," he embraced him, "this is a sad time."

"Safwan how is Suheera? She must be so distraught," the home secretary asked.

"She is with our sisters; she has hardly stopped crying," Mr Khan said.

The home secretary turned to look at Manjitt, "And who is this?"

"This is a police officer, Detective Virdee," Mr Khan said.

"Detective Constable Virdee, Sir. I am here taking statements from the family."

"How do you do, Officer? I hope the enquiry is progressing."

"Yes, Sir, but it's early days and we have a lot to follow up," she said.

"This is Assistant Commissioner Walker," the home secretary said, introducing the other man.

The home secretary sat down with his two brothers and began talking to them.

"Who is your commanding officer?" the assistant commissioner asked Manjitt

"Chief Superintendent Smith, Sir," she said.

"Ah, Smith, yes I have heard of him – drives flash cars. I hope you have made some progress on this case," Walker said.

"Well, we are checking on the girl's background and that of her friends," Manjitt replied.

"What have you found out? Are there any leads yet?" he asked.

"I have only been sent to take the family statements. Sir, I don't know much about the wider case," Manjitt said.

"Well, I hope you're being discreet," Assistant Commissioner Walker said. "The home secretary is the first Muslim to hold such a high office in government and there is talk that he could be prime minister one day, so we don't want any silly scandals – you know what the press are like. This needs to be cleared up as soon as possible."

"We are doing all we can to find whoever did it, Sir," she said.

"Well, if you have any problems I can help you with, just ring me at the Yard. I know it's not always possible to get the officer in charge of a case to listen to the ideas of junior officers," Walker said.

"Thank you, Sir," Manjitt said. "I will bear that in mind."

"That's good, we can always use bright talented officers like you," AC Walker said, "and I'm sure promotion would come soon in the right environment."

"Yes, Sir, thank you."

Manjitt looked over to Mr Khan, who was still talking to his brothers, and said, "Mr Khan, sorry to interrupt you, but could I speak to your wife now?"

Mr Khan looked up, "Of course, Detective." He stood up. "I will be back shortly," he said to his brothers. "Follow me, Detective."

"Goodbye, Sir," Manjitt said to the home secretary.

"It was nice to meet you," the home secretary said.

Manjitt turned to follow Mr Khan.

"Don't forget," AC Walker said, "anything that comes up that I can help with, just call me at Scotland Yard. Take my card, Officer." He handed Manjitt his card.

"I will, Sir, thank you."

Mr Khan led Manjitt from the room, closing the doors behind him.

★★★

Charlie arrived back at the police station and decided to call in on Caroline Myles. He knocked on her door and entered.

"Hello, Caroline," he said. "I thought I would pop in and have a catch up."

"Hello, Charlie, come in and sit down."

"How's the case going?" she asked.

"Things are a bit hard at the moment," Charlie replied. "We can't seem to find many leads that we can follow."

"How's Inspector West getting on?" she asked.

"He seems a very good officer," Charlie answered. "Knows his job."

"That's good," Caroline said. "I have had a few calls from the press to the station wanting a story."

"Well, we have a press officer coming over Monday," Charlie said, "and there is going to be a press conference Monday afternoon. I was going to ask if there was somewhere the press officer could use while they're here, as I don't have the space for them in our offices."

Caroline looked at Charlie with a smile on her lips. "I take it the press officer is not your choice?" she said.

Charlie smiled. "We do our best with the staff we are given by the gods above us," he said.

"I will find a spot for your press officer away from your offices," she said.

"You're a mind reader, Caroline," he said. "I will have to be careful when I come into this office."

"I like to think we are on the same side, Charlie," she said.

Charlie stood, "I will keep that in mind. Speak to you later."

"Okay, Charlie, bye for now."

★★★

Charlie climbed the stairs to the squad's offices. He saw Pelé sitting in one at a computer; in another, Harry was at his desk, which had papers and files all over it.

"Harry," Charlie said, "your filing system leaves a lot to be desired."

Harry looked up. "Hello, boss," he said. "This is a foolproof system. I don't have to leave this chair to put my hands on what I need."

"Well, don't pass it on to the rest of the squad," Charlie said. "This place would look like a tip. What's happening?"

"Everybody's at it," Harry said. "Manjitt is at the family's, Danny should be plotted up outside with his camera, Pelé is next door chasing up info on the family, Jordan's on his way back from Oxford and West is on the local CCTV."

"And out of that lot, do we have anything?" Charlie asked.

"Good and bad," Harry said. "West and his boys have given us a potential lead – a black BMW, which might be the car the body was moved in. It's the only car seen to enter the vicinity of the murder scene and leave in the time frame for when the body was dropped off. I have phoned Doctor Taylor to ask if the girl has any fibres on her clothes that could match the seats used in a BMW. He said he would check, but it might take time, as he would need to get information from the manufacturer. Bad news from Jordan – those two supposed police officers have the laptop. However, he has some CCTV of the two and is bringing it back with him for us to see."

"I have been thinking about the autopsy report," Charlie said. "We have assumed she went to meet someone at a house or something, but what if she met someone in a car or more than one person? When she got in the front seat, the person sitting in the back could have leant forward and grabbed her by the neck, which would have left the driver free to stab her."

"It would fit with the angles, boss," Harry said, "and might explain why we have no CCTV of her walking in the area in the early evening, as well as no eyewitness sightings."

"So that makes that BMW very important, Harry," Charlie said. "Make sure West knows just how important it is, but we still search the house. Let's not tip our hand to anyone. I see you got the locks done…" He held out his hand, and Harry opened a draw, took a key out and passed it to him.

"I called in at the Yard on the way over, saw the big chief," Charlie continued. "I don't think he knew anything about the strange things going on around this case."

"How's his suntan?" Harry asked.

"He's looking as good as ever," Charlie said. "I also had a couple of visitors to my house, claiming to be from the gas suppliers, but Mike didn't let them in. So, I have a couple of things for you to check for me, Harry. Get in touch with the gas supplier and ask if there is a problem in the area with leaks. Mike is going to ring you if they turn up again; he will let them into the house, but put the security cameras on. Take someone with you and go over to my house – you know how to work the cameras – to check what they were up to."

Oscar knocked and came into the office. "Hello, boss," he said.

"Hello, Pelé," Charlie replied, "have you got anything for us?"

"Well, boss, Manjitt got a lot of stuff on the family; their parents came over to this country in the early sixties, appear to have worked hard, sent their kids to university and they have all done well. No record of any trouble with them, though there are a few flags on other members of the family: Mr Khan's brother, Khurram, has a son with a warning for possession of a small amount of cannabis; while his sister, Hibba, has a son who was arrested at an anti-war demonstration, but was released without charge. Apart from that, nothing."

"Okay, well done," said Charlie. He took the pictures he had printed from the security camera from his pocket, "I want you to check this van out, run the registration number through the system and print off copies of the two men. I want one for everyone." He passed the pictures to Oscar.

"These are lovely and clear," Oscar said, looking at the prints.

"Are you hungry, Harry?" asked Charlie.

"Yes, could do with a bite to eat."

"What about you, Pelé?"

"Yes, boss, starving."

"Okay, take my car and go get us some sandwiches and some biscuits for the office."

"What, the Bentley, boss?" Oscar said.

"No, afraid not. It's the Ferrari," Charlie said, smiling.

"Harry, do you have another camera?" said Oscar. "I want a few pictures of me in the car. I'll send them round my family, show them how well I'm doing and get one blown up to give to Jordan."

"On your way, Pelé," Harry said, "and bring the boss's car back without a scratch."

Oscar left the office.

"Harry, we have a press officer joining us Monday morning," Charlie said.

"Not in here with us?" Harry said.

Charlie laughed, "No, I spoke to Caroline."

Harry smiled, "Caroline?"

"Chief Superintendent Myles," Charlie said. "She said she would find somewhere away from us."

"Seems like a good officer to me," Harry said, still with a smile on his face. "You should look after her."

"You are not indispensable, Harry," Charlie said.

* * *

Mr Khan led Manjitt left out of the door and along the hallway, when she noticed Raju standing by the bottom of the stairs. They passed one door to the left that was closed, before coming to another closed set of double doors. Mr Khan stopped, knocked lightly on the doors and opened them. Manjitt followed him into the room, where she was met with seven women.

"Suheera," Mr Khan said.

The woman in the middle stood up. She was wearing a long black dress and a dark headscarf covered her hair.

"This is my wife, Suheera," Mr Khan said, looking at Manjitt. "Detective, please try not to upset her too much."

His wife's eyes were red and she looked very tired.

"Of course, Sir, I will try and be as easy as I can," Manjitt said.

"The detective is here to take a statement from you, Suheera," Mr Khan said. "Answer all the questions you can, and try and recall anything that might help catch the wicked person who killed our daughter."

Manjitt saw her eyes start to water at the words.

"These are my sisters, Mysha and Hibba," Mr Khan said, pointing to the two women closest to his wife. Both were also dressed in black with dark headscarves on. "This is Mysha's daughter," he pointed to a young girl of about sixteen seated behind the women, who was dressed in a similar fashion to her mother, "and my other sister Hibba's daughter." Seated to one side by the window overlooking the garden, the girl was in a full hijab and her dark eyes looked directly at Manjitt – there was nothing to tell her age. She nodded at Mr Khan's words. "Finally, this is Diana, my brother Khurram's wife." He indicated the woman standing by the table, tea cup in hand, dressed in a dark two-piece suit and whose blonde hair was not covered. She was a strikingly good-looking woman.

"Thank you, Sir," Manjitt said.

"I will leave you now. When you are finished, one of the women will bring you back to the study," he said. Mr Khan turned and left the room.

"Please come and sit down," Suheera said.

"Thank you, I will try and be as quick as I can," Manjitt said. "All I need to know is how your daughter was and what she did around the house on Friday."

After fifteen minutes, Manjitt felt she had coaxed all that she could out of Suheera. The answers all seemed genuine. No one else had uttered a word. Manjitt stood up.

"Thank you for your help," she said to Suheera, whose eyes were again showing tears. "Can I give you my card in case you think of anything else that may help us?"

Suheera nodded, taking the card.

"Could someone take me back to your husband?" Manjitt asked.

"I will," Diana said.

"No, I will take the detective back to the study," the girl in the hijab said.

Standing up, Manjitt saw she was about 5 feet 6. Diana stood back, not saying a word.

The girl walked past Manjitt. "Follow me," she said, opening the doors.

Manjitt followed her out, pulling the doors closed behind them.

"Have you been in the police long?" she asked, as they walked along the hallway.

"About eight years," Manjitt said.

"Do you enjoy your job?" the girl asked.

"Yes, I find it rewarding," Manjitt replied.

They got to the study door and Manjitt noticed Raju had not moved from where he had been standing before. The girl knocked on the door and opened it. "Uncle, the detective has finished," she said.

Mr Khan stood up. He had been seated talking to the home secretary and his other brother. Assistant Commissioner Walker was standing just behind the home secretary. "Thank you, Abrar," Mr Khan said.

Abrar was about to turn and go, when the home secretary stood and said, "Abrar, we are going now, we have work to do. Go and say goodbye to your mother, then meet us at the front door in a minute."

She went out, closing the doors behind her.

The home secretary embraced his brother. "I will be in touch, but if there are any problems you can ring me on my private number."

"Thank you, Mahbeer, for all your help," Mr Khan said.

The home secretary embraced his other brother and said goodbye. He then walked towards Manjitt, with Assistant Commissioner Walker close behind. They both stopped in front of her, "I hope you are able to get this nasty business all sorted soon. Have you finished with my brother's family?" he asked.

"Not quite yet, Sir," Manjitt answered.

"What else is left to do? They have helped you fully. I think they need to have some peace to grieve as a family," the home secretary said.

"Yes, Sir, but there are a number of things that have to be done," Manjitt said.

"I'm sure they're just loose ends that can be tied up another time," AC Walker said.

"No, Sir, they are important to the enquiry," Manjitt replied.

Mr Khan came and joined them. Manjitt was feeling quite outnumbered.

"What is the problem?" Mr Khan said.

"I don't think there is a problem, as Detective Constable Virdee was just finishing here. She will ring and make an appointment to clear up any outstanding questions, won't you?" AC Walker said, looking directly at Manjitt.

Manjitt thought for a moment, *Boss, I hope you're there to catch me.*

"No, Sir, these are things that need to be done as quickly as possible to ensure the enquiry is not hindered."

"What is it you want, Officer?" Mr Khan said.

"I still need to take a statement from your son and Raju," Manjitt said.

"Oh, that is not a problem," Mr Khan said.

"You will do that quickly and leave the family in peace," AC Walker said.

"And there is one other thing that has to be done," Manjitt said. "The house has to be searched."

The three men in front of her stood silent for a few seconds, before the home secretary spoke first. He turned to Walker and said, "Surely, that won't be necessary."

"I can't see any need for that," Walker said. "Officer, you will leave the house now. I will be in touch with your superior officer to sort this nonsense out. You are overstepping the mark."

Manjitt stood quite calmly.

"Home secretary," she said, "a girl has been murdered. Part of the investigation is to eliminate any possible avenues of enquiry that we don't need to follow, and searching the house would do that."

"I am sure you can see my family have been completely open and honest with you. There is no need for a search of the house. It would cause them great distress," the home secretary said.

"I understand that, home secretary, but it has to be done as part of this investigation," Manjitt replied, standing her ground.

"I don't think you understand at all, Detective Virdee," AC Walker said. "You will leave the house now, that is a direct order, and you will report to my office tomorrow with your commanding officer at 10am. Do you understand that?"

"Yes, Sir," Manjitt said, as she put her satchel over her shoulder, turned, opened the door and went out. As she got to the front door and was putting her shoes on, Abrar appeared.

"I hope you catch the criminal who killed my cousin," she said.

"We will do our best," Manjitt replied.

"If there is any help I can give you, please let me know," Abrar said. "I am working for my uncle, the home secretary, as his private assistant. Here's my card."

"Thanks, I will bear that in mind," Manjitt said.

Raju suddenly appeared from nowhere and opened the front door. Manjitt walked to her car, got in and pulled out of the drive past the waiting press. There seemed to be lots more of them now and a couple of television cameras had joined the throng.

They must know the home secretary is there, she thought.

★★★

Jordan arrived back at the station. He had just got out of the squad car and was walking across the yard, when he heard a roar and turned to see a red Ferrari bearing down on him. He leapt to one side as the Ferrari stopped just past him. The door opened and Oscar got out.

"Hello, peasant," he said to Jordan.

"I would remind you that's no way to speak to a senior officer," Jordan said, "and how did you manage to get the keys off the boss to drive that, you jammy sod?"

"The boss has his favourites," Oscar replied, "and as its common knowledge that you only became a detective sergeant because of your good looks, he's not going to lend it to an airhead, is he?"

Both spent a few minutes looking over the car, and then went into the station and up to the office. They found Charlie and Harry there, sitting with Inspector West.

"Hello, boss," Jordan said.

"How was your trip to the countryside?" Charlie said, as he took some sandwiches and his car keys off Oscar.

Jordan pulled a chair up and sat down beside West, while Oscar gave some sandwiches to Harry.

"I got the numbers for the two friends," Jordan said. "I phoned and spoke to the girl, Leanne Trumain, who basically told me the same as the others – that Ashadieeyah was a lovely girl who worked hard and was a good friend. I have the address of the German boy that she went on the walking holiday with, Karl Bauer. I will try and chase him down and speak to him, too. I also have a copy of the CCTV that shows our two supposed police officers coming and leaving with the girl's laptop."

"Will we get any good still pictures off the CCTV?" Harry asked.

"Don't know how clear they will be," Jordan replied, "but it gives us a reasonable look at them."

"Well, whoever they are," Charlie said, "they knew the girl was dead and were in Oxford four or five hours before us – just bear that in mind. Oscar will give you a picture of two people who turned up at my house and tried to get in saying they were gasmen, so we might have at least four people wandering around the outside of this enquiry who know something that we don't or want to find out what we know. With that in mind, Inspector West has got us a little chink of light."

He nodded to West.

"We have identified a black BMW that fits with the time span for the murder," West said. "We have eliminated all the other cars that were in the area at the time the BMW leaves the road near the murder site at 23.50. We have had cameras along the main roads close by checked and we have a BMW driving down the A3 towards New Malden at five past twelve. Seven minutes later, it turned off the A3 and headed into New Malden. It appears again going past New Malden station, but doesn't appear on any other cameras around that area or any major roads coming from that area again."

"Have we got a make for the car?" Harry asked.

"Well, it's not definite," West said, "but one of the officers checking with me said it was a series five BMW. He thought he could identify it by the shape."

"Well done, Inspector," said Charlie, "but we keep this BMW between us. No one outside the squad must know we might have a lead, as that car could be the key to this case. Inspector, the two officers you had going through the CCTV footage must be made to understand that they can't say a word to anyone about it – put the fear of God into them to keep their mouths shut. I want you to follow it up. I know it is going to be a bit of work, but take New Malden station as the centre and work your way out from it. Get all registered owners of black BMW 5 series within 5 miles, and then start checking them out."

"Yes, Sir," said West.

"Pelé, don't forget to give those pictures out I gave you," Charlie said, "and hurry up and check that van registration."

"Will do, boss," Oscar said.

"Hello everyone, can I join the party?" Manjitt said as she came into the office.

"There's no sandwiches left," Oscar called out.

"Manjitt, how did you get on?" Charlie asked.

"I think you are going to love this one, boss," Manjitt replied.

"Jordan, shift your carcass and give the lady a seat," Harry said.

Jordan stood up, saying, "So much for sexual equality."

Manjitt slipped into the chair he had just vacated and then went through everything that had happened at the house.

"Well, I look forward to meeting Assistant Commissioner Walker tomorrow," Charlie said. "So, we have the son and our strange man Raju outstanding on the statement front. Okay, everyone get on with what needs to be done, but get a key off Harry for the doors first. Manjitt, you get off home, I will meet you at the Yard tomorrow at nine. We will pop in and see the big chief first."

Everyone got up and left the office, each taking a key that Harry passed out.

"What do you think, boss?" Harry said.

"Well, if I am being kind, I think our AC Walker is trying to impress the home secretary," Charlie said. "But you know me, Harry, I have a suspicious mind, so here's what we will do. When that press officer turns up in the morning, give them a report on the case, stress we need to find witnesses who may have seen the girl on the Friday evening etc, don't give them anything we don't want them to know and let them arrange a press conference for whenever they want. I will speak to Superintendent Myles."

"Caroline," Harry interrupted.

Charlie looked at Harry, "You have just lost your Christmas bonus." He continued, "In terms of arranging to have the press conference somewhere away from the station, put Chief Superintendent Myles and the press officer together. It should buy us some time while they are phoning round to arrange things. Now, I will be at the Yard with Manjitt tomorrow for this meeting at ten with AC Walker. So, why don't we do what we do best?"

Harry looked at Charlie. "We upset people," he said.

"Good thinking," Charlie said, "I want you to pick up the search warrant from the magistrate and get a team together, but don't tell them what they are going to do. At about nine, send a couple of uniforms over to the house and get any of those press that Manjitt said were hanging around moved about 50 metres down the road – tell them it's because the family want some privacy and the neighbours are complaining. When they are out of the way, I want you to get the search team into some unmarked vans. Once they are in the vans, you can tell them what they will be doing – and take West with you. I want you knocking on Mr Khan's door at 10am exactly. Be as discreet as you can, Harry, but do the house top-to-bottom and the garden and any sheds. Sit Mr Khan down and have a quiet word with him, because he might understand what we are trying to do without AC Walker there. I look forward to seeing how long it is into our meeting with AC Walker before he gets a phone call."

Harry laughed, "Boss, are you sure? Walker is going to be upset."

"That's what we do best, Harry," Charlie said. "Get Danny back from the house now and make sure he goes through the pictures he's taken. Tomorrow, he can go with you. Right, I'm off, but ring me if anything pops up. Leave Oscar on duty till nine, get everyone else off home in an hour, and make sure the front desk has your number in case anything comes up while we are not here." Charlie got up. "See you tomorrow, Harry."

"Okay, boss," said Harry.

***

Outside, Charlie got into his car and rang Chief Superintendent Myles before starting the engine. The phone was answered on the third ring.

"Hello Caroline, this is Chief Superintendent Smith."

"Oh, hello Charlie. How is the case going?" she said.

"Well, it should get a little more interesting tomorrow," Charlie said, "but I wanted to ask you a favour."

"Yes, what's that?" she asked.

"Well, the Yard are sending over a press officer tomorrow," Charlie said. "I think they will be arranging a press conference, but I have to be at the Yard for a ten o'clock meeting and my chief inspector has an important job in the morning. Could you look after whoever comes over? They will need a hall or large room to hold their press conference, so your local knowledge would help out."

"Yes, that's no problem. Anything to help," she said.

"Thank you," Charlie said, "I will get my chief inspector to bring whoever turns up to you."

"By the way, Charlie, what have you done to my Inspector West?" Caroline asked. "Whenever I ask him how the case is going, he tells me he's not allowed to talk about anything."

"He has the makings of a good copper," Charlie said. "You'll get to see that in the years to come. I will pop into your office when I get back Monday and get you up to speed on the case."

"Okay, Charlie. See you tomorrow."

"Bye, Caroline," Charlie said.

***

Harry got to the police station at 7.30am on Monday. He unlocked the office and was just sitting down after making some tea, when Jordan popped his head in the door.

"Morning, Harry, I am going to chase up the German boy. We have to rule him out of the enquiry and I know you don't like loose ends."

"Are you after promotion or something?" Harry said.

"I was thinking more of a holiday," Jordan replied.

"Promotion would be easier to get," Harry said, "but you're right, though. He had a two-week walking holiday with the girl and now he's nowhere to be found. Keep me up to date with how you get on."

Jordan left Harry's office and went to the other, which the rest of the squad were using. He sat down and turned on one of the computers. Inspector West was the next to arrive.

"Morning Harry," he said. "Has anything come up or should I chase down that car?"

"Morning Inspector. Grab yourself a cup of tea from over there and sit down," Harry said. "I need to go over a couple of things with you."

Harry started pulling various bits of paper from different piles on his desk and arranging them, while Inspector West came and sat down opposite him. *If my desk was like that,* he thought, *my boss would slaughter me.*

"Morning Harry, Inspector," Danny said, as he poked his head round the office door. Harry and the Inspector both looked over to the door.

"Hippie, don't go away. Get in here, grab a cup of tea and join us," Harry said.

"Invited in for tea? That means you have a dodgy job you want me to do," Danny said. "Ah, I see the Inspector's got a cup, too, so at least I know I won't be alone when I get in to trouble."

"Hippie, shut up, get your tea and sit down," Harry said.

Danny got himself a cup of tea and sat down next to the Inspector, opposite Harry. He turned to the Inspector and said, "Well, at least he hasn't given us the biscuits that the last officer he had in for tea and biscuits had. He's never been seen again."

"Have you finished?" Harry said. "Now, we are going to plan a few things this morning that only we three are going to know about until the last minute. First, though, did you speak to the officers looking into the BMW?"

"Yes, I left them in no doubt that their careers were at stake if I heard a whisper about it from anyone else."

"Good, I think you should keep them on that until we have found the car," Harry said. "Now, today we are going to search the Khan family home."

"I thought AC Walker told Manjitt we had to stay away from the house," Inspector West said.

"He doesn't run this investigation, the boss does. If he says we search the house, we search," Harry said. "Do you have a problem with that, Inspector?"

The Inspector sat still for a moment, "No, Harry, search it is."

"I think he has the makings of a good senior officer," Danny said.

"By the way, Hippie, good work on the CCTV," Harry said. "When we finish at the house, I want all the pictures you took yesterday printed. Check that none of the faces have popped up anywhere else."

"Harry, you just told me I did a good job," Danny said. "That means you might have a real shitty one for me to do next – you have to understand how things work around here, Inspector?"

"You're getting too smart, Hippie. Right, here's what we are going to do." Harry then ran through the plan that Charlie and he had worked out.

"You got that, Inspector?"

"Yes Harry, I will get a team together ready downstairs for nine thirty," West said.

Harry turned to Danny.

"Hippie, I want you to go here," he passed an address to Danny. "You will pick up a search warrant for the Khan's address from the magistrate who lives there. Come back here after – then we are ready to go. Remember, the two of you, not a word till we are ready to move off."

Danny and the Inspector left the office. Harry put a call through to the front desk telling them to call him if a press officer turned up asking for Chief Superintendent Smith. When he put the phone down, he started to write up a report for the press officer. When he had finished, he went next door to see Jordan.

"How're things going?" Harry asked.

"I have tried the number for the German boy a few times, but nothing," Jordan said. "So I got onto the German police and spoke to a detective over there, explaining that we needed to speak to the boy. I gave him the phone number and address. When he gets something, he will phone me back."

"Good," Harry said, "and you're coming out with us later. We are going to search the house."

"I knew the boss would not let someone tell him what he can and can't do," Jordan said.

"Jordan, when we get to the house, there are two officers from diplomatic protection outside. Whatever I tell you to do, just do it."

"Harry, I know better than to not follow your orders," Jordan said, smiling.

The phone rang in Harry's office.

"Be downstairs at nine thirty," he told Jordan and went to answer the phone. He spoke on the phone for a minute, then left to go down to the front desk.

When he arrived, the constable behind it pointed to a man in a dark blue suit sitting in the waiting area.

"Has Chief Superintendent Myles come in yet?" Harry asked the constable.

"Yes, Sir, about ten minutes ago."

"Thank you, buzz the door open," Harry said.

Harry went through the door and up to the man, "Hello, I am Chief Inspector Davis and I am on the murder investigation. Chief Superintendent Smith is not available at the moment."

The man stood up. He was a couple of inches taller than Harry, with dark, well cut hair.

"Hello, Chief Inspector, my name's Christopher Wade. I have been sent over from the police press office to help you."

"That's very nice," said Harry, though he thought the sarcasm was lost on Mr Wade. "I have a report of what we know so far and what we would like to get help on."

Harry passed him the report he had put together.

"Thank you. How is the case progressing?" Wade said.

"It's only been a couple of days, so it's not clear yet," Harry said. "That's why your help will be vital. If you'll follow me, I'll take you upstairs to meet Chief Superintendent Myles. She is going to help you with the organisation of the press conference."

Harry waved to the constable behind the desk, who buzzed the door. Harry took Wade through it and up the stairs to the first floor and to Myles' office. Harry knocked, opened the door and led Wade in, closing the door behind him.

"Hello, Ma'am, I'm Chief Inspector Davis. I work for Chief Superintendent Smith, who asked me to make sure Mr Wade from the press office got to meet you."

Caroline looked up. *Charlie must have the worst-dressed squad of police in the country*. The chief inspector in front of her looked like he slept in his clothes; his hair was all over the place and his shoes had seen better days. She stood up. "Thank you, Chief Inspector. Hello, Mr Wade."

She held out her hand and Wade stepped forward to shake it.

"Call me Christopher, please. It's a pleasure to meet you."

"If you don't need me, Ma'am," Harry said.

"No, that's fine, Chief Inspector."

Harry went out the door and back upstairs to their offices.

"Harry," Jordan called. "Dr Taylor rang and the fibres on the girl's clothes match the velour used in some BMW models. He will send over a report. He did ask how you knew, but I told him I knew nothing."

"Well, that puts that BMW top of the list," Harry said. "After we get back from the house, we will sit down with everyone and have a chat. Oh, and the press officer just arrived – a Mr Christopher Wade."

"What's he like?" Jordan asked.

"The boss is going to love him," Harry said.

Jordan laughed, "See you downstairs at nine thirty."

* * *

Charlie arrived in the Bentley at Scotland Yard at 8.50am. He went through the security procedures and found a space not too close to the other cars and went up in the lift to the ground floor. He scanned the waiting area and saw Manjitt, caught her eye and she stood up and walked towards him. He noticed the admiring glances she was getting off of the male officers.

When she reached him, he said, "Come on, let's go up and see the big chief." They went up in the lift to the seventh floor and Charlie took Manjitt to Assistant Commissioner Crick's office. He knocked and entered. Crick looked up from his desk.

"Charlie," he said, "I only saw you yesterday. Twice in a week – this is a record. Who is this?"

"Detective Constable Virdee, one of my squad," Charlie said. "I brought her over to see you because we have run into a bit of a problem with the case."

"Nice to meet you, Virdee," Crick said. "Well, both of you sit down." He indicated the chairs opposite him at his desk, "Tell me what the problem is."

* * *

Danny had taken the search warrant to Harry, who had checked it over to make sure the address and everything else was correct. He and Danny then made their way down to the station car park, where they found West and Jordan waiting by two vans. The back doors of both vans were open, with half a dozen officers in each.

"Did you send two uniforms to the house to move the press away?" Harry asked West.

"Yes, Harry, fifteen minutes ago."

"Check with them and make sure they got them well down the road," Harry said.

Inspector West went off and Harry turned to Jordan and Danny. "Now, you two, this could be tricky, so be on your toes."

West was back within a minute. "They have them 60 metres down the road. The officer said there was a lot of moaning, but they did as they were told in the end."

Harry looked at his watch; it was 9.35am. "How many female officers do you have on the search team?" Harry asked West.

"We have four, is that enough?"

"Yes, that's good. Right, let me have a quick word with them and then we can get off."

The four off them walked over to the vans.

"Listen up you lot, Chief Inspector Davis is going to speak to you," West said. The officers in the vans went quiet.

"Now, we are going to carry out a search warrant on the house of the murdered girl," Harry said.

"I want everyone to be as professional as you should be. The family are very upset about their daughter, but we have to search the house. Whatever happens when we get there, you are following my orders – no one else's. Does everyone understand?"

Everyone nodded in the vans, although there were a few looks exchanged over the orders.

"Do you want to say anything, Inspector West?"

"Yes, this is a very delicate operation," West said, "so you will make sure we carry out this search like the textbook says. If you are not sure about something, you ask one of us. Do you all understand?"

A collective 'Yes, Sir' was heard from the back of the vans.

Harry checked his watch; it was just coming up to 9.45am.

"Right, let's get going," Harry said. "Jordan, you go with Inspector West in that van; Danny will come with me in this one. Inspector West, you're the lead van. I want us to come in from the end of the road away from where the press have been put."

⋆⋆⋆

Charlie finished relating what had happened to Manjitt when she had met AC Walker at the Khan's house.

"Well, Charlie, I will join you at this meeting," AC Crick said. "I would like to hear why AC Walker thought a search of the house was not necessary – it does seem a bit strange, as it is basically standard procedure. Shall we go to his office? It's on the ninth floor and its 9.55 now."

They all stood up and AC Crick picked up his hat from the table. Charlie and Manjitt followed him out of the office and down the corridor to the lift. They had to wait a few seconds for it to arrive, but the doors opened and they got in. On the ninth floor, the doors opened and they turned right, eventually coming to a wooden door with Walker's name on it. Charlie glanced at his watch; it was one minute to ten. AC Crick knocked and they went in. Inside, there was a desk just to the left of the door, which had a uniformed policewoman sat behind it. She looked up as they entered.

"Can I help you?" she said.

"We are here to see Assistant Commissioner Walker," Charlie said. "I am Chief Superintendent Smith."

"Wait one moment, I will see if he's ready to see you," she said and went through a door at the far end of the office. She was back within a minute. "Assistant Commissioner Walker will see you now."

The three of them entered the office. It had lots of wooden panelling and a long bookcase along one wall with what looked to be law books on it. There were also a number of framed awards hanging on the walls, along with pictures of AC Walker and various people.

Walker was standing when they entered, and Charlie noticed his expression change when he saw AC Crick was with them. Sitting to Walker's side was another man, who looked to be in his forties.

"What do we owe the pleasure of your company?" Walker said to Crick.

"I thought I would come up with my officers and see why someone from another department thought it was okay to summon them here without speaking to me first."

Charlie had a sideways glance. *Well, that's a good opener from the chief.*

★★★

The vans pulled into the drive at Mr Khan's house. Harry was happy that West had got the press far enough away for them not to see what was going on. He glanced at his watch – two minutes to ten. The vans came to a halt and all the doors opened and bodies piled out. Harry and Danny went to the head of the group, joined by Jordan and West. As they approached the front door, the two police officers came forward.

"One moment please, what are you doing here?" said the one on the right.

Harry looked at him and said, "I am Chief Inspector Davis. I have a warrant to search this house, so officer, please step aside."

The two officers exchanged glances. "I am sorry, Sir, but we are under orders not to let anyone in."

"I will ask you once more," Harry said. "I have a signed warrant from a magistrate. You are obstructing an officer in the execution of his duty, please step aside."

"I am sorry…"

The officer got no more words out before Harry said, "Nick them, Jordan." Jordan jumped forwards. Grabbing the first officer, one of West's men joined him and quickly got him under control. Danny and West, along with one of West's men, quickly got the other officer restrained.

"I am sorry this has happened," Harry addressed the two officers being held. "Danny, cuff them and stick them in the van. Take their firearms and radios off them. Inspector, leave two of your men out here. No one is to enter the house while we are searching it."

West ordered two of his officers to do what Harry had said. Danny took the two handcuffed officers to the back of one van, helped them up and said, "Make yourself comfortable, boys. You may be here for a while," and shut the doors behind them.

Harry, Jordan and West approached the door. West rang the bell.

"Harry, when we get in," Jordan said, "make sure everyone takes their shoes off."

"Pass that on to everyone, Inspector," Harry said to West.

The door was opened by a man who Jordan remembered was Raju.

"We have a warrant to search these premises," Harry said to him and quickly pushed past him into the house. Danny grabbed Raju, while everyone followed Harry in and removed their shoes.

"Where is Mr Khan?" Harry asked Raju.

"I will take you to him," Raju said.

"Jordan, you and the inspector start the search," Harry said. "Begin upstairs. Jordan, you find the girl's room; Inspector, bring anyone you find down here to join us. Remember you lot," Harry said, addressing the rest of the search team, "treat everyone with respect. I don't want anybody upset. You two…" he pointed at two uniformed officers, "stay with me."

Jordan and Inspector West led the search team up the stairs.

"Okay, Sir, if you would lead us to Mr Khan," Harry spoke to Raju.

Raju led Harry and Danny to a set of double doors to the left of the staircase, knocked on the doors and pushed them open. Harry and Danny followed him in.

"The police are here," he said.

Mr Khan had been seated, but stood up as they entered.

"Mr Khan, I am Chief Inspector Davis. We are here to search these premises to obtain any evidence for our enquiries."

"What? This is not right. I thought the police were not going to disturb us," Mr Khan said.

"I am afraid that is not how we work," Harry said. "Is there anyone else in the house, Sir? I want them all in this room."

"My wife and sister are in the kitchen and my son is upstairs. Raju will get them," Mr Khan said.

"I am afraid he stays in here, Sir. Danny, you go and get Mr Khan's wife and sister from the kitchen." Danny left the room. "Some officers are upstairs, so I'm sure they will bring your son down in a minute. Now, we are going to be as quick and as careful as we can. We do not want to upset you or your family in anyway, Sir, but please work with us and it will all be over in no time."

"Can I make a phone call to my solicitor?" Mr Khan asked.

"Yes, Sir, if that's what you want to do," Harry said.

* * *

AC Crick sat in the middle of Charlie and Manjitt, facing Walker across the desk. The other man had still not been introduced to them and sat quietly behind and to the left of Walker.

"Well, would you like to tell me what this is about?" Crick said to Walker.

"I was not happy with the way your officer behaved at the home of Mr Khan, the home secretary's brother," Walker said.

Dropping in the home secretary's name, Charlie thought. *Trying to show he has friends in high places.*

"And how did she behave?" Crick said. "The report I got from Chief Superintendent Smith said that she followed his orders correctly."

"I was standing with the home secretary at the time and she demanded that the house should be searched. When I pointed out that she would have to wait because the family were very upset, she was very disrespectful. I thought it was only right that I sent her away before she made a fool of herself," Walker said.

"Well, that's not the version of events that has been related to me," Crick replied.

"I think, as a junior officer, she may have felt under pressure from her commanding officer," Walker said, "to put pressure on the family, rather than work with them. After all, their young daughter has been murdered. I expect they thought they could get the case solved quickly, but I do think the commanding officer should have been there to supervise as it is a delicate case."

"Sir, if I may just say something?" Charlie spoke to Crick.

"Yes, go ahead, Chief Superintendent," Crick said.

Charlie turned and looked directly at Walker, "Sir, I have every faith in my officer to behave respectfully and with tact. I don't believe for one minute she behaved in the way you have described. She has worked for me for a number of years and has been an exemplary officer. She, along with another officer and myself, visited the family on the day of the murder. We only spent a small amount of time with the family and I arranged with Mr Khan that we would come back the next day to take formal statements. Now, as they are a Muslim family, we have to respect their religion and I thought it was best that a female officer should question Mr Khan's wife rather than a male officer. She was going to point out to Mr Khan that we would need to search the house to eliminate the family from the investigation, but your intervention has put us back. As for Mr Khan being the home secretary's brother, I don't feel that gives him any special rights to avoid having his house searched."

No one said anything for a minute. Walker was staring back at Charlie, who still held his gaze. The sound of a mobile phone going off broke the silence, and the man seated behind Walker took his phone from his pocket and answered it.

"Chief Superintendent," Walker finally said, "you may have every faith in your officer, but you were not there – I was. I always feel junior officers mimic the behaviour of their senior officers and you are an officer whose attitude and, shall we say, extravagant lifestyle gives rise to speculation."

The man behind Walker finished his phone call, got up, lent over and spoke quietly into Walker's ear. Charlie saw his face tense up, after which the man sat back down.

"Sir, I don't know about my attitude," Charlie said, "so you will have to ask my commanding officer." Charlie pointed at Crick sitting beside him. "As for an extravagant lifestyle, it's not a description I recognise. I would hope my officers do follow my example as I always do the best to solve every case that comes my way."

Crick held up his hand. "I think we are straying from why we are here," he said.

* * *

Mr Khan finished talking to whoever it was on the phone, while Danny had brought Mr Khan's wife and sister in from the kitchen and they sat down next to Mr Khan. Another officer brought their son in and he sat at the table near Raju.

Harry went over and spoke to Mr Khan. "Sir, I am sorry we had to come here today like this," Harry said, "but I can assure you we will be quick and try not to make any mess."

"You could have asked; we have nothing to hide," Mr Khan replied.

"Our officer who came yesterday asked and was sent away," Harry said.

"The young female officer?" Mrs Khan asked. "She was a very nice girl."

"Yes, Officer Virdee," Harry said. "Now, Mr Khan, I have been asked to tell you by my Commanding Officer, Superintendent Smith, who you met on Saturday, that he does not feel any of you are involved. However, if we didn't search the house, it could lead to trouble for us and for you. People might speculate that because you're the home secretary's brother, we were giving you special treatment. They might even think your brother had put pressure on us, which might leave him open to rumours in the newspapers."

Mr Khan looked at his wife. She spoke first, "They are right, Safwan, you should have told Officer Virdee that they could come back and look round the house."

"I didn't get a chance, the policeman who came with Mahbeer sent her away," Mr Khan replied.

"Well, if one of my officers could get a statement from your son and the other man sitting over there, we will get out of your way as quickly as we can," Harry said.

"Yes, of course," Mr Khan said. "Mahir, come over here," he called to his son.

His son came over and stood by his mother, while Harry signalled to Danny to join them.

"This is Detective Constable Kane," Harry said. "If you go with him, he just wants to ask you a few questions about your sister and what happened on Friday."

"It's alright, you go with the officer and tell him all you can remember," Mrs Khan said to her son.

Danny led the son away to one side of the room.

"Would you like some tea?" Mrs Khan said to Harry.

"That would be very nice, thank you," Harry replied.

"Raju, get us some tea please and bring three cups. It is alright if he goes to get the tea?" Mrs Khan asked.

Harry nodded.

★★★

An hour later, Harry stood by the open front door. All the officers had left the house and were now in the vans. He had checked they had not made a mess in any of the rooms. Mr and Mrs Khan stood just inside the door.

"I am sorry for all the trouble," Harry said, "and I do hope you understand why we had to come here today."

"Yes, we understand, I should have realised yesterday," Mr Khan said.

"Thank you for the tea, Mrs Khan," Harry said. "If we get any news on the case, I will send Officer Virdee to tell you personally."

"Goodbye officer and thank you," Mrs Khan said.

They shut the doors as Harry walked away. Jordan, Danny and Inspector West were standing by the vans.

"Well done, Inspector, your officers did a great job," Harry said.

"We didn't find anything, though," West replied.

"I never expected to, Inspector. Let's get back to the station," Harry said.

"What about the two officers who we have in the back of the van?" West said.

Harry looked at Jordan and Danny, "Oh, sod it, let's take them back to the station and do them for obstruction."

"Are you sure, Harry?" West said.

Harry gave West a look.

"Okay, obstruction it is," West said.

★★★

Arriving back at the station, all of the officers piled out of the vans. Harry got them together, thanked them for a good job and sent them off to carry on with their normal duties.

"Inspector, you and Danny take those two into the custody suite," Harry said, pointing at the two officers from the Diplomatic Protection Squad. "Charge them with obstruction and let them make a phone call. I dare say someone will come and get them, but we have to make a point. Then, come up to the office. Jordan will make us all tea and we can sit and chat."

"Two sugars, tea boy," Danny said.

"It's not the sugar in your tea you should worry about," Jordan said.

Danny got the two officers out of the van. Inspector West buzzed the custody door and they took them in. The sergeant behind the counter looked up.

"Hello, Inspector West, how are you?" he said.

"Fine thanks, Sergeant. These two here," the inspector pointed at the two officers, "are being charged with obstruction."

The sergeant looked at the two officers and back at Inspector West, "Is this a joke, Sir?"

"No, Sergeant. Once they are processed, let them have a phone call and stick them in a cell," West said.

The sergeant had thought he had seen it all, until now. "Okay, Sir."

★★★

AC Crick looked at Walker.

"I think there may have been a misunderstanding on your part about how the investigation was being run. I'm sure all Detective Constable Virdee was doing was trying to explain what needed to be done, but you assumed she was being unfeeling towards the family."

"I am sorry," Walker interrupted, "but I know what went on at the house and this officer's behaviour fell well below the standards I expect – and from the tone of her commanding officer," he pointed at Charlie, "I can understand why."

"That being the case," Crick said, "you should have contacted me with your observations and I would have dealt with it. I don't think it is right that my officers should be summoned to your office for a dressing down."

"You may be right on that point," Walker said, "but I felt her behaviour in front of the family and the home secretary needed addressing. I had also said that the home of Mr Khan should only be searched with a prior arrangement, yet I have just been informed that a search of the house has taken place this morning, with officers turning up in vans. I hope they had a proper warrant."

Crick looked sideways at Charlie. "Is that true?" he said.

"Yes, Sir, a magistrate issued a search warrant," Charlie said. "The search was led by Chief Inspector Davis, my second in command. I felt the inquiry was being held back; the girl was not killed where she was found, so we needed to rule the house out as a place of the murder." Charlie looked directly at Walker, "Just good simple policing, really. Any enquiry would follow the same procedures."

Walker said nothing, but his eyes bore into Charlie who returned his gaze.

"If I might ask one question of AC Walker," Charlie said. "Sir, may I ask if your department has any interest in our case or the murdered girl, or if her family are of interest to you?"

Charlie saw Walker sit back slightly in his seat, "The only interest I have is your officer's attitude at the family home."

He didn't answer my question, Charlie thought.

Crick looked at Charlie, then to Walker. "I think I will sort this out with my officers," Crick said. "I feel there may have been a misunderstanding. If you would leave it in my hands, I will deal with it."

Walker looked at Crick, "I hope you will send me a note of what decision you have taken regarding your officer." He turned and looked at Charlie, "I hope, Chief Superintendent that you will take this as a word of caution and in future give a better lead to your officers. Some people think your lifestyle does not fit in with good policing, especially when doubts have been raised in some quarters about your, shall we say, spending power. Rumours start."

Charlie looked at Walker, smiled and said, "Thank you, Sir, for your words of advice. As for rumours, I don't give them much thought. I only buy something if I can afford it and I always try to give a good lead to my officers."

Crick stood up, "We won't take up any more of your time."

Charlie and Manjitt stood, "I will inform you of the outcome of my chat with my officers," Crick said.

Crick and Manjitt turned to go to the door, while Charlie stood still for a moment. "It was nice meeting you, Sir," he said, "I dare say our paths might cross again in the future."

Walker looked at Charlie, "Who knows? Let's hope for your sake they don't."

Charlie turned and followed Crick and Manjitt out of the door.

* * *

Nothing was said between the three as they made their way back down to the seventh floor to AC Crick's office. When they entered, Crick laid his hat on his desk and took his seat.

"Okay, you two. Sit down," he said.

Charlie and Manjitt took a seat.

"Well, that was a strange meeting," Crick said. "Detective Constable Virdee, I will deal with you first. I don't attach any blame to you in this incident, as I feel that AC Walker was not aware of the full facts regarding the investigation. In any case, he should have come to me with his complaint."

"Thank you, Sir," Manjitt said.

"If you would like to wait outside now, while I speak to the Chief Superintendent," Crick said.

Manjitt got up and left the office.

Crick looked at Charlie. "I don't really know what to make of that meeting," Crick said, "but I get the feeling there was more going on than just him tearing a strip off Virdee."

"He didn't answer my question about his department being involved with the family or girl," Charlie said. "I think there is something else going on that we don't know about yet."

"Well, Charlie, I get the impression you're not his favourite person, so tread carefully," Crick said. "He is an officer known for being a bit ruthless when it comes to getting his way."

"I will bear that in mind," Charlie said, "and thank you for supporting Virdee at the meeting."

"I quite enjoyed it. I always know anything involving you or your officers is never uneventful," Crick said. "Be on your way, Charlie, and keep me up to speed."

"I will, Sir."

Charlie rose to leave, but as he got to the door, Crick called him, "Charlie, watch your back. Walker is not a person to cross."

Charlie left the office. Manjitt was waiting outside.

"Come on then, let's get back and do some real police work," he said to her.

Up on the ninth floor, Walker had been quietly fuming at the attitude of the Chief Superintendent. He made a couple of calls, and then put a call through to the home secretary to arrange a meeting.

* * *

Harry was seated in his office, after returning from searching the house. Jordan gave him a cup of tea.

"That all went to plan, Harry," Jordan said. "I checked the girl's room and it was all neat and tidy – nothing out of the ordinary in there."

"I think the boss is right," Harry said. "There is something not quite right about this case, but let's keep beavering away and see what turns up."

Danny and Inspector West came into the office.

"Where's my tea?" Danny said. Jordan passed him a cup. "Hope I don't wake up with stomach pains after this."

Danny sat down opposite Harry. West stayed standing and Jordan passed him a cup, too.

"Did you get anything from talking to the son and that man, Raju? He must be their butler or something," Harry said to Danny.

"The butler was not very helpful," Danny said. "He saw her on Friday around the house and when she left in the late afternoon, nothing else. The son was more interesting. He said he spent quite a bit of time catching up with her. She was telling him all about university – he wants to go to Oxford, too. Anyway, he said she got two phone calls, he was not too sure of the time, and she also made one. He said it was about ten minutes before she left and she knew the person she had been talking to because she had joked with them. He didn't know whether it was a man or woman though."

"Well, we now know she had her phone when she left the house," Harry said. "I will get onto the mobile phone company about her call record – they must have done it for me by now."

"May I join you?"

They all looked towards the door. Chief Superintendent Myles was standing there. Harry and Danny stood up.

"Yes, Ma'am, can I help you?" Harry said.

"Chief Inspector Davis, I have just had a commander from the Diplomatic Protection Squad on the phone to me, asking why I had arrested two of his officers. Of course, I could not tell him, as I did not know. He then asked what sort of a station I was running when I did not know my officers were arresting his. I take it there's an explanation for this."

"Yes, Ma'am," Harry said, "they were obstructing us in our duty of carrying out a search of the murdered girl's house, with a warrant obtained from a magistrate. I thought it right to arrest them, otherwise vital evidence may have been tampered with or destroyed in the house."

"A very nice answer, but you could just have asked them to move out of the way," Myles said.

"I did and they didn't, so they left me no alternative, Ma'am," Harry replied.

She looked around at the others standing in the room, "Inspector West, were you there?"

"Yes, Ma'am," West said.

"And is that what happened?" she asked.

"Yes, Ma'am," West replied.

Turning back to Harry, she said, "Well, Chief Inspector, in future if you arrest anyone in the course of this enquiry, you will inform me – and I mean anyone. Is that clear?"

"Yes, Ma'am," Harry said.

"And Inspector West, I want to see you in my office in an hour."

"Yes, Ma'am," West said.

She turned and left the office. No one said anything for a while, and then Jordan said to West, "I think you're going to get your bottom smacked."

"Can you imagine if the boss and her got it together, what their kids would be like?" Danny said.

"Listen, Inspector," Harry said, "whatever she says to you, just blame me – say I told you this and I told you that. When the boss gets back, I will have a word. He can go and see her, smooth things over."

Oscar came into the office. "Hi all," he said. "Inspector, I just saw your boss on the stairs and she didn't look too happy. Who's upset her?"

Danny and Jordan pointed at Harry.

"Why did I bother asking?" Oscar said.

"Listen, Pelé, you better have something for me," Harry said, "or I will have you on late duty for the rest of your career."

"Well, I do Harry, but it's a bit strange. The van that was outside the boss's house, I ran the number plate and it doesn't exist. Now, I know that's not strange, a couple of bad boys in a van with dodgy number plates, but I have been sorting through all the pictures Danny took yesterday outside the house and look…"

He passed Harry two photographs.

Harry took them, had a look and turned to Danny. "This picture here," he gave it to Danny. "Where did this bloke come from?"

Danny had a look at it. "I think he arrived in the support car that was with the home secretary. He got out, wandered back to the road and had a look up and down it. I suppose he was checking for anyone following them."

"Okay, everyone," Harry said. "Go and get on with what you were doing. Jordan, you get on to the Germans – we have to get hold of that boy. Inspector, you and Danny get on and find us that BMW – that's the priority now. Remember, whichever officers you use, I don't want a whisper getting out. Danny, don't forget to type up the statements you took."

They left the office.

"Sit down, Pelé," Harry said. "Did anyone else pop up twice in any of the pictures?"

"Only Manjitt – Danny took quite a few of her. Oh, and a Mr Wade came up to the office earlier. I think I upset him a bit."

"The press officer," Harry said.

"Yes, he told me he was, but I said he could not come into any of these offices without your permission and chucked him out. He did say I had to tell the boss that there is a press conference at five."

"Where is the press conference being held?" Harry said.

"I don't know, I shut the door before he told me," Oscar said.

"Well, do me a favour and go and find out."

"Where's his office?" Oscar said.

"I don't know," Harry said, "find that out, too."

Oscar got up and left the office. Harry picked up the phone.

★★★

Assistant Commissioner Walker was sitting talking to two of his junior officers. They were in the waiting area of the home secretary's office. An assistant to the home secretary was at her desk, working at a computer.

"When we go in to see him, I will do all the talking unless I ask either one of you to confirm something," Walker said. The two officers nodded. "I don't want him thinking we don't have all the facts. We have to make him think we are trying to help him to keep things under wraps."

The assistant stood up and called to Walker that the home secretary would see them now. She opened the door to let Walker and the two officers into the home secretary's office.

The home secretary stood up from behind his desk.

"Hello, Walker, please take a seat. Would you and your officers like some tea or coffee?"

"No thank you, Sir," Walker said.

The home secretary waved his hand and the assistant closed the doors and left.

"Well, what is it you wanted to discuss with me that was so important?"

"Well, Sir, something has just been brought to my attention concerning your brother's daughter," Walker said.

"What? You have information about her murder?" the home secretary asked.

"No, Sir, I am sorry to tell you this, but we believe she may have been mixed up in a terrorist plot," Walker said.

The home secretary sat silent for a minute or two, his mind trying to take in what had just been said. Walker watched him. He knew he had the home secretary were he wanted him; he would play it slow and make it seem like he was trying to help.

The home secretary asked Walker what evidence he had.

"Well, Sir, since earlier this year, we have been picking up rumours of a terrorist plot," Walker said. "What made this unusual were the rumours it was being run by a woman. Now, we have not seen this before, so we thought it might be a ruse to throw us off the scent of a real plot. However, we then got a photo of an Englishwoman who had appeared in Pakistan according to our contacts out there. They said she had met up with some known al Qaeda sympathisers and disappeared into the tribal areas. Four days later, she reappeared in Peshawar and stayed there one day. She then took a plane to Iran and onto Turkey, where she stayed three days before flying back to London."

"Surely you're not telling me it was my niece?" the home secretary said. "I find that highly unlikely. I have seen her grow up and have spoken to her many times. She was never interested in politics; whenever her father and I would start talking about it, she would leave saying how boring it was."

"I understand it has come as a shock to you and I had it double-checked as soon as this information was brought to my attention."

Walker held out his hand and the man to his left gave him a large envelope. Walker pulled a photograph from it and passed it to the home secretary. It showed a young woman dressed in a Shalwar Kameez, with a headscarf covering long dark hair that hung down her back. She was with two men in what appeared to be a crowded market.

. "That picture was taken in a market in Peshawar," Walker said. "The two men with her are al Qaeda operatives."

"It's not a very good picture; it could be any young girl," the home secretary said.

"Yes, but our Pakistani colleagues say it's her," Walker replied. "When we got this information from them, we checked the flight she had taken from Turkey back to this country." He took another picture from the envelope. "We got this from the CCTV at Heathrow." He passed the picture to the home secretary.

The home secretary looked at the picture. It showed a young woman passing through customs. It looked like Ashadieeyah, but was grainy and not the best of pictures.

"I still can't believe that's her," he said. "What else have you got?"

"Well, we have been watching her on and off for a few months now," Walker said. "She must have been well trained because she never tipped us off that she was up to anything. However, that's not to say she hadn't been in contact or met others who are involved – so many people come and go from the university, it's hard to keep track of who's who. When we heard she had been murdered, though, I sent some men to search her room at the university in case anyone she was connected to tried to cover their tracks. We recovered her laptop, which is being examined. We hope to get some information off it that will give us some leads."

"What are you going to do next?" the home secretary asked.

"I understand this is very delicate for you," Walker said, "but hopefully we will get some information from the laptop on what the target of the plot was and who else was involved. You may have been the target."

"I can't believe that for one second," the home secretary said. "You are talking about my brother's daughter, who I have watched grow up."

"I can understand your reluctance to believe that, Sir," Walker replied.

"So, do you know why she was murdered?"

"We think there may have been a falling out with some of the terrorists she was working with," Walker said. "Maybe they resented her being a woman and the leader, or somehow they discovered we were onto her and killed her before she led us to them. We might know more when we have gone through her laptop completely. I would like to have a chat with your brother and his wife about any old or new friends she met – if you could speak to them. We want to keep it as quiet as we can. I don't want to cause any embarrassment to you."

Walker and the two officers with him stood up.

"Sir, we don't want to stop the ongoing inquiry into her murder, as it might tip any terrorists off that we know about them. If they think it's just a murder investigation that the police are carrying out, it keeps us ahead of them. I will keep you informed of any developments."

* * *

Ten mintues later, they were in the car heading back to Scotland Yard.

"I think that went very well," Walker said. "Now, I want us to find out how far Chief Superintendent Smith and his team have got with their inquiries. We need to be one step ahead." He spoke to the officer in the front seat, "We need to see what information they have gathered, so have someone check out their office. You might leave something behind, so we can keep up to date with what they're up to."

The officer in the front nodded, "I will get something from the technical boys."

Walker turned to the officer sitting in the back of the car with him.

"I want something on Chief Superintendent Smith."

* * *

Charlie and Manjitt arrived back at the station and made their way up to the offices.

Seeing them as he looked up from working, Harry said, "How was your meeting, boss?"

"Harry, you would love AC Walker, he's a first-class idiot. What surprised me is how Manjitt didn't give him a taste of her karate when she had the chance," Charlie said. "What's been happening here?"

"Well, the house search went as expected – we found nothing," Harry said. "I had a word with Mr Khan. I think he understood what we were doing and I think Mrs Khan has a soft spot for Manjitt. Danny got a statement from the son, who told us she got two phone calls and made one about ten minutes before she left the house. It seemed she knew who she was talking to according to the son, but he didn't know if it was a man or woman."

"Well, that makes the phone records vital," Charlie said.

"Oscar has discovered something, too. Here's your picture of the van outside your house." Harry passed the picture to Charlie. "We had no luck with the registration as it's on false plates, but here's a picture Danny took of people outside Mr Khan's yesterday." He handed over the second picture to Charlie. "The man in the picture Danny took yesterday got out of a car that was escorting the home secretary," Harry said.

"Well, we know what one of our gasmen does in his spare time," Charlie replied.

Charlie passed the pictures to Manjitt. "What would he be doing at your house pretending to be a gasman?" she asked Charlie.

"Now, that's a good question, Manjitt. Harry, ring Mike and tell him to switch all the cameras on inside and outside the house," Charlie said.

"Will do, boss," Harry said. "Also, I think you should pop in and see Chief Superintendent Myles. There's going to be a press conference at five."

"How are we doing on the BMW?" Charlie asked.

"They're still chasing it down – might take a bit of time, but West and Danny are on it," Harry replied.

"What about Jordan? Has he had any luck with the German boy?" Charlie asked.

"He's in there now…" Harry pointed at the other office, "trying to track him down."

"Okay, I am going to go down and see Caroline," Charlie said.

"Find out about the press conference; Manjitt, get hold of Pelé and I want you two to see if you can find out who he works for."

He handed Manjitt the picture Danny had taken. Charlie stood up and was just about to leave the office when Harry said, "Boss, I nearly forgot, Chief Superintendent Myles, or Caroline to you, was a bit upset about the way we did the raid on the house this morning."

Charlie turned. "Why? What happened?"

"I told you, the search was perfect. It's just we had to arrest the two coppers outside to get in and no one told her," Harry replied, smiling at Charlie.

"Thank you, Harry, for leaving the best news till last," Charlie turned and left the office.

* * *

A short time after, Charlie knocked on Caroline Myles' office door. Entering, he said, "Hello, Caroline, I understand there is going to be a press conference."

"Hello, Charlie," she said. "Yes, at five o'clock we are borrowing a hall at the school along the road from the station. I will give Mr Wade a call, ask him to come up to my office and go over it."

She picked up the phone and called Wade. After putting down the phone, she said, "Charlie, I had a problem with your team today. It slipped their mind to inform me that they had arrested two police officers and put them in the cells downstairs. I had an irate commander on the phone giving me hell about something I had no idea about."

"Yes, Chief Inspector Davis has told me that he forgot to tell you," Charlie said. "He's very sorry about it."

"Charlie, I have my doubts whether your chief inspector would know what sorry was. Does he ever look like he's not been dragged through a hedge? I can't believe your team's dress sense."

"I don't have them on my team for the way they dress," Charlie said. "They are some of the best coppers I have worked with and I know Harry can seem a bit off, but he's as sharp as a knife and keeps the team on their toes. He seems happy with your Inspector West."

"Why? What has he said about him? I have West coming to my office in a few minutes. He should have informed me what went on this morning," she said.

"Harry has not said a word about him, which means he's a good one. If he goes on about someone, it means they're no good at their job – and I bet I can tell you what your inspector says about this morning," Charlie said.

"Well, I hope he tells me what went on," Caroline replied, looking at Charlie.

"Oh, he will, but in what our team know as 'Harry speak'," Charlie said, smiling back.

There was a knock at the door. Caroline said 'Come in' and Inspector West popped his head round the door.

"You wanted to see me, Ma'am?"

"Yes, come in, West."

The inspector walked to her desk and stood in front of it. "Hello, Sir," he said to Charlie.

Charlie nodded.

"West, I was surprised that you did not bring me up to speed on what had occurred this morning," Caroline said.

"Yes, Ma'am, but Chief Inspector Davis said he was going to do that," West said.

"But you arrested two police officers and put them in the cells downstairs. Didn't you think you should have at least informed me of that?" she said.

"Well, Ma'am, Chief Inspector Davis told me to do that and I thought he would tell you what we had done," West said.

Caroline looked over at Charlie, who smiled.

"Okay, West, you can go. In future, I want to be informed about what is going on in my station."

"Yes, Ma'am."

West turned and left the office.

"I take it from that answer that was 'Harry speak'," Caroline said.

Charlie smiled. "Yes, he is a good officer, your West."

★ ★ ★

Jordan came in to see Harry.

"I have spoken to our German friends. The officer I have been speaking to went to the boy's address and it seems his father had died and the boy is nowhere to be found. He asked the neighbours, but they have not seen him since the funeral. He told me he put a bulletin out to all police stations, so if he turns up anywhere, he will be informed. There's not too much else we can do."

"Ring the other friends," Harry said, "and ask them that if he should get in touch, they should give him your number and get him to call you."

Jordan nodded. "Will do, Harry," he said.

★ ★ ★

Christopher Wade sat with Caroline and Charlie, outlining how he thought the press conference should go.

"Now, I will stress the need to find out about the girl's movements," Wade said. "Do we have a picture we can give them?"

"Yes, I will make sure you have it," Charlie said.

"I am not going to have any of the family there, but if we need to, we can do another press conference and get them to make a plea in front of the cameras. "Have we made any more progress with the case? Any new leads?"

"No, not too much. We've done house-to–house, but nothing. The report you got is just about everything we know," Charlie said.

"I understand you searched the family home this morning; was anything found?" Wade asked.

"No, nothing," Charlie said.

"Okay, I will read a statement on what we know so far and ask for help from the public," Wade said. "I will then invite questions. I will try and take most of them, but might ask you to make a comment on a specific point, Chief Superintendent. Is that okay?"

"Yes, fine with me, Mr Wade," Charlie said.

"Well, I will get back to my office," Wade said. "Oh, I had a run-in with one of your officers this morning. He didn't take kindly to me walking into his office, so he threw me out, told me I could not come in without being asked and shut the door on me."

"Well, I'm sure it wasn't personal and he was only doing what he had been told," said Charlie.

"Well, I will see you downstairs at about 4.40. We can walk down to the school," Wade said as he stood up. "Chief Superintendent Myles, I have asked a couple of your officers to go down there early and see the school caretaker and get the hall set up."

Charlie and Caroline both nodded. Wade left the office.

"Are you coming to the press conference?" Charlie asked Caroline.

"No, I will watch you on the news," she said.

Charlie stood up. "Caroline, before I go, there are a few funny things turning up in this case. I can't say anything about them yet, but if you get any funny phone calls from an outside force asking about our investigation or any of the officers working for me, will you let me know?"

Caroline looked at Charlie. "Yes, of course. If you think there's anything I can help with, just let me know."

Charlie left the office and went back upstairs. He found Harry still sorting through mountains of paper on his desk.

"Harry, did you ring Mike?" Charlie asked.

"Yes, boss," said Harry. "I have also got the girl's phone record on its way over to me, so hopefully we might get something from it. Jordan's not had a lot of luck chasing the German boy, but he's still working on it."

Charlie sat down, picked up his phone and dialled. The phone rang twice, before it was picked up, "Hello, Julian Squires speaking."

"Hello, Julian, it's Charlie."

"Charlie, good to hear from you. How have you been? Haven't heard from you for over a month," he said.

"Yes, been very busy lately, but I would like to get together for a chat soon," Charlie said.

"Well, I don't have too much on this week," Julian said.

"What about Wednesday evening? I will book a table at the usual place," Charlie said.

"That's good for me, Charlie. I will bring some papers that need signing and bring you up to speed on things."

"Thanks, Julian, see you there."

★★★

The school hall was like Charlie remembered from his childhood school, with the wooden floor and pictures painted by pupils decorating the walls. He was seated next to Wade on the small stage at one end of the hall. Seats were laid out in rows in front of them, and he realised now what it must have been like for the teachers during morning assembly looking down on the children. There were also a number of journalists seated with notebooks in hand and a couple of television crews positioned in the middle front of the floor.

Wade asked if everyone could settle down, introduced himself and Charlie, saying he would read a statement and then take questions. The press listened to Wade run through the report Harry had given him and when he was finished, he invited questions. Charlie listened; they were what he expected and Wade answered them easily. However, one journalist towards the back then asked,

"Is it true the home secretary tried to stop you searching the house of the murdered girl's family?"

Charlie couldn't see who asked the question, as the lights from the television cameras obscured his sight. He looked across at Wade, who held up his hand to him. "We have no comment to make on that matter," Wade said.

Charlie leaned in and whispered to Wade, "What do you mean? The home secretary never put any pressure on us."

Wade whispered back, "Please leave it to me, Chief Superintendent, I know how these things work."

Charlie sat back.

"So, are you saying that he did or didn't?" the journalist asked.

"As I said before, we have no comment to make on that matter," Wade replied.

Another journalist near the front asked if it could have been a kidnapping. Wade asked Charlie to answer, which he did and explained why they felt it wasn't.

The news conference went on for another ten minutes, until Wade called an end to it, saying they would hold another one in a few days to give an update on the investigation. He said he had pictures of the girl that he would pass out and anyone with information should contact them.

★★★

When they had got back to the station, Charlie pulled Wade to one side.

"Mr Wade, I don't like the way that press conference went and the thing about the home secretary. You should have just said there was no pressure on us."

"Chief Superintendent," Wade said, "I have done many press conferences. Believe me, when someone tries to bring politicians into the mix, it's best to make no comment."

"But that's being ambiguous. Surely the press will translate your 'No comment' as meaning that he did," Charlie said.

"I don't think so; they have to find something that says he did and us being non-committal doesn't give them anything," Wade replied.

Charlie shook his head. He wondered if Wade was listening to what he was saying. Charlie said he was going to go and see how his squad were progressing.

"Keep me up to date with everything," Wade called out as Charlie climbed the stairs.

When he got into the office, Harry was sitting with his hands behind his head. Charlie went and sat down at his desk.

"A good press conference, boss," Harry said.

Charlie looked over to see Harry smiling at him. "I have had some arseholes to work with before, but this one takes the biscuit. I just think he's opened a can of worms and he doesn't seem to know, or he does but is playing the dope. Do you think I am reading too much into it, Harry?"

"Boss, I watched it and I think every paper in the morning will be speculating about the home secretary interfering with the investigation," Harry said. "The appeal for help finding the killer will be lost."

"Surely it was not deliberate," Charlie said, "but it puzzled me nonetheless. Up to that point, all the questions were routine, then that one comes out of the blue. I didn't see who asked it, as they were at the back of the hall."

"You want me to do anything?" Harry asked.

Charlie sat for a minute. "Wade said he had done lots of press conferences; Harry, see if you can find out who he has worked with previously. I'm off home, see you in the morning."

★★★

Later that evening, the home secretary called at his brother's house. He stayed for over an hour, telling him all that he had been told by Assistant Commissioner Walker. He said it might be a good idea if the family went away for a while, because if the news broke, there would be lots of press and the house was likely to be besieged by reporters.

When he left the house, the home secretary phoned the prime minister's office. He was told the prime minister was at a reception, but he would be pencilled in for a private meeting first thing in the morning before the full cabinet met.

★★★

Manjitt was at her flat in Stratford. She lived on the fifth floor and was in the kitchen, making herself a sandwich. From the window, she could see the Olympic Stadium. She remembered the crowds that packed the area at the time of the Olympics and the trouble she had getting in and out. Thankfully, things had settled down now.

Her mobile phone suddenly went off. She picked it up along with her sandwich and walked through to her living room. She glanced at the number that came up, but it was not one she recognised.

"Hello," she said.

"Officer Virdee, this is Mrs Khan, can I talk to you?" she heard.

Manjitt thought she sounded a little distressed. "Yes, of course, Mrs Khan, but we don't have any news to tell you yet."

"But my brother in-law was here earlier and he told us." Mrs Khan began to sob down the phone.

"Mrs Khan, what's the matter?" Manjitt said. "Honestly, we have no new leads. I would tell you if we did. Please tell me what's happened and I will try to help you in anyway I can."

Mrs Khan calmed a little, but her voice was still breaking. "Could you come and see me tonight? I need to speak to you."

"Yes, of course, I will be there as soon as I can," Manjitt said.

When Manjitt rang off, she put a call through to Charlie. He told her to go to the house and call him back as soon as she discovered what the problem was.

* * *

Charlie had been sitting in his front room going over the case and all they had gathered so far, when he had recieved the call from Manjitt.

When she rang off, he got all the statements from the family together and reread them. He couldn't see anything that had been missed and all the verbal reports from his team who had come into contact with the family were of the opinion they were not involved. However, Mrs Khan's phone call worried him. *Had they missed something?* He would wait until Manjitt phoned him again.

He rose and went to the kitchen. His three greyhounds stood up as soon as he came in, so he pushed open the door and off they went into the dark of the garden. He stepped outside and the security lights automatically came on, turning night into day. He watched the dogs chase and race each other across the grass.

* * *

It took Manjitt just over an hour to get to the Khan's house. The traffic had been relatively light, so she had met no hold ups. She pulled onto the drive of the house, where the two police officers were again stationed outside. She got out of the car and walked to the front door.

One off the officers asked who she was and she showed her warrant card. He asked her what her business was with the family, so she told him it was none of his and to get out the way. He moved to the side; Manjitt knocked on the door and Raju opened it. She entered, slipping her shoes off. Raju said Mrs Khan was expecting her and she followed him to the main room.

Reaching the door, Raju knocked, pushed it open and Manjitt went in, Raju closed the doors behind him as he left them. Mrs Khan was seated with Mr Khan, and they both looked at Manjitt as she walked in. She could see that Mrs Khan had been crying, as her eyes were very red and she had a handkerchief screwed into a ball in her hands. They both stood up.

"Thank you for coming so quickly," Mrs Khan said.

"That's okay, what's the problem?" Manjitt said.

"Please come and sit with us," Mr Khan said.

Manjitt went and sat in the chair opposite them, and the Khans sat down and looked at each other for a moment. Mrs Khan then turned to Manjitt.

"As I told you, my brother in-law came this evening. He told Safwan that our daughter is a terrorist and had been plotting with others."

Manjitt was stunned by what she had heard. "What did he say exactly?" she asked Mr Khan.

He related everything his brother had told him. Manjitt thought for a moment.

"There must be some mistake, as all our enquiries have not shown anything of the sort," Manjitt said.

"You are not keeping anything from us, are you?" Mrs Khan asked.

"No, I promise you, I have been totally honest with you," Manjitt replied.

"But your senior officers might know something and not told you about it," Mr Khan said.

"No, it's not the way my senior officers work," Manjitt said. "I can assure you of that, Mr Khan."

"My brother wants me to take the family away," Mr Khan said, "to avoid all the press he says will be around the house."

"Would you mind if I made a phone call?" Manjitt asked.

She stood up and went to the far side of the room. She then

phoned Charlie and spent five minutes talking to him. After ending the call, she came back and sat with the Khans.

"I have just spoken to my boss and he has told me to tell you that he does not suspect your daughter of any form of terrorism and that we will get to the bottom of it."

Mrs Khan said, "I am sorry, I didn't offer you some refreshment, would you like some tea?"

"That would be nice, thank you," said Manjitt.

Mr Khan pressed the bell and Raju came in. "Bring tea for us please, Raju," he said.

Raju nodded and left the room.

"Where will you go if you have to get away for a while?" Manjitt asked.

"We have relatives in the Leicester area, so we will go and stay with them," Mr Khan said.

"My parents live in Leicester and that is where I was born," said Manjitt.

"Where are your parents from?" Mrs Khan asked.

"They came to this country in the 1970s from Uganda, to get away from the trouble out there," Manjitt replied. "My father was an engineer and got a job with a local company. My mother worked for a building society."

"Safwan's family," Mrs Khan pointed to her husband, "came from Kenya, also in the 1970s, while my parents are from Pakistan."

"Had your daughter travelled abroad much?" Manjitt asked.

"No, never," Mrs Khan said. "We were planning a holiday to Pakistan to visit all my relatives. We had been waiting till our son had had his sixteenth birthday and then we would go. I spoke to Ashadieeyah about it and she was looking forward to meeting all the family she had only ever seen in my old photographs."

Raju came into the room with the tea.

* * *

After Charlie got off the phone from talking to Manjitt, he phoned Harry. Next, he put a call through to Assistant Commissioner Crick and arranged to meet him tomorrow.

This case is running in some strange directions, Charlie thought. There were still some loose ends to tie up, before they could start to see what was really going on. He would speak to Mike in the morning and make sure he knew to be aware of any strange goings-on around the house.

★★★

Harry got to the station early, just past six in the morning. After Charlie's phone call last night, he wanted to get everything sorted and all the team on the ball. He had spoken to Jordan and told him to be in early, as he had a job for him to do.

Making his way up the stairs, he was surprised to see the lights on in the office and a man standing on a chair fiddling with the light bulb.

"Can I help you?" Harry said.

The man looked at Harry in the doorway. "I have been sent to check the electrics, apparently there have been a number of problems with shortages on the system. I am just checking the wiring."

"Who asked you to do that?" Harry said, "We've had no problems in here."

"I don't know, I just got asked by my office to run the checks," the man said.

"And who is your office?" Harry asked.

The man got down from the chair, took a card from his pocket and handed it to Harry. "I'm all done here now," he said. "Your wiring all seems okay."

Harry sat down in his chair, "Just wait a minute while I check." He started to dial the number on the card, "Who gave you the key to the office?"

"I got it from the front desk," the man said. "Is there a problem? I am only doing what I was asked."

"I am sure there's not, but these offices are connected to a murder investigation and no one should come in here without permission," Harry said.

The phone was ringing at the other end, but no one answered.

"I don't know if anyone will be in the office yet, might be a bit early for them," the man said.

"How many more offices have you got to check?" Harry asked.

"I have checked all I need to. It's why I get in early to do it, so there's no one in my way and I can get round without any hassle," the man said.

Jordan appeared at the office door.

"Morning, Harry," he said. He looked over at the man standing by Harry's desk, confused.

"He was sent to check out our electrics; there's been some shortages on the system," Harry said, pointing to the man. "They gave him a key at the front desk to get in."

"Sorry if it's caused a problem," the man said, "but no one told me I needed to check before I came in."

"That's okay," said Harry. "I will get hold of your office later. What's your name?"

"Jamie, Jamie Grant," the man answered.

"Well, Jamie, if you have finished in here, we have a lot to be going on with," Harry said.

"Yes, of course," Jamie said. He picked up his bag, left the office and went down the stairs.

Harry quickly got out of his seat, grabbed Jordan by the arm and took him out of the office. At the top of the stairs, he whispered in Jordan's ear, "Follow him, I want to know where he goes. Don't lose him."

Jordan disappeared down the stairs. Harry went back into the office and stopped by the door, knelt and had a look at the locks.

Standing up, he started to slowly search the office. After, he went to the front desk, checked with them who had made the appointment for the electrician to come in and if he had been given any keys for the offices that were locked. Yes, he had been, but not Harry's, as the front desk did not have any.

Harry went out into the station car park and phoned Charlie.

***

After speaking to Harry, Charlie left the house and stopped briefly to speak to Mike. He then put a call through to Julian, who said he would get back to Charlie as soon as he had made a few calls. Charlie next put a call through to Assistant Commissioner Crick, putting their meeting off until later in the day. He would drive straight over to the station and speak to Harry and the team first. Harry had rung all the team, telling them there was going to be a debrief at 9.30am, but to meet in the canteen.

Charlie arrived at the station at 8.30 and found Harry sitting in the small canteen, where he had said he would meet him. On the door, a sign said, 'Closed. Do not enter unless invited. Do not even open this door or you will face a disciplinary.'

"Morning, boss," Harry said. He got Charlie a cup of tea and sat back down. "I rang everyone and told them to meet us in here and not to go near the offices. I have locked them all up again."

"It's lucky you got in early, Harry. What do you reckon?" Charlie said.

"He was a pro, not a sign on the locks that they had been tampered with, but he had no idea we had changed them," Harry said. "He said he got the keys from the front desk. I double–checked and they don't have any of our keys, so we just have to make sure everyone on the team has theirs with them."

"What about the case?" Charlie asked.

"Well, we don't know how long he had been in there, but we

have to assume he got a look at everything we have written down," Harry said. "The only thing that there's no report on yet, is our BMW, so he won't know anything about that. Everything else, however, is compromised."

"How much do you want to bet I know where our so-called Mr Grant leads Jordan to?" Charlie said.

"I think I will keep my money in my pocket, boss," Harry said, "as I have a feeling I know as well. Oh, I did find out that our Mr Wade has worked on a number of cases for the Anti-Terrorism Squad as their press spokesman."

★★★

The team all arrived one by one. By 9.30am, they were all there except Jordan. Harry asked everyone to show their office keys – all had them and all said they had not given theirs to anyone else.

Charlie addressed the team, "Now, we are meeting in here and I am not going to go over everything with you, as there have been a few strange happenings lately. I aim to get everyone together later and we will be in a position to put you in the picture. For now, I want everyone to get on with what they were doing on the case, but don't use the offices and don't phone in to speak to anyone until Harry or I tell you. Okay, get on with things. Manjitt, you stay here for a moment."

The rest of the team left and they filled Manjitt in on what had been going on that morning.

Charlie's phone rang. He spoke for a couple of minutes, "Thanks, Julian, they are to ask for Chief Inspector Davis when they arrive. Are they bringing those other things I asked for? Great, see you Wednesday", before ringing off. As he did, Jordan appeared at the canteen door. Harry waved him over to join them. Jordan sat down next to Manjitt.

"Morning, boss," he said to Charlie. "Well, Harry, our Mr Grant took me all the way back to Scotland Yard. I watched him go through security and drive down into the car park. I left it at that and came back."

"I saved my money, I think," Harry said to Charlie. He turned to Jordan, "Do you have your office key?"

Jordan fished his key from his pocket and held it up.

"Listen, you two," Charlie spoke, addressing Manjitt and Jordan, "we have to assume that our investigation is compromised. Why, we don't know yet, but I think we can say people who are working for Assistant Commissioner Walker of the Anti-Terrorism Squad are taking a strange interest in us. I am meeting AC Crick later and will fill him in on what's been going on. Let's see if he can get some answers."

"I picked up a paper on the way back," Jordan said. "Have a look at the headlines." He pushed the paper across the table and the headline read, 'Home Secretary pressures police enquiry'.

"We will see what our press officer has to say about that later," Charlie said. "Now, Harry and I will sit down with the rest of the team later, but there are a couple of loose ends around the family we have to tie up. Manjitt, I want you to go back to the family and see if they are going to move in with their relatives for a while.

"Also, I know Mrs Khan said her daughter had not been abroad, but we know the home secretary told them she had been to Pakistan, supposedly plotting with terrorists. What I want to know is, can they find out when she was supposed to have gone? The only time we cannot place her is the two weeks of the walking holiday with our German friend, so ask Mr Khan if he can get the dates from the home secretary. I think we will have to take them into our confidence and explain what we are trying to do. Tell Mr Khan to be as careful as he can when he asks for the dates; perhaps work something out with him when you're there. If he's not too sure, ring me and I will speak to him."

There was a knock at the canteen door. They all looked up to see a constable standing there, who Harry signalled to come in.

"Sir, there are two men downstairs to see you," he said to Harry.

"Shall I bring them up here?" Harry said.

Charlie nodded and Harry left with the constable.

"Harry is going to bring some people up who are going to, shall we say, give us a bit of technical support," Charlie said. "I want you to listen to them carefully."

Harry appeared at the door with two men in dark suits, each carrying a large briefcase. Harry invited them to sit down, closing the canteen door behind him. Harry introduced them to Charlie. The older of the two, who had a tightly cut beard, spoke to Charlie.

"Our company was contacted by Mr Julian Squires, who is one of our valued customers. He said we could be of service to you."

He spoke with a foreign accent, but Charlie could not place it.

"Did you bring everything he asked you to?" Charlie said.

The younger of the two placed his briefcase on the desk and opened it. He handed Charlie a mobile phone, "We have eight of these as requested, and all eight numbers are listed on each phone. They are all encrypted, so anyone one listening in will not be able to decipher the conversations. They are state-of-the–art."

He placed the other seven on the table in front of Charlie.

"I also have four of these interceptors to check for audio or visual bugs." They were small, about hand-sized. "These are the latest models; they can detect GPS tracker devices, wireless cameras or mobile phone tracking where a burst signal is being used to transmit a signal, which would be missed by normal detectors. It gives off an audible noise when something is detected, but you have an earpiece so no one will know that you have found whatever's there."

"Thank you," Charlie said, "will you run through how to use them with my officers?"

Over the next ten minutes, he went over the full use of the devices, showing how they are operated and what could be detected.

"Harry, will you take the two gentlemen up to the office? I will join you in a few minutes," Charlie said. The two men left with Harry. Charlie turned to Manjitt and Jordan. "Now, I know this all seems a bit over the top, but I have a horrible feeling that someone wants to know our every move."

Charlie gave them one of the new phones each, noting the telephone number down by their name. "I want you to use these to talk to anyone on the team about the case. I will get Harry to ring you with everybody's number, but also use the normal phones for normal conversations – as if anyone is listening in, we want them to think we don't have any idea what's going on. Now, you two will each take one of these." He handed them each an intercept detector. "Manjitt, I want you to sweep the Khan's house with this. Jordan, you keep this on you and I will go over with you in a while what I want you to do. Manjitt, you get off now to the Khan's."

Manjitt left the canteen. Charlie asked Jordan to help him take the rest of the phones and detectors up to the office, where they found Harry seated with the two men.

"Was there anything?" Charlie asked.

Harry held up a small device. "It's not working now, but it was in the wall socket over there," he said.

Charlie and Jordan placed the phones and detectors on the table, and Charlie spoke to the two men, "Thank you, gentlemen, for all your help. If we should need you again, I will be in touch through Mr Squires."

The two men stood.

"Anytime we can be of service," the older one said.

"Harry, will you take them down to the front desk and see them out?"

Charlie shook their hands and they left with Harry.

"Well, Jordan, now you can see," he held up the small listening device that had been placed in the wall socket, "that someone wants to know everything that's going on in here."

Charlie sat down, before continuing, "Harry and I have been thinking about this German boy. I want you to get onto the phone to that German officer you spoke to and see if he has had any luck finding him, but also drop into the conversation the question of whether anyone else has been asking about him. Then, phone all the friends up again and see if they have any idea where he might have gone – ask them if any other police have been in contact and the dates of the walking holiday. If Manjitt gets a date from Mr Khan, we can see if they match."

Jordan got up and left the office. Charlie put the bug that had been discovered in his pocket, and Harry came back in and sat down.

"Those two characters you got in are a bit scary," Harry said. "It just shows the things that can be done without you even knowing. Where did you find them?"

"Julian's firm has used them in the past and their company put the security system in at my house," Charlie said. "I will have to go down and talk to Caroline about what went on this morning. Call the others in, have a word with them about what has gone on and issue them with a phone each. We have to find that BMW, Harry – it's the key to this and the longer it's missing, the less chance we have. Put all the rest of the team on it. I also want a result on the German and what's happened to those phone records? Once I've spoken to Caroline, I am off to see Crick at the Yard."

"I will get everyone shifting, don't worry," Harry said.

* * *

The home secretary sat in a side room of the main cabinet meeting room at Number Ten, waiting for the prime minister. The newspapers on his lap did not make for good reading and the headlines were sure to have been badly received. How had the papers come by the story? To make it worse, the police not denying he had interfered in their enquiry at their press conference was not a great help, and now he had to discuss with the prime minister that his niece might be mixed up in a terrorist plot.

The doors opened and the prime minister came in, followed by the party chairman and the chief whip. The home secretary stood and they exchanged pleasantries. They all sat down at a table.

"Well, home secretary, I see you have the morning papers," the prime minister said. "Would you like to explain to us how you got into this position?"

The home secretary proceeded to go through everything that had happened at his brother's house.

"And you have had no other contact with the police carrying out the investigation into the girl's death?" the party chairman asked.

"No, none at all," he replied.

"Well, that should be easy enough to clear up," the prime minister said. "We can get hold of the chief investigating officer and he can issue a statement clarifying what went on. However, I understand you have a more pressing matter you want to speak to me about."

The home secretary then ran through everything Assistant Commissioner Walker had told him.

The prime minister turned to the chief whip.

"What do you think?" he asked.

"Well, in the short term, as long as nothing gets into the press about it, we can wait and see where the enquiry goes – but I think we should keep in contact with the Anti-Terrorism Squad, in case we have to decide on any action the home secretary needs to take," the chief whip said.

The prime minister turned to the party chairman, "What are your thoughts?"

"It could be a delicate matter if something did happen. Especially if it came out that we knew about it," he replied.

"I will speak to the commissioner later and see if he can tell us more," the prime minister said. "If you want to go and join the rest of the cabinet, home secretary, we will be in shortly."

The home secretary stood and left the room.

"This could turn into a disaster if we are not careful," the prime minister said.

"We have the new terrorist legislation coming up for a vote soon," the chief whip said. "We don't need any bad publicity, as we only just have enough support to get it through parliament."

"We may have to ask the home secretary to write a resignation letter, just in case we hear some bad news and need to move fast," the party chairman said. "We might have to dissuade him from running for the leadership."

"I agree with the party chairman," the chief whip said. "We can't have him running with this over his head. If he wins and then it came out that his niece was a terrorist, it would be a disaster for the party."

"Let's sort out the first problem," the prime minister said. He turned to the party chairman, "Speak to whoever is running the murder investigation and get the interference bit clarified; get a statement from them pointing out the home secretary has not interfered in the investigation."

The prime minister rose. "Now, let's go into the cabinet meeting and I shall make my announcement about stepping down. Have you got the press conference scheduled for straight after?"

The party chairman nodded.

* * *

Charlie was sitting opposite Caroline.

"I told you the other day I thought this investigation had some funny things going on in it. Well, this morning has confirmed our suspicions."

He got the listening device from his pocket and put it on the table.

Caroline picked it up. "What is it?" she said.

"It's a bug; it was placed in our office to listen in on everything we say about the case," Charlie replied.

"Who put it there, the press or a private detective? And how did he get into the building?" Caroline asked.

"No, none of them. Harry actually walked in when the man had just finished placing it. He had Jordan tail him when he left the police station," Charlie said, "and he followed him all the way to Scotland Yard."

Caroline sat silent for a minute. "This is all a bit too strange – you're telling me the police are spying on the police?"

"I will take you into our confidence, Caroline, and tell you all we know about this case and the strange happenings that have happened along the way," Charlie said, before relating everything from the beginning.

When he had finished, Caroline said, "It does seems that there is something else going on in the background. You think our press officer, Wade, is mixed up in it, too? Why don't we get him in? He needs to explain how he is going to deal with what has come out in the papers this morning anyway, and I think he wants to hold another press conference in the late afternoon."

"I am going to Scotland Yard first. When I am finished there, I will ring you. If you can get him up to your office for when I get back, we can see what he's got to say – but we must be careful that he doesn't know we suspect him."

Charlie took the last of the eight phones and gave it to Caroline.

"When I call you or you need to get hold of me, only use this phone. No one will be able to monitor our conversations."

Caroline took the phone. "It's all getting a bit cloak and dagger, Charlie," she said.

"All I am worried about, Caroline, is a murdered girl and I don't want anyone interfering in that. I will call you when I am finished at the Yard. Can I ask that you speak to all your officers and tell them that if they have contact from anyone from an outside force regarding our case, they are to report it to you immediately Tell them there's a corruption case against some officers and they should avoid getting mixed up in it."

Charlie stood and left the office.

Caroline phoned the duty desk sergeant and told him to come up to her office. She wanted to know who had authorised the checking of the electrics.

***

Harry had got in touch with Danny, Oscar and Inspector West. They had all arrived at the office and were now seated around the desk.

"Right, you three, give me some good news," Harry said.

"I think we have some for you," West said. "We have got 125 BMWs registered in the geographical area that we have been looking at. Out of those, thirty-two are series 5s – we are getting a list together for addresses."

"Well, run the series 5s first, but you will have to check the others just in case we got the description wrong," Harry said. "How many men do you have on it with you?"

"Apart from us, just three other officers," West said. "There is a big demonstration up in London and all the spare coppers have been taken to that."

"Well, you are going to have to split it between you three," Harry said. "Each take one of the spare officers with you. Now, we don't want to tip off whoever has this car, so let's find out that a car does belong at those addresses and then run background checks on whoever lives there. We will see what we come up with. Good work, though. Now, here is a new phone for each of you."

Harry wrote their name beside the number of each phone, then ran through all that had happened and how they should contact each other. When they left the office, Harry rang the mobile phone company to find out what had happened to the phone records of Ashadieeyah Khan.

Jordan had managed to catch the German officer he had spoken to previously, who told him he had found out the boy had gone to the Alps to do some hiking. The officer had spoken to one of the boy's aunts, who said that after the funeral he had wanted to go away for a while. He would be calling in on some family that lived around the German-Swiss border, but she could not say when as he had not given any precise dates.

Jordan had asked if anyone else had been in touch about the boy. The German officer had said yes, but it was strange as his office had had a call from the BND, which is part of the German Anti-Terrorism Police. Jordan said he didn't know why they would be interested in the boy, but thanked him for all his help.

He then set about trying to contact Ashadieeyah's friends to see if he could get a date for the walking holiday and if Karl had been in touch.

★★★

Charlie was in AC Crick's office at Scotland Yard. He had just finished briefing him on all that had gone on. The photos and the listening device were on the table.

Crick spoke, "This is a strange one, Charlie. We had that meeting with Walker and he must have known all along what we had come to see him about. I have had a call from the prime minister's office this morning, too, about making a statement that the home secretary has not interfered with the investigation."

"Well, that's true. He hasn't," Charlie said. "That's down to Wade."

"Well, I will get one out saying he has not and has been extremely helpful – or words to that effect," Crick said. "But how are we going to play this, Charlie? There seems to be a lot going on."

"I want to see where it leads us," Charlie said. "We have a couple of things going for us, like the fact they don't know we are onto them with all their spying. They also don't have the information on the car."

"Okay, Charlie, but be careful. Walker is a hard nut and has a lot of friends in high places," Crick said. "I will write up a report on everything you have told me, just in case we need it, and I will keep it locked away."

Charlie gathered all the pictures together and slipped the listening device into his pocket. "I will keep you updated on anything else that happens," he said.

"Be very careful, Charlie," Crick said.

Charlie left the office and made his way back to the car park and climbed into his Bentley. When he was seated, he took the scanner out of his pocket, turned it on and waved it all over the car, nothing. He switched it off, took out his phone, called Caroline and arranged for her to get a meeting with Mr Wade. She told him that Wade had phoned her and he was holding another press conference at 6.30pm. She said she would tell Wade to come to her office at 5.30pm for a planning meeting.

* * *

Danny, Oscar and Inspector West each took one constable with them, split up and went searching for the black BMW. They each took a third of the list, on which were the details of the cars' registered keepers and the addresses. It would take some time as people might not be in or may have moved, sold the car and not updated their information with the DVLA.

Oscar was on his sixth address. He pulled up in front of a normal terraced house, like thousands of others in the outer suburbs of London. He looked along the road, but didn't see any BMW parked. He walked up the path, rang the doorbell and waited, but there was no answer. He turned to leave, when his eye caught a face at the window on the first floor. He turned and rang the bell again, keeping a watch on the window. The face didn't appear, but there was still no answer. He walked back to the car where the constable was sitting.

"I thought I saw someone at the top window on the left," he said.

The constable looked up, "Don't see anyone there."

"Give me the list with the names on it," Oscar said.

The constable passed him the list. Oscar read down it until he came to the name: Mirla Fournier, registered keeper of a black series five BMW. Oscar didn't know if the face had been a man's or a woman's. He put a circle round the name. He would do some more background checks when he got back to the station, but they would press on with the list as they still had a lot to get through.

* * *

Charlie got back to the station and walked into the office to find Harry and Jordan sorting through reports.

"Tell me we have some leads to follow," Charlie said.

"We have a list of BMWs and addresses," Harry replied. "The team are out visiting them now, but there are 125 on it. It might take some time, but it's a start."

"How did you get on with the German boy?" Charlie asked Jordan.

"Not so good, he's gone off walking in the Alps. He was upset after his father's funeral and needed to get away. The German policeman spoke to one of his aunts, so if he turns up, she will get him to call. One strange thing, though, the German told me he had a call about the boy from the BND – who are their Anti-Terrorism Police. I also managed to get hold of a couple of her other friends. One said she was not sure when Ashadieeyah went away, but the other two thought it was the second week in July."

"Well, at least we have a little nugget to go on," Charlie said, "but someone must have been asking for him to be checked out too, by the sound of it, we won't be taking any bets on who that is. Harry, what about the phone records? Tell me you got them."

Harry held up the list, "I have a strange tale to tell as well, boss."

"Now, why am I not surprised?" Charlie sat down.

"I got onto the phone company again today and they told me they had sent it over already. After a few heated words, they came back to me and said that an officer, a Constable Jamie Grant, had said that they should be sent over to Scotland Yard and not to us. You remember our Mr Grant, boss? He happens to have the same name as our electrician from this morning. Might just be coincidence, but call me suspicious. Anyway, I have them now."

Charlie looked at Jordan. "Jordan, run a check on the system and see if there is a Constable Jamie Grant."

Jordan got up and went next door.

Harry continued, "On the day the girl went missing, the last two calls she made were to the same number and the last call she received was from the same number. I've checked it out and the phone is a pay-as-you-go. It was bought two weeks ago from a phone shop in the Bentall Shopping Centre in Kingston. I put a call through to them and they are going to check their CCTV for the day of the phone purchase. I told them how important it was, so hopefully we will get something."

"At least we are starting to get a picture together," Charlie said, "if a little hazy. We know from Ashadieeyah's brother that he thought she knew whoever it was she was talking to on the phone. The phone was purchased from a shopping centre not too far away, so I'm guessing whoever it is lives close. Remember, Harry, that Jamie Grant's friends know about her phone, too. Send Jordan over to the shopping centre; he needs to get any evidence from there before our Jamie Grant turns up."

Jordan came back into the office, "No Jamie Grant on the force."

"Maybe it's just a common name used by our friends at the Yard," Harry said.

"I have a meeting with Caroline and our friend Mr Wade, and there is a press conference at 6.30pm. I will come back and check in with you before I go to it. Chase everyone up, Harry. Get them back here for six and we will have a quick catch up before I go."

"Do you go into make-up before you go in front of the cameras, boss?" Jordan asked.

"With my handsome good looks, I don't need to," Charlie said, as he left the office.

***

When he got to Caroline's office, he found Wade was already there. Charlie sat down.

"I have just been going over what the papers ran with this morning," Caroline said. "Mr Wade was just about to tell me how we should handle it later."

"I read the papers, but I don't think it's too much to be worried about," Wade said. "Lots of speculation. They will probably try and get us to elaborate on it, but we will just 'No comment' any of their questions on the home secretary. It is nothing to do with us."

"Mr Wade," Charlie said, "in all the papers you read, did you see our appeal for witnesses with any information or the phone number they should ring? Because I didn't."

"Yes, I was disappointed about that, too," Wade replied. "I will emphasise that they should include that appeal in their next additions. Do we have any new leads that we can tell them about?"

"No, we seem to have run into a brick wall – that's why we need to get an appeal for help out," Charlie said.

"That is what we will concentrate on this evening, then. I will ask them to make sure they put the girl's picture in the papers tomorrow. Anyway, I will see you at the school hall later – until 6.30 then."

Wade stood up and left the office.

"He's a smooth sod," Charlie said, "but I forgot to tell him a press statement is coming out from the Yard about how the home secretary has never interfered in the case. If he is asked about it and says 'No comment', I think he will be digging his grave."

Caroline smiled, "I will watch just to see that."

"Oh don't worry, I'm sure there will be a reporter who asks it," Charlie said.

"I also got all my senior officers and sergeants in earlier and told them about not speaking to anyone from an outside force who is asking about the murder investigation," Caroline interjected. "They are to report any enquiries and make sure all their constables know, too. I mentioned a corruption investigation, so I think the winds up them. Although, as they left the office, I heard someone say that anyone who drives a car like he does must be on the take. You don't know who they were referring to?"

"I have no idea, but I will check – see if any of my team has bought a new one," Charlie smiled as he said it.

* * *

When Charlie got back to the office, all the team were there except Jordan.

"Well then," Charlie said as he sat down, "who is going to start?"

Manjitt spoke first, "I got Mr Khan to ring the home secretary, but he wasn't available. He left a message for him to call when he was free. I checked the house for any listening devices – nothing. There are still two coppers outside and a lot more press on the pavement. I also explained what you said and Mrs Khan was very grateful."

Charlie nodded at Manjitt, and then turned to the others. "Okay, you three, well done on getting the list of cars. Tell me how it's going."

"We have got about halfway through it," Danny said, "but we

will have to go back to some of the addresses we have already been to, as no one was in. Tomorrow, we will have a few extra bodies to work with us as there is no demonstration – Inspector West said he will sort them out in the morning."

West nodded.

"Alright everyone, you can all get off home," Charlie said. "I will see you in the morning."

They all left the office.

"What do you reckon, Harry?" Charlie asked.

"Well, boss, I get the feeling we are making progress slowly, but we do have some decent leads to follow," Harry said.

"Don't stay too late, Harry. I am off to the press conference," Charlie said. "You could do me one favour, though, before you go. You still got a couple of old friends in Fleet Street?"

Harry nodded.

★★★

Charlie sat in the same seat as he had at the first press conference. Looking out, he noticed that there seemed to be more press and television this time.

Wade started off the conference by making an appeal for witnesses to come forward and asking all the press to use the girl's picture and the phone number the public could call in on. He then asked for questions. The first few were just general and he passed them to Charlie to answer. Then, one reporter asked if they could now comment on the role of the home secretary in the enquiry. Wade said they still had no comment to make.

The reporter asked again, "Are you saying that the home secretary has not interfered in the enquiry? Or he has, but you're not willing to say anything?"

Wade said they were not willing to comment on the home secretary's role in the investigation, as it was not relevant.

The reporter then asked if he therefore disagreed with the press statement given out by Scotland Yard a little earlier, which had said the home secretary had not interfered and had been helpful to the police in getting his family to answer all police questions.

Wade looked a little stunned, but ploughed on, "I don't think that's relevant, as I said we have no comment."

"Are you saying you disagree with Scotland Yard's assessment?" the reporter asked.

Wade said he just wished to talk about the girl and the help that was needed from the public, but the press were having none of it.

A few more then joined in, asking Wade to expand on his answer regarding the home secretary. Charlie waited a little while longer as Wade continued to flounder, but finally stepped in to explain that only one of his officers had met the home secretary at the home of the murdered girl's family and that they had found the home secretary nothing but helpful. He had had no other contact with anyone else on the investigation.

One of the press then asked Charlie, "Has anyone from the home secretary's office been in touch about the enquiry, if not the home secretary?"

Charlie replied that no one from the home secretary's office or anyone they knew connected to the home secretary had been in touch with them. He then asked the press to remember they were investigating a murder of a young girl and needed all the help they could from the public and the press. He thanked them for coming and said they would hold another press conference on Friday.

* * *

As Charlie and Wade walked out of the hall, making their way back to the station, Charlie said, "I don't think that went too badly, do you? The press seemed to get the message in the end."

Wade did not answer straightaway, but as they entered the police station, he said, "Did you know that Scotland Yard had put a press statement out?"

The police constable saw them come through the doors and buzzed the security lock. Charlie thanked him, turned to Wade and said, "Yes, I did know they were putting a statement out about the home secretary's involvement, but I thought you would have known, too – seeing that you have some important connections at Scotland Yard and that they might have kept you informed."

Charlie left Wade at the bottom of the stairs, walked through to the car park, climbed into the Bentley and started the journey home.

★★★

Jordan had got back to the station and found Harry still behind his desk. He noticed Oscar next door on the computer.

"Give me some good news," Harry said.

Jordan took a CD from his pocket, slipped it into a player and pressed fast forward. "This is for the day that the phone was brought. It was paid for with cash at 3.20 in the afternoon. I dare say if we check the address they gave, it will be false."

He stopped the CD at 3.15pm and pressed play. Harry and Jordan watched the screen for several minutes, before Harry switched it off.

"Well, what you make of that?" he said to Jordan.

"It's not the greatest picture, but we can see him clearly and what he was wearing," Jordan said.

Harry nodded and said, "We can get a few stills off that tomorrow. Then, I think it might be worth going back to the shopping centre and seeing the security manager for the whole site and asking if he has the CCTV for the day the phone was bought – see if we can spot our man coming and going from the shop. Was he with anyone else? Did he go to the car park? More importantly, did he have a black BMW? Remember, too, that our friend Jamie Grant might be looking to get the same information."

"He might not have any luck there," Jordan said. "I told the shop manager we have been having trouble with the press ringing people up trying to get information on the murder by pretending to be police officers. I said that if anyone else asks about this CCTV footage, he should say the cameras were not working that week. He will let us know if anyone does ring."

"You are going to make a good police officer one of these days," Harry said.

"Don't go giving me compliments, Harry, I will start to think you like me," Jordan said, smiling.

Harry laughed. "Go on, get yourself home and take Manjitt with you in the morning."

Harry stood up, left the office and went next door.

"What are you up to?"

Oscar looked up. "I am just running a few checks on an address and a name that caught my eye today. I will be done shortly and go back to check it out tomorrow."

"Turn the lights out and lock up when you leave. See you in the morning," Harry said as he left.

* * *

The home secretary was sitting with three other MPs from his party in a room in the House of Commons. They were all friends and part of the team that were backing him to become party leader when the prime minister stepped down. He had just explained what he had learnt from his meetings with Walker and the prime minister.

"I can't believe what I have been told," he said. "I know my brother's daughter like she was my own and never once have I heard her speak in any way politically. All she wanted to do was get her degree and take up law."

"It might sound strange, but do you think it could be a dirty tricks campaign against you? To stop you becoming prime minister?" said one of the men.

"I think that might be a bit farfetched," he said. "What have we gathered talking to other party members?"

"Well, there is still widespread support for you, but I have heard whispers that you are being seen as damaged by the rumours," the man replied.

"Do we have any idea who is behind the rumours?" the home secretary asked.

"Well, from what I have been told, they are coming from the chief whip's office. He has never been a fan of yours, so it wouldn't be a surprise," the man said.

"He has the prime minister's ear, so we must be careful," the home secretary said. "I will try and get a meeting tomorrow with the prime minister – see if I can sound him out about things. Do we have any good news?"

"Well, there was a press statement from Scotland Yard denying you had interfered with the investigation. Also, on a televised press conference, the chief superintendent leading the investigation said you had been nothing but helpful to his officers, so hopefully that will put a lid on that," the man replied.

"I am going to speak to my brother later," the home secretary said. "I will ask him if he has heard any news on the investigation and we will meet again tomorrow after I have spoken to the prime minister."

⋆⋆⋆

AC Walker was at his desk, with two of his officers seated opposite him.

"How are we progressing?" he asked.

"I have the Germans looking for the boy, but he's disappeared," one of the men said. "They are running a background check on him for us. He might be mixed up in the plot, so they are more than anxious to make sure they don't have an al Qaeda sympathiser running round. The bug we put into their office must have been a dud as it's not working, but from what we gathered from their files, they seem to have hit a brick wall. We are checking to see if there have been any new emails between Pakistan and anyone we have under watch regarding the girl, but we have no idea as to the plot or who is behind it, yet."

"What about Chief Superintendent Smith? What have you gathered on him?" Walker asked.

"Lots of rumours," the second man said, "but nothing concrete. He does live well and has a very big house sitting in its own grounds. He comes from the East End – not rich parents, so he must have done something to acquire his money. I ran a check with the lottery people, but he has never won that. His bank account shows nothing. He gets his wages paid in, but nothing else. The house was bought without a mortgage and the cars are the same – no finance. It's a mystery."

"I watched his press conference earlier and he gave a clean bill of health to the home secretary," Walker said. "That is no good to us; if he was to be prime minister, we know he would want us to go soft on questioning and the amount of time we can hold suspects without charge and god knows what else he would want to tie our hands with. I am going to meet up with our friends in parliament tomorrow and see if they can help us with anything. In the meantime, I want to know if Chief Superintendent Smith has anything at his house that might tell us more about him."

"We went there once, but couldn't get in. He has a man who lives in the gatehouse," the officer said.

"Well, do what you have to do to get in," Walker said, "and if you don't find anything, you might want to leave something behind that a policeman shouldn't be found with. We can then arrange for a search on some accusation that has been made against him."

"Okay, I will take someone with me tomorrow," the first man said. "We also have the phone records from the girl's phone; I will get them checked out in the morning."

"Put a call through to Wade; he must have heard something by now," Walker said.

★★★

Charlie was sitting in the front room, with his three greyhounds lying at his feet. He had been writing up some reports and was reading a few letters he had received. His house phone suddenly rang and he reached over and picked it up.

"Hello, Charlie, it's Julian."

"Julian, how's things? Are we still on to meet tomorrow?" Charlie asked.

"Yes, I always enjoy our nights out. I just thought I would ring you as I have a bit of information. Can you call me back on your new mobile?" Julian said.

"Yes, ring you back in a second."

Charlie put the house phone down and went to his jacket to get the phone. The three dogs all looked up.

"No, you lot, stay there. It's not walkies."

Charlie went into the kitchen, sat on a stool and phoned Julian.

"Charlie? Good, at least I know we can talk freely now," he said.

"You're getting as bad as me thinking someone might be listening in," Charlie said.

"I think that's why you asked for the phones and the other things, Charlie. I hope they have come in handy for you," Julian said.

"Very much so, Julian. Now, what is it you wanted to talk about?" Charlie asked.

"I got a call from someone who works for the bank where you hold your account," Julian said. "They said they had been asked to check up on your finances."

"Well, I expected something like that, but there's not much for them to see," Charlie said.

"No, all your main assets are in other accounts run through our firm and are mostly abroad. If anyone sniffs around them, we would know straightaway, but I thought it was best to let you know," Julian said.

"Thanks, Julian, I will make sure your favourite wine is on the table tomorrow."

"Charlie, I would expect nothing else. See you tomorrow."

Charlie went and put the phone back in his jacket. The dogs looked up as he came back into the room.

"Okay, come on. Let's go."

The three dogs jumped up, nearly knocking him over as they rushed through towards the kitchen and the back door. He would walk them up to Mike and Maggie's and have a word with them.

* * *

Jordan and Manjitt arrived at the Bentalls Shopping Centre at 9 o'clock. They found their way to the security office and were introduced to the duty manager. They explained to him what they needed to do and he took them to his small office away from the main surveillance room.

"We will be able to concentrate better in here with no distractions," he told them.

Jordan told him the times he wanted to check, starting with the time before the phone was bought – in order to catch the man arriving at the shop. He next planned to work back to where he had come from, then would try and follow him after he had bought the phone, so as to get a complete picture of his movements.

Jordan and Manjitt pulled up chairs either side of the manager and started to watch the screens.

* * *

Harry was in his office, trying to put a picture together of all they had gathered, where it was leading them and what was missing. The missing list was much longer.

West and Danny arrived. "Morning, Harry," they both said.

"Have you got us some more bodies to work on the case today?" Harry asked.

"We have another six officers. Danny and I are going to sort the list out and get things covered quicker," West said.

"What line are you spinning when you knock on the doors, so that you don't tip off what we really want to know?" Harry asked.

"We are saying a BMW was involved in a hit-and-run on Friday night," Danny said. "Then we ask the usual questions: were they driving Saturday? Can we check the car to make sure it's not damaged? Can we check all the documents? Can anyone corroborate their story? Then, see what we get."

"Make sure you give a good briefing to the new ones working with you today," Harry said. "I don't want anyone tipped off that we are looking for them. These might help; they are pictures of a man who bought the phone used to call Ashadieeyah Khan."

Danny and West took the pictures.

"Make sure everybody gets copies and studies them," Harry said.

Oscar came into the office and said, "Danny, you look extremely sunny for the middle of November. What a lovely shirt."

"This shirt cost a good few quid from Camden market," Danny said.

"But bright yellow flowers on a green background? Your taste was always bad, but it's getting worse. Harry, you are not letting him out in public dressed like that?" Oscar asked.

"If he gets results, he can wear a dress for all I care," Harry said.

"Don't put ideas in his head, Harry," Oscar replied.

Danny and West left the office, with Danny giving the finger to Oscar as he did.

"Well, Pelé," Harry said. "What have you got for me?"

"It's nothing concrete, it's just about one house I visited yesterday," Oscar replied. "I don't know; I just got a feeling. The car is registered to a Mirla Fournier at that address, but I ran a check and she's not on the voting register or on the council tax list. She comes up as a French citizen – came here nine months ago according to immigration records – but found nothing else on her. I could have sworn someone was in the house when we called yesterday."

"There was no car near the house?" Harry asked.

"No, we had a drive around the block – nothing," said Oscar.

"How many more addresses have you got on your list to visit?"

"I still have about ten to check," Oscar replied.

"Well, get some of those out the way, then swing by that address and see if you get an answer this time," Harry said. "If you don't, have a sneaky look round the back and a root in the bins. See if you turn up anything and take the picture of the man who bought the phone."

Oscar went off to collect the constable he had worked with yesterday.

There was a knock on the office door and Harry looked up to see Chief Superintendent Myles standing in the doorway. Harry stood up.

"Can I come in, Chief Inspector?" Caroline said.

"Yes, Ma'am, what can I do for you?" Harry asked.

"I tried to call your boss this morning, but he must have been busy. I have to go out today, so I wondered if you would pass a message on?" she asked.

"Yes, of course, I will pass it on as soon as he gets in," Harry said.

"Will you tell him that Mr Wade has left us? Apparently someone thought he wasn't doing a good job and he's been recalled to the Yard," Caroline said.

"I know the boss will be heartbroken at the news, Ma'am," Harry said.

Caroline smiled, "And how is the investigation coming along?"

"It's early days yet, Ma'am."

"Do you have many leads?"

"No, none yet."

"Any suspects?"

"No, none yet."

"Any thoughts on what may have happened?"

"No, none yet."

"Well, thank you, Chief Inspector, for being as informative as ever."

"Always glad to help, Ma'am."

Caroline turned away, smiling.

Harry sat back down and went back to making his list up.

★★★

Charlie had driven from home and decided he would call in at the Khan's house to have a talk to them about the case. When he pulled onto the drive in front of the house, he saw that Manjitt was right – there were far more reporters standing around now, A few moved forward and took a few pictures of him; some who recognised him called out questions, but he just waved a hand and ignored them.

The two officers outside the door saw him and nodded. He pressed the bell and Raju opened the door. He was invited in, slipped off his shoes and was shown in to see Mr Khan. Charlie shook his hand.

"Mr Khan, I called in this morning to bring you up to speed with the investigation. Is Mrs Khan able to sit in with us?"

Mr Khan excused himself and went to get his wife. Charlie had a look round the room while he waited. There were lots of family pictures – many with their daughter in, and the home secretary featured in several.

Mr Khan came back into the room with his wife. He asked Charlie to sit down and they sat opposite him. Charlie began to go through all they had been doing and the progress they were making. He asked Mr Khan if he had been able to speak to his brother about the dates their daughter was apparently in Pakistan. Mr Khan told him that his brother had phoned and said he would try and get the exact dates, but Mr Khan said he did not believe his daughter had ever been to Pakistan.

Mrs Khan then spoke, "You have a very nice officer working for you, Officer Virdee."

"Thank you, she is good at her job," Charlie said, "but I can assure you that any officers I send to see you are completely trustworthy. However, we are worried that some strange things have been happening with your daughter's case. It's why I came here. I would like to meet the home secretary, but I don't want anyone else to know. It has to be private, because I want to fill him in on what I think is going on."

"We will do all we can to help," Mr Khan said.

"Is it possible you could get your brother to come to the house?" Charlie asked. "He must not know that I will be here, so you will need to make up a reason for him to come."

"I will arrange that," Mr Khan said. "He told us he is very busy at the moment and is under some pressure, but I am sure we will be able to get him to call in."

"You have to make sure he comes alone. No secretaries or anyone else with him must come to the house," Charlie said.

Mrs Khan asked, "Do you think Safwan's brother is mixed up in our daughter's murder?"

"No, not at all, Mrs Khan," Charlie said, "but I think people around him are mixed up in trying to stop us finding the answers to your daughter's murder. I also get the feeling they are trying to damage the home secretary in the process."

"What about the policemen at the front door?" Mr Khan asked.

"I will deal with them when you let me know the home secretary is going to be here," Charlie said.

"Should I ring you and let you know when it's been arranged?" Mr Khan asked.

"No, Mrs Khan will ring Officer Virdee and have a general conversation," Charlie answered. "Say you would like her to come over and tell you how the investigation is going, giving her a time to call in. I know this must seem a little strange, but I can assure you that our main intention is to catch the person who murdered your daughter."

"Thank you, Chief Superintendent, we will do all you ask," Mr Khan said.

Charlie said goodbye and that he hoped to see them again soon. He then left the house and set off for the police station.

★★★

When Charlie arrived at the office, he found Harry writing on the whiteboard.

"How's it looking to you, Harry?" he said.

"Morning, boss. I have been looking at everything and the car seems to be the key. Now, whoever it is doesn't know we have the car on our radar, so it's one up to us. We still have to show our hand a little with knocking on people's doors and asking about it, though. We have to hope they don't get suspicious when we do, but we have to assume they will and will try to get rid of the car, or just try and disappear. At least we have a picture of the man who bought the phone."

He handed one to Charlie.

"Jordan and Manjitt are at the shopping centre now, trying to see if they can pick him out and follow his movements. Everyone else has the picture, so you never know; he might open the door to some of the team when they're knocking on doors."

"We can only hope it's that easy, Harry," Charlie said. "Harry, I want you to put together a dossier of all the strange goings-on for me."

He took the listening device from his pocket and passed it over.

"Collect any pictures we have of our Mr Jamie Grant and write up all the interference etc. I am trying to get a private meeting with the home secretary to let him know all we have about Walker and his team. I think it's time we hit back."

"It will be a pleasure, boss," Harry said, "and I have a message for you from Chief Superintendent Myles – or Caroline to us. She said that Mr Wade has been taken off the case as press officer. Apparently, the Yard recalled him."

"What terrible news," Charlie said, with a smile. "I thought AC Crick wouldn't put up with him. Do we know if they are sending anyone else over?"

"She never said; let's hope they don't."

* * *

AC Walker had just left a meeting at the House of Commons, where he had been briefing the Home Affairs Select Committee on the current terrorist threat. He was now with one of his officers, who had told him how Wade had been removed as press officer on the orders of AC Crick.

"Let's not worry about that," Walker said. "He had not managed to get anything for us anyway. Just make sure there's no trace of communication from us to him."

They came to a door in one of the long corridors, whose sign read 'chief whip's office'. They knocked and went in. The chief whip was seated at his desk with the window behind him. When he saw them enter, he stood and shook hands with Walker. He told his secretary to leave them alone for thirty minutes, and the secretary got up and left the office.

"Thank you for coming to see me, Assistant Commissioner," the chief whip said. "We are very worried about the information concerning the home secretary and we are hoping you can help us resolve it."

"I am sure we both want the same outcome to this problem," Walker said. "From our point of view, having someone in charge of anti-terrorism who might in some way be mixed up in it puts us in a delicate situation."

"Yes, I can see that, so we will work together to get the best result for us all. However, I watched the press conference yesterday and the lead officer seemed to give him a clean bill of health on not interfering in the case. I thought we had arranged the opposite," the chief whip said.

"The press officer, who was supposed to make things happen, let us down. I think we might find that the officer who is backing the home secretary up will be under a cloud of his own soon," Walker replied.

"Oh, you have some doubts about him?" the chief whip asked.

"There have been lots of rumours about him and checks are being carried out, so I think we will have him out of the way in a few days time anyway," Walker said. "It might be good if a few papers could mention his backing for the home secretary – you know the thing, crooked cop who backed the home secretary."

"I will have a word with a few journalists I know; tell them I might have a big story for them in a few days."

"It might be a good idea if rumours of the girl being tied to a terrorist plot started to leak out. Though none of my officers can confirm any questions being asked about it, it might prove troublesome for the home secretary and the police officer in charge of the murder investigation," Walker said.

"Well, let's hope it doesn't get out," the chief whip said, smiling.

* * *

The home secretary had just finished a meeting with his immigration minister and was now walking with him and two assistants back to the main lobby of the House of Commons.

They had just turned into a corridor when the home secretary saw AC Walker coming out of the chief whip's office. Walker didn't see him as he had turned and was walking away from him. *Why would Walker be having a meeting with the chief whip? He has nothing to do with anti-terrorism.*

He would speak to a few colleagues see if they had any idea.

★ ★ ★

Manjitt and Jordan came back into the office.

"Well, how did you get on?" Harry said.

Charlie looked up. "They're smiling, Harry. They must have got something," he said.

Jordan spoke first, "We did, but it's strange."

Manjitt took the CD from her bag. "It gives us some idea, but then asks us a bigger one. We went over the thirty-two cameras they have in the place and have put together the best picture we can of the man's movements in and outside the building. They're not all great shots, but we think it shows as much of him as possible."

"Let's see it and we can talk about it after," Charlie said.

Manjitt put the CD in and they all sat watching as different views of the man's movements through the shopping centre and the car park showed on the screen. There was about fifteen minutes worth and when it was finished, Harry said, "Play it again."

After the second viewing, Harry was the first to speak again, "It doesn't give us a better picture of the man other than the one from the shop, but who does he meet when we see him go into the car park?"

Jordan spoke, "Well, it's a girl with long black hair. It could be our murdered girl."

"Impossible," Charlie said. "You have her up in Oxford, but you can double-check. Get onto her tutor straightaway and find out if she was absent that day."

Jordan got up and left the office to go next door.

"They do leave in a black BMW. We see it driving out of the exit of the shopping centre and there appears to be two people in it," Manjitt said.

"We might be able to blow that couple of frames up and get a registration number off the car," Harry said.

"Do it right away, Harry," Charlie said.

Jordan came back into the office. "I spoke to her tutor, Professor Kinbury, and he will get back to us as soon as he has the information on her attendance."

"Manjitt, what do you make of it?" Charlie asked.

"I don't think it gives us much of a picture, as all we have is a girl meeting the man. It could be our victim, but it could as easily be me. All we know is that he met someone in the car park and they drove off together," Manjitt replied.

"Manjitt, check on the DVLA database and see if Ashadieeyah Khan had a driving licence. It's the girl who's driving the car when it leaves," Harry said.

Manjitt went next door and got onto one of the computers. The phone rang next to her and she called Jordan in. Harry stood in the corner as the printer started to throw out the copies of the car registration, one of which he gave to Charlie.

"What do you make of it, boss?" he said.

"It's not very clear, but i think can make out a seven," Charlie said.

"I will see if I can get someone at forensics to try and clear it up for us," Harry said.

Manjitt came back in, "She didn't have a licence."

"Manjitt, get onto the rest of the team. Tell them to go and check all the cars on the list with a seven in the car registrations. Tell them to be cautious," Charlie said.

Manjitt left as Jordan came back into the office. "Ashadieeyah Khan was at all her tutorials on that day."

"So, we have two people in the car we are looking for and

forensics told us that two people could have been involved in the murder. Let's hope the rest of the team get some luck. Harry, have a look on the list they made up and how many of the cars have a seven in their registration."

* * *

Mike had just finished clearing the leaves from some of the drains around the cottage, when he saw a van pull up outside the front gate. He went into the cottage and told Maggie he would be going up to the house. He heard the bell from the front gate, so walked out of the front door and approached the man standing there.

"Can I help you?" he said.

"We came a few days ago about your gas," the man said. "We have to get in today, otherwise we will be getting the police involved and you could get into trouble."

Mike stood for a while and finally said, "Alright, do you have to check the big house and the cottage?"

The man turned, walked back to the van and said something to the driver. He walked back to Mike and said, "No, only the big house."

Mike said he would open the gates and they could follow him up. He then went back to the cottage, picked up his car keys and mobile phone, and walked to his car. As he climbed into the front seat, he tapped a number into his mobile.

"Tell Charlie he has visitors at the house."

He put the phone down, started the car and drove onto the driveway. Pressing the key fob, the main gates started to open and he signalled the van to follow him.

* * *

"There are twenty-nine on the list with a seven in the registration," Harry said.

Charlie thought for a moment. "Why would they go and buy a phone?" he said. "They must have had Ashadieeyah Khan's number in the first place because they phoned her first. They either knew her number all along or they met her somewhere and she gave it to them."

"Or they got it off one of her friends," Jordan said.

Harry's phone rang. He listened for a couple of minutes and then put the phone down. "You have visitors at the house," he said to Charlie.

Charlie nodded to Harry. "Well, whatever way, she knew one or both of them – but if she's been at university most of the year and only got back Friday, and never went out till late that afternoon, how have they got her number?"

Manjitt came back into the office. "I passed on the message to everyone and told them to be extra cautious," she said.

"Harry and I are going to stay on this. I want you two to go to my house," Charlie said to Jordan and Manjitt. "Pick up a change of clothes on your way, as you'll be staying the night. I will let Mike know you're coming. When you get there, Mike will show you the surveillance footage from inside and outside the house. Right at this moment, a couple of men, one who I expect has a name like Jamie Grant, are pretending to be gasmen or something in my house. I want you to look at the film of them and find out what they were up to."

"Will do, boss," Jordan said. "Manjitt, make sure you bring some attractive pyjamas."

"I will be doing some karate practice before bed; you're welcome to take part," she said.

"You don't know what you're missing," Jordan said.

"Make yourselves at home," Charlie interrupted. "I will get Maggie to come up to the house about 8am to cook something for you. Ring me when you have discovered what they have been up to and Manjitt, you might get a call from Mrs Khan passing the time of day with you. She'll then ask you to come over and tell her how the investigation is going, giving you a time that you should go and visit. Don't worry; it's just something I have arranged for her to do. Let me know the time and day she gives you."

Manjitt and Jordan got up and left. Charlie made a quick phone call to Mike.

"This phone gives us a new problem, boss," Harry said.

"Yes and no, Harry. I know the pictures are not great, but we should still take them round to all her family and friends. If they don't recognise them, we still ask if they have given Ashadieeyah's number out to anyone for whatever reason. Harry, get onto the phone company and see if they can give us a list of the numbers that pay-as-you-go phone called. If they can, I want it without delay. I have had a thought, Harry; see if the network can trace whereabouts the phone is now. We might get lucky if they still have it. I am going to check in with the rest of the team and see how they are getting on. I will pick us up some sandwiches as well."

Harry was already on the phone when Charlie left the office. As Charlie went down the stairs, he met Caroline coming up.

"Hello, Charlie," she said. "Have you got a minute?"

"Yes, if you don't mind me making a few phone calls," Charlie said.

Charlie followed Caroline to her office, while already talking to Danny on the phone. He sat down and then called Inspector West, but could not get hold of Oscar. He would try again later.

"Sorry about that, Caroline, but things are just getting interesting on the case," he said.

"That's okay, Charlie, I just wanted to check that you got the message about Mr Wade," she said.

"Yes, I was so upset when Harry told me," Charlie laughed.

"I thought you would be, but how are we going to cover the press conferences if we need to have another one?" she asked.

"I will have a word with my boss, but do you have any thoughts?"

"No, not really, as long as we get someone who sings from the same song sheet as us. I had a chat with your Chief Inspector Davis this morning."

"Harry? I bet that was a long conversation," Charlie said.

"I have to admit, I have an admiration for him. He can answer a question by telling you the truth and not actually have told you anything," Caroline said.

"Caroline, I couldn't work without him," Charlie said. "He gets things done. He's also got old friends all over the place who owe him favours; a sharp mind and the rest of the team respect him."

"Well, you couldn't have anyone better guarding the investigation's secrets," she said. "I don't think Saint Peter could get anything out of him."

"Only if I told him it was okay to say something," Charlie said.

⋆⋆⋆

Manjitt and Jordan had stopped off to pick up some clothes and were now outside the gate at Charlie's house. They saw Mike coming towards them; they had met him and his wife on a couple of occasions when they had come over on a Sunday to have dinner with all the team together. Manjitt waved at Mike and the gate started to open. They drove through and stopped beside him.

"Hello, Mike," Manjitt said, "the boss sent us over to check things out."

"The two men left about an hour ago," Mike said. "They were in the house for about twenty minutes. I stayed with one of them in the kitchen, but the other said he had to go check out some appliances elsewhere in the house."

"Well, climb in the back, Mike. We will go take a look. The boss said you would show us the security footage," Manjitt said.

Mike got in the back of the car and they drove up to the house.

"Park at the front, then we won't bother the dogs," Mike said.

★★★

A short while later, all three stood in front of the large television screen in the front room. Mike had the security remote in his hand and a list with numbers on it beside the names of rooms. They watched as it showed Mike coming in the back of the house with the two men.

"Ha! Our electrician Jamie Grant has turned into a gasman," Jordan said.

"These pictures are as clear as day – the BBC would be proud of them," Manjitt noted.

They watched as the two men went through the motions of looking at a few pipes and things; the three greyhounds had stood watching them until it appeared Mike had shooed them outside. Then, one of the men got up, took his tool bag and left the kitchen. Mike pressed a button and it showed the man walking through the hall to the stairs, button after button pressed, until it showed him opening a door and disappearing into a room. Five minutes later, he came out and they followed his progress back to the kitchen. Five minutes after that, they got up and left the house with Mike.

"What room did he go into?" Jordan asked.

"It's a bedroom; I will take you up and show you," Mike said.

They followed him upstairs to the bedroom that the man had disappeared into. "I will let you two get on with things. You will find me in the kitchen when you're done. I'll make some tea."

Manjitt and Jordan went into the bedroom. Manjitt held her fingers to her lips took the scanner from her pocket and went round the room checking for listening devices.

"All clear," she said.

"You know this bedroom is larger than my whole flat," Jordan said.

"Well, it's going to take longer to search then," Manjitt said, "but I bet it's a lot cleaner."

"I will start in the bathroom; you begin in here," Jordan said.

They had been methodically searching the room for twenty-five minutes, when Jordan said, "I can't find anything out of the ordinary."

"He was in here for five minutes, so he wouldn't have been able to take the floor boards up," she said.

"But he did have a tool bag with him, so let's look at anything that can be unscrewed or prised open," Jordan replied.

They went back to searching the rooms again.

"Manjitt, in here," Jordan called from the bathroom.

When she went in, Jordan was standing on the edge of the bath. "It looks like the air extractor fan has been messed around with. There's a screw missing and if you look down under the sink, you will see it."

Manjitt knelt down, reached under the sink and picked up a tiny screw. She passed it to Jordan, who placed it in the empty hole and twisted it with his fingers.

"It fits," he said.

"Well, let's check it out. I will go see Mike and get him to get some tools."

★★★

On his return to the office, Charlie had finally got Oscar on the phone and explained about the car registrations. Oscar told him he had fourteen on his list still to check.

Once back, Harry said to Charlie as he walked in, "Boss, West just called. They went to one house to check on the car and apparently when the door was opened, they smelt cannabis. They went in and found that nearly every room had been turned into a cannabis factory, so they've nicked two people in the house. West said it would have a street value of over a hundred grand, but it's not our car."

"It will do Caroline's crime figures the world of good and crosses another of the addresses off our list. Here, have a sandwich. Any luck with the mobile phone company yet?" Charlie asked.

"They did a quick check on it, but no signal – so it's either switched off or has been gotten rid of. They are seeing if any other calls were made from it and will get back to me."

"Well, we can only hope they used it," Charlie said.

★ ★ ★

Manjitt returned to the bedroom with a toolbox and went into the bathroom where Jordan was sitting.

"You know the shower in here is computerised," he said. "I had a look at it and it apparently has twelve jets that massage your body with the water sprayed at different pressures as you stand. I hate to think what it cost, but I'll ask the boss if I can have one for Christmas."

"Stop dreaming and take the toolbox," Manjitt said as she passed it to him.

He took two screwdrivers from the box.

"One of these might fit," he said, as he stood up on the side of the bath and switched the extractor fan off. He put the screwdriver into the first screw and turned it, and it slipped and came away easily. He passed it to Manjitt and tried the second screw, which he twisted and it started to move – as did the remaining screws. When they were all out, he reached up and pulled the front of the extractor away, so that it hung just below the main casing.

Jordan had a look inside, placed his hand in and pulled a brown package from the right-hand side, before taking a further look.

"There's something else in here, too." He reached in a little further and pulled a small handgun out. "What people keep in their bathrooms."

He stepped down from the bath. Manjitt laid the brown package on the dressing table, pulled at the brown tape that was binding it and a small tear appeared, through which white powder could clearly be seen.

"I bet that's not talcum powder," she said.

Jordan laid the handgun beside it.

"Get your phone out and take a couple of pictures. I will put the extractor back together; you ring the boss," Jordan said.

⋆⋆⋆

Harry answered the phone on his desk, wrote a number down and looked up at Charlie.

"That mobile phone was only used two other times," he said. "It called the same number twice. I will run a check on it and see what we get."

Charlie's phone rang and he listened to Manjitt tell him what they had found. He gave her some instructions and said he would see them later. He then called AC Crick at Scotland Yard and spent five minutes talking to him.

Harry looked across the desk. "Good news, boss?" he asked.

"Yes, Harry, we are one step ahead of our friends and they don't know it yet. We need to keep it that way for a few days more, so I have asked Crick to do us a favour."

Charlie looked at his watch. "Put a call through to the rest of the team and see how they're getting on, Harry."

⋆⋆⋆

Oscar had visited six houses, where they had found four BMWs parked outside. He had spoken to the owners and looked over the cars, but all had had reasonable explanations as to where they had been on Friday evening and all said they had witnesses to prove it. He had no doubt they were telling the truth.

Now, he was being driven along the high street in New Malden by a young constable who he found good company and seemed good at the job. The traffic was quite heavy, being the start of rush hour, but he wanted to get back to the address where he had seen the face at the window. However, just as they were close, they were stopped at some traffic lights by a car turning across the traffic, which struck a motorcycle coming across the junction in front of them. Oscar saw the rider thrown over the car bonnet, hit the tarmac and slide for another 10 yards along the road. He and the constable immediately jumped out the car and ran to the rider.

Checking him over, Oscar thought he looked in a bad way. Oscar left the constable to attend to the rider and went back to the car. He called an ambulance and reported the accident, then returned to the injured rider. The constable was kneeling with him and trying to get him to speak, so Oscar found the car driver and told him to stay in his car until more officers arrived.

It was about ten minutes before a local police car was able to get through the traffic to them. Oscar explained what he had seen to the officers, pointing out the car driver, and told them to chase up how long the ambulance would be. He spoke to the constable he had worked with all day and said that he should stay here and help out, while he would go and check the address they had been heading to.

Oscar climbed back in the car, put the siren and emergency lights on and slowly inched his way through the traffic until it thinned out a bit. He then turned the emergency lights and siren off, noticing the time was 5.30pm. *Hope there's someone home*, he thought.

★★★

Charlie was listening to Harry relate what the team had told him of their progress.

"At least we are thinning the possibilities down, Harry," Charlie said.

Harry's phone rang; he listened for a minute and put it down. "Got an address for the number the pay-as-you-go phone rang. It's a farm in leatherhead. I will run a few checks on who owns it."

"Let's hope we get some breaks on that," Charlie said. "I am off now to meet Julian for dinner. I will be calling in at the Yard in the morning, but ring me if you get anything."

"Night boss. I will stay and chase up a few of these things."

Charlie left Harry, walked down the stairs and called in to see Caroline.

"I hear there was a good result on the drugs front today," he said as he looked round her door.

"Yes, a great find, your mob should come over this way more often," Caroline said. "One of the biggest we have had in a long time, but how's the rest of the investigation going? I have had the press onto me for an update."

Charlie went through how they were progressing and asked Caroline if she would organise a press conference for tomorrow afternoon. He explained he would be at the Yard tomorrow morning and would try and get a new press officer. Caroline told him not to worry she would sort things out until then.

* * *

Oscar pulled up outside the house, where a black BMW was parked in the driveway. He got out and walked up the path to the door; he could see lights on at the windows. *Someone's at home,* he thought.

He rang the doorbell and stood back. Out of the corner of his eye, he saw the curtains move in the window. A few moments later, the door was opened by a woman. Strangely, she looked like a smaller version of Manjitt.

"Can I help you?" she asked.

"Yes, I am sorry to bother you. I am a police officer," he showed her his warrant card, "and we are investigating a hit-and-run accident on Friday evening in which a black BMW was involved." He pointed to the BMW, "Is that your car?"

"Yes, but I have not been involved in an accident," she said.

"Could I have your name please and do you mind if I look round the car to check there's no damage?" he asked.

"Mirla Fournier. No, go ahead, but I can assure you I have been in no accident," she said.

Oscar walked to the car and started to pretend to check it over. The woman had an accent; it wasn't French, but sounded like it could be Australian or from that part of the world. He walked around the car and came back to the door.

"Do you have the car's insurance and your driving licence, as I noticed the tax disc is out of date?"

"Surely not," the woman said.

"I am afraid so, take a look," Oscar said.

The woman came out and looked into the windscreen. Oscar followed her.

"Do you mind opening the car so I can check the tax disc, please?"

The woman looked at Oscar. "Is that necessary? I can see it's out of date and I will get a new one tomorrow."

"Sorry, but I have to check it," he said.

The woman turned and went back into the house. She was gone a couple of minutes. Oscar was starting to wonder if she would come out again, when the door opened and she returned.

"I had trouble remembering where I'd left my keys," she said.

The BMW locks clicked as she pressed unlock on the key fob. Oscar opened the passenger side door and reached in for the tax disc. It was too dark to make much out inside the car. He stood up with the tax disc and walked back to the door.

"Do you have your insurance and driving licence?" he asked.

"Oh yes, sorry. Come in, I will find them," she said.

She stood aside and Oscar went in. She closed the door behind him and asked him to follow her. She led him to the front room, which was where the curtains had twitched when he had first rung the bell. A man was seated watching the television with his back to them.

"I have my licence in my bag," the woman said, "and I think my insurance is in one of these drawers." She knelt down, pulled a few drawers open and found it.

Oscar checked her licence. "I see you're French; have you been in the country long?" he asked.

The woman stood up. "A few months now. I can't seem to find my insurance documents, but I am sure they're here somewhere," she said.

"Well, you will need to find them. If you don't, I will have to impound the car and have it towed away – that's the law now," Oscar said.

"I know I have them somewhere here," she said.

"If you tell me who you are insured with, I will go and check that your insurance is up to date. I noticed you don't have a very strong French accent," he said.

"No, I lived a long time abroad from when I was young. My brother might know where the documents are."

She said something in a foreign language to the seated man, who stood and turned to face them. Oscar recognised him straightaway as the man in the pictures from the phone shop. He felt a sharp pain in his side and looked down to see the woman's hand pressed against him. *She's punched me,* he thought. He then watched her hand pull away from him as if in slow motion and he saw a long silver blade. He felt his legs begin to buckle and he fell forward, crashing into the drawers that the woman had opened. He felt another sharp pain as he lay there.

★★★

Harry stayed late in the office, finishing off the outstanding reports and running a few checks on the farm that had been called by the mobile phone. When finished, he took his jacket from his chair and walked out of the office, locking it behind him.

He then went into the office next door to turn off the computers, but noticed there was a message on one of them. He pulled it up; it was for Oscar from the French police regarding an enquiry about Mirla Fournier. She had reported her passport lost or stolen eighteen months ago while on holiday in Egypt. She was living in Paris and was still there.

He would let Oscar know that he should check this woman out in the morning.

* * *

Charlie pulled into the entrance of the Romford greyhound stadium, drove up and parked outside the main stand. He waved to the parking attendants, who knew his car, as he walked through the doors leading to the pavilion restaurant, which served some of the best food you could get. He always met Julian here. Charlie had owned a number of greyhounds; in fact, the three he had at home had all raced for him with varying degrees of success.

Charlie walked into the restaurant and was met by Sandra, the manager. She welcomed him and asked him how he had been, while showing him over to a table by the big window that looked out onto the first bend. It was a great place to see the dogs come racing by at such speed and power – it was this that he liked about greyhounds; they had such physical power, but such laid back temperaments.

He asked Sandra if she had the wine he had phoned and asked for. She said she had and would bring it to the table. He was just looking through the race card for the evening, when he saw Julian come through the doors. Julian spotted him and walked over.

Charlie stood. “Hello, mate,” he said.

"Hello, Charlie, hope things are going well," Julian replied.

"Yes, sit down," Charlie said. "Let's have some wine and a chat, then we can watch some racing while we eat and try and find some winners."

Sandra returned with the wine and menus, and Julian looked at the bottle

"Charlie, how do you manage to find this? Some of my friends would kill to drink this."

"Well, enjoy it and let's talk, because I want to concentrate on the racing soon," Charlie said.

They ordered their meals, while Julian took some papers from his briefcase. He explained that the scholarships Charlie had set up in his parents' name at six local schools had enabled twelve of their pupils to go to university that year. He just needed his signature to sign off the payments to cover all their fees for the coming year. He then explained how Charlie's other investments were doing.

When Charlie had first gone to Julian's office and been told he had come into £150 million, it had taken him some time to work out what to do. He quickly realised, however, that he was happy staying in his job as a policeman. Julian had given him advice on what to do with the money, so he had asked Julian to manage it for him. According to Julian, he was now worth even more – even after spending on whatever he wanted. They went through a few more papers as they ate, until Julian eventually put the papers back into his briefcase.

"That's the last of them," Julian said.

"Good, let's get studying the form of the next race," Charlie said.

* * *

Manjitt and Jordan were seated at the table in the dining room of Charlie's house, eating the last of the meal Maggie had cooked for them. Jordan poured them each a glass of white wine.

"Do you ever wonder where the boss got his money from?" Manjitt asked.

Jordan looked over the table at her. "I did and I asked Harry once," he said. "What did Harry tell you?" Manjitt asked.

He told me the boss was the most honest and loyal copper he had ever met or worked with," Jordan said.

"And what else?" Manjitt asked.

"If Harry tells me that, I am not going to argue," Jordan replied. "In all the years I have worked with the boss, Harry has been proved right. The boss has got my arse out of a few scrapes several times."

"It makes you wonder, though," Manjitt said.

"You can ask him when he gets in tonight," Jordan replied as he took a drink.

"No, I will take Harry's word for it," she said.

Manjitt's phone rang, "Hello, Mrs Khan."

She spoke for a few minutes, placing the phone into her pocket when she had finished.

"Well, what did she have to say? Jordan asked.

"I have a message for the boss. She said she's found Ashadieeyah's diary in her coat in the laundry basket. I told her I would pick it up and have a look through it – you never know, there might be something in it to help us."

"I'll tell you one thing," Jordan said, "the boss is not going to be happy that it wasn't found in the house search."

He picked up his glass and held it up, "On the other hand, I didn't search the laundry. Cheers."

* * *

The home secretary had spoken to his brother, who had sounded worried and arranged to meet him at his house. He was now seated with a couple of fellow MPs and was relating what had happened at the meeting he had had with the prime minister.

He told them the prime minister had not been forthcoming with any information regarding the chief whip, so had decided he should give some press interviews next week setting out his ideas as if he was prime minister and openly come out as a prospective leader. It would then be clear who was against them.

He phoned AC Walker and asked if he could tell him the dates his niece was supposed to have been in Pakistan. Walker had told him he would call him back with the exact dates when he had them to hand. The home secretary asked him about the ongoing enquiry. Walker said they had made no further progress, but would keep him informed.

He made no reference to his meeting with the chief whip.

⋆⋆⋆

When Charlie arrived home, he stopped at Mike and Maggie's cottage. Mike told him he had followed the instructions Charlie had given him earlier. They had the dogs at the cottage and would bring them back up to the main house in the morning. Charlie then drove up to the house and parked the Bentley in the garage. Going inside, he found Manjitt and Jordan in the main room watching the news on television.

"Hello, you two, thanks for sorting out my little problem," Charlie said.

"It was easy enough with your security boss and we know we have no chance of stealing the knives and forks," Jordan said.

"Well, let's have a look at the video of it," Charlie said as he picked up the security remote. They watched the recording. When it had finished, Manjitt and Jordan took him upstairs to show him exactly where they had found the planted gun and package.

"Why do you think this is going on, boss?" Manjitt asked.

"I am not too sure of all the reasons, but our murder investigation has crossed over into someone else's investigation.

They feel that instead of getting together to work it out, we are part of the problem – but what I do know is that our murdered girl was not part of a terrorist plot."

"Mrs Khan rang me earlier," Manjitt said, "and she said the home secretary will be calling at their house at midday tomorrow. He has a meeting on the south coast, so said he would drop in on his way. She has also found Ashadieeyah's diary, which was apparently in her jacket in the laundry basket. I said I would pick it up in the morning."

"How was that not found in the house search?" Charlie said. "I will speak to West in the morning. Manjitt, when you get the diary, have a good read through and see if it throws up anything for us. Right, you two, I am tired and we have a busy one in the morning. Let's get our heads down and be up at seven. I will do a breakfast of tea and toast."

"You spoil us, boss," Jordan said.

⋆⋆⋆

Charlie arrived at Scotland Yard, parked his car and made his way to AC Crick's office. He had told Manjitt and Jordan to stop off at Mr Khan's to pick up Ashadieeyah's diary and take it back to the station to see if it told them anything. He knocked on Crick's door and went in.

"Good morning, Charlie," Crick said, "I think it will be an interesting day ahead."

"It might have its moments. Did you get the package I sent over to you?" Charlie asked.

Crick reached and opened a drawer. Taking out a small box, he placed it on the table and took out a small handgun, a brown package and a CD disc.

"I can see what these are," he said, "but what's on the disc?

"That's how they were delivered to my house," Charlie said.

Crick pushed the CD into his computer and watched the screen. When it came to an end, he looked up at Charlie. "Do we know who that man was?"

"We believe he's a police officer working for AC Walker in the Anti-Terrorism Squad and we have him in the pictures I showed you before," Charlie replied.

"Well, I have got a meeting arranged with AC Walker at 9.30am for us," Crick said. "I told him we wanted to discuss your case with him. He asked me which aspects of it, but I said I was not up to speed and you would put him in the picture."

"Thank you, Sir. I don't want him to know anything about what we have discovered his team has been up to, but I want to see how he reacts to a few request I make. I expect you will be contacted shortly by police complaints about me and how they are intending to raid my house on information they have received."

"I expect so, but they'd have to inform me before launching an investigation," Crick said.

"You can demand to know where they got the information from," Charlie said, "before they go ahead with their enquiries."

"I like it Charlie, but don't worry, I will make sure I have every bit of information they have been given on you before I say anything."

Crick looked at his watch. "Shall we go up to Walker's office?"

He put the package back in his desk and they left to get the lift to the ninth floor.

★★★

Manjitt and Jordan had stopped at the Khan's house to pick up the diary. Mrs Khan had told Manjitt that everything was still arranged for her senior officer to meet the home secretary at midday.

They walked into Harry's office.

"Morning, you two. How was your night of luxury?" Harry asked.

"I'm going to ask the boss if he'll take in a paying lodger," Jordan said.

"We got a call from Mrs Khan last night to give us a message for the boss, but she also told us she'd found Ashadieeyah's diary in the laundry," Manjitt said. "I have had a quick scan through and there are a couple of interesting entries."

"Well, get on with reading it thoroughly. I want to know everything that gives us a lead and I also want to know why it wasn't found in the house search," Harry said.

Manjitt went into the next office to go through the diary.

"Jordan, get hold of Pelé for me – he's not come into the office yet – and find out if he went straight on to the car search. When you get him, let him know there's a message from the French police for him."

Jordan left and Harry went back to making some checks on the farm that had been called from the mobile.

* * *

Charlie and AC Crick sat opposite Walker. As usual, a man was seated behind him, though Charlie noticed it was not the famous Jamie Grant.

"What is it you think I can help you with?" Walker said, looking at Charlie.

"It's very nice of you to see me, Sir, as I know how precious your time is, but it has come to my attention that you have information that may help my murder investigation. Whilst questioning Mr Khan, he mentioned that you had his daughter's laptop."

"I'm not sure who could have told him that," Walker said.

"It might have been his brother, the home secretary. Are you saying he was misinformed?" Charlie asked.

Walker sat silent for a moment. "Yes, it has come into our possession, but I don't know how that affects your investigation. If we had discovered anything relevant, we would have informed you," he said.

"How do you know what's relevant to our investigation?" Charlie asked.

"Chief Superintendent, if we had found anything about a boyfriend or a threat from anyone to the girl, we would have told you," Walker said.

"But we have wasted valuable time searching for it when you could have told us you had it. Can we have a look at it now? I can get one of my officers to go through it," Charlie asked.

"That's not possible, as we need it for an ongoing inquiry," Walker replied.

"Do you have her mobile phone?" Charlie asked.

"No, we don't," replied Walker.

"Sir, can I ask whether you are investigating the girl for any reason that may affect how I am conducting my investigation?" Charlie asked.

Walker was quiet. He turned and spoke softly to the man seated behind him, before turning back.

"Her name did come up in an enquiry, but we are not sure how much it means yet and it is only in a minor way. It probably means nothing – we get lots of names that crop up, but once we have checked them out, it is usually a false alarm."

"So there's nothing I should worry about that may conflict with my investigation?" Charlie asked.

"No, you have nothing to worry about there," Walker said. "If we did find anything we think can help you, we would tell you straightaway."

"You could have told us that your officers had been to her university and taken her laptop in the first place," Charlie said.

Walker again turned and spoke to the man seated behind him. When he turned around, he said, "I was not informed where her laptop had been recovered from and in any case, we would not inform the local police or any other departments in case any news of our investigation leaked out."

"But once you had it, you could have let us know," Charlie said.

"Chief Superintendent, I don't want to repeat myself," Walker said. "You don't seem to be listening to what I have told you. I didn't know we had got the laptop from the university, but I did ask my officers once I knew about it if they had any information that may have helped you. There wasn't any."

Walker turned and spoke to AC Crick, "I don't think your officer seems to understand the bigger picture. We are dealing with national security, which I know you appreciate, so maybe you should have a chat with him and explain. I know the commissioner is fully supportive of the work we do."

AC Crick said, "I am sure the commissioner is, but we are investigating a murder. I know he would want cooperation between departments and, I have to say, I think that has been lacking on your part."

Walker smiled at Crick. "I think you will find that national security comes first, but if you wish to take it up with the commissioner you can. Now, if there is nothing else, I have work to do."

Charlie and Crick stood up, and Charlie said, "Thank you for taking the time to see me. You have put my mind at ease."

Walker looked at Charlie. "It's good to see a senior officer who appreciates the bigger picture."

AC Crick interrupted the exchange, "I'm glad we had this meeting and that you have been so open and helpful to my officer. He can get on with things now, without worrying he has not been told everything."

Charlie and Crick turned and left the office. Once they were out of the room, Walker turned to the other man, "I think it's time the rumours of the chief superintendent's suspected dealings with criminals got to the relevant department, and they understand that action is needed quickly."

★★★

When Charlie and Crick were back in his office on the seventh floor, Crick spoke first, "What a despicable man. I want to go to the commissioner with this straightaway."

"If you could just hold off until a bit later," Charlie said, "I think we may get a powerful ally on our side."

He then explained what he was going to do. Crick agreed to wait until he got his phone call and Charlie left to go to the Khan's house for his meeting with the home secretary.

★★★

Jordan walked into Harry's office.

"I can't raise Oscar. I got hold of Danny and Inspector West, and he's not out with their teams looking for the car. I also rang his home phone and there's no answer," he said.

"Get hold of West, find out which constable he was with yesterday and find out what they covered," Harry said. "I will give his phone a few more calls. He might have gone out dancing and overslept."

Harry then called Oscar's house a couple of times, letting it ring for a few minutes. He also tried the mobile, but there was no answer.

Manjitt came into the office. "Harry, I think we have something that ties it all together."

Harry told her to sit down and run through it for him.

"In her diary, she wrote that earlier in the year she had met an old school friend she hadn't seen for years, who had immigrated to Australia with her family. Ashadieeyah had said that the friend was visiting family here with her parents, before they went onto Pakistan to see other relatives. Ashadieeyah suggested that they could spend some time together and asked if she wanted to go on a walking holiday with her and some friends from university. Anyway, the friend got in touch with her again at the beginning of July and said that she was worried her parents were trying to organise an arranged marriage for her in Pakistan that she didn't want. She asked if she could borrow Ashadieeyah's passport to use to get out of Pakistan if she had to, because her parents held her passport – in Ashadieeyah's diary, she says how much they looked alike. Anyway, Ashadieeyah gave her the passport and her friend said she would return it when she got back."

Harry sorted through some reports on the table.

"Here it is, Pelé checked out her old school friends and the only one we couldn't get was a girl who had emigrated to Australia, whose name was Shiza Akmal. Manjitt, get onto the Australians and let them know how important this is to us.

Stay on the phone until you get some information on her and make sure you get something."

Charlie came into the office and Harry briefed him on what had been going on. "Let's hope Manjitt gets something for us, but where's Oscar, Harry? Find him. I will be at the Khan's house, so phone me if anything turns up. Have you got that dossier you put together for me?"

Harry passed over a file. "I have put everything in there."

Charlie left to go to his meeting with the home secretary.

Jordan then came back into the office and told Harry he had spoken to West, who said the constable working with Oscar yesterday had explained what had happened, and that Oscar had gone off alone to do the final check while he was tied up at the road accident.

"Dig the address out that Pelé was going to," Harry said. "Get Danny to meet you there and check it out. It's just not like Pelé to go missing."

* * *

Charlie was seated with Mr and Mrs Khan in their front room, drinking tea and going over how the case was progressing. He was hopeful that the discovery of the diary might give them new leads to follow up. Just after midday, the home secretary arrived. He came into the room and was greeted by his brother.

"What is the problem you called me about?" he said.

"It is not really a problem, but the chief superintendent asked us to get you here," Mr Khan said.

The home secretary turned to Charlie. "Why did you ask me to come to my brother's? You could have contacted me at my office or phoned and made an appointment to see me. I have already had a hard time from supposedly interfering in your investigation; I don't need to be implicated in secret meetings."

Charlie asked the Khans if he could speak privately to the home secretary, and they left the room. Charlie sat down and the home secretary took the seat opposite him.

"Home secretary, I understand all your reservations, but please allow me to explain and show you some evidence I have gathered – after which, I think you will understand why I did not want our meeting to be known about."

"Alright, Chief Superintendent, but I don't have a lot of time. I have to be at a meeting on the south coast this afternoon."

Charlie started to go through what had been happening to the investigation from the beginning and the strange things it had suffered from, passing documents and photographs for the home secretary to see as he did. He also explained what had been found at his house and been given to Assistant Commissioner Crick.

When he had finished, the home secretary sat back with the dossier of evidence Charlie had passed to him.

"This might tie in with some strange things I have also been experiencing," he said. "I will cancel my meeting this afternoon, get onto the commissioner and call him to a meeting at the Home Office to see me. I will have to inform the prime minister, as this could have far-reaching consequences. May I take all your documents with me?"

"Yes, of course, and you might like to get Commissioner Crick along to your meeting as he has been to the same meetings as I have. He also has the items that were planted at my house," Charlie said.

"Thank you, Chief Superintendent. I will be in touch when I have had the meeting and have gotten to the bottom of this."

"Thank you, Sir," Charlie said. "All we are trying to do is find out who murdered your brother's daughter."

★ ★ ★

Jordan had got the address of the house Oscar had been going to and phoned Danny, telling him to meet him there. When Jordan turned up, he saw Danny and a constable standing beside their car. Jordan got out and went over to them. Danny pointed to Oscar's car parked further along the road.

"I had a look and it's all locked up."

"Let's knock on the door and see what we have," Jordan said. "Constable, you go round the back and have a look."

Jordan and Danny walked up to the front door and rang the bell, but there was no answer. Danny tried to look through the curtains, but they were drawn and tightly closed. The constable returned from looking round the back of the house.

"Nothing round there," he said.

Jordan knelt down and looked through the letterbox. There was no movement inside. He called out, but there didn't seem to be anyone in.

"There wasn't a window open round the back?" he asked the constable.

"No, it's all locked up," he said.

"Well, Danny, what do reckon?" Jordan said.

"Oscar's car is sitting over there and we have a house all locked up, which he was supposed to be checking out. I don't like it," Danny replied.

"No, me neither. Have you got anything in your car to get the door open?" Jordan said.

Danny went back to his car and Jordan phoned Harry to let him know what they were going to do. Harry told him to take the door off its hinges if he had to. Danny came back with a large metal ram with two handles on it.

"Give it to me," Jordan said.

Danny and the constable stood back, while Jordan swung the ram. It crashed into the door just above the lock; the door gave but didn't open. Jordan swung again, landing the ram right on the lock. The door crashed open. Jordan quickly dropped the ram and entered the house, followed by Danny and the constable.

"You check upstairs," Jordan said, pointing to the constable. "Danny, do the kitchen."

Jordan opened the door to his left. The room was in darkness because of the drawn curtain. He felt for a light switch, found it and flicked it on. He stood in the doorway and remained frozen for a second – across the room, lying over some partially opened drawers, was Oscar.

"Danny! In here!" Jordan cried out.

He went to Oscar to check for any sign of life, but found none. Danny entered the room and looked at Jordan kneeling beside Oscar's body.

"Oh shit, not Oscar," Danny said.

Jordan looked up. "Call Harry and let him know what's happened. Tell him we'll have a look round and to get forensics over here."

Danny called the constable to come outside with him and call Inspector West to come to the house. Danny called Harry and told him what they had found. Harry said he would be over as soon as he could and would call Charlie to tell him. He got up, went next door to Manjitt and told her about Oscar, but said she was to stay there and get the information from Australia as it could be vital.

Harry then called the boss – Charlie had been driving to the station but said he would go straight to the house.

* * *

When Charlie arrived, he found Harry and Inspector West standing outside the front door.

"In here, boss," Harry said.

Charlie followed him into the house and the room where Oscar's body lay. Jordan and Danny were standing in the room. Charlie looked down at Oscar.

"What was it?" he asked Jordan.

"It looks like he was stabbed and fell across the drawers. There's no blood anywhere else," Jordan said.

"Right, seal the house up until forensics have been," Charlie said.

All four walked outside to join West.

"Inspector, I want the road blocked off at both ends. No one is to come in, unless they live on the road – and they have to prove that they do. Harry, as soon as forensics have finished, I want that house torn apart. Find anything that might give us an idea of who was there when Oscar went in. I don't want anything missed," Charlie said. "We have to assume that Oscar had found something or someone here. There's no car, but it might have been here. If it was, then we have to believe the people in the house are the same people who killed Ashadieeyah."

"We have the phone calls made to the farm in Leatherhead," Harry said. "That's the only lead we have to this place if it's the same people."

"Get back to the station, Harry, and take Jordan with you. I want to know all there is to know about it. I want a map of the place, too. Let's not hang around; whoever these people are, they are not frightened of killing if they need to. Jordan, find out how the rent or rates were paid for this house. If it was from a bank account, check that out," ordered Charlie.

Harry and Jordan left.

"You all right, Hippie?" Charlie said to Danny.

"Yes, boss, it was just a shock seeing Oscar lying there," he said.

"I know, but we have to stay focused. Oscar was doing his job and we have to do ours, otherwise we won't catch who did this," Charlie replied.

Meanwhile, Inspector West came back, more marked police cars turned up and a forensics team drove onto the driveway.

"Danny, brief the forensics on what we have."

Danny walked over to the forensics team.

Charlie turned to West, "Inspector, when the forensics have finished, I want a team to search the house. Listen, the last house search missed a vital clue. I don't want that happening again so choose the search team carefully. Before you start, let Harry know and he will speak to them."

"Yes, Sir," West said. "Nothing will be missed."

Danny came back over. "I asked them to give us a preliminary as soon as they can."

"Danny, you and the inspector organise a quick house-to-house along the street and find out who lived here. Did anyone see much of them? Can we get any descriptions? Was there a BMW parked here? Do every house and also the ones backing onto the garden. If no one's in, keep a check on it – when they turn up at the road block, question them before they're allowed through."

Charlie then put a call through to Assistant Commissioner Crick and told him what had happened. Crick asked if Charlie needed any more help, as he could have as much as he wanted. Charlie said he would let him know when they were clear about what had happened. Crick told him he had been called to a meeting that evening at the Home Office, but would ring Charlie later and let him know how things had gone.

Catching up with West and Danny, who were sorting out the house-to-house, Charlie said, "I'm going back to the station; keep me informed if you turn up anything."

★★★

When Charlie got back to the office, the first thing he did was get Oscar's file from Harry. He checked the address of Oscar's parents and told Harry he would be gone for a couple of hours as he was going to break the news to them about their son.

Meanwhile, Harry had gotten hold of an Ordnance Survey map of the farm in Leatherhead and the surrounding area. He had run a Land Registry check on it and found out it was bought two years ago by a company based in Switzerland. He had checked the council records and they showed that there was one person living on the farm – a William Hartnall. However, Harry couldn't find any other trace of him on any records or bank accounts.

Manjitt was still on the phone to Australia. Harry told her to inform them that a police officer had now been killed and he wanted a picture of Shiza Akmal from them soon.

Jordan came back in. "There's a direct debit set up to pay the rent on the house," he said, "and I have the details coming through soon. I have also been onto the people who own the house to give me a description of the person renting it from them – it sounds like our phone buyer. I will get one of West's men to shoot over there and see if they can identify him from the picture."

Harry then took a call from Danny, who said two neighbours had seen a black BMW parked outside the house often, but had not seen who lived at the address.

Jordan came back into the office. "The rent is paid from an account in the name of Mirla Fournier," he said, "who we know is living in France – it's a good possibility that Shiza Akmal and Mirla Fournier are the same person."

"Put an alert out to all airports and ports to stop Mirla Fournier or Shiza Akmal if she tries to leave the country. She might have already gone, but let's do it anyway," Harry said.

Manjitt came in. "Harry, I spoke to the Australians. They have quite a bit on Shiza Akmal; it seems she was mixed up in a number of radical Islamic groups out there and had been questioned, but never charged, in connection to terrorist plots. They said she had disappeared about a year ago. They are emailing me the details and a picture now."

"Well done, Manjitt. Get the picture printed as soon as it comes through."

Harry then took a call from forensics, who told him they had a lot of fingerprints and possible DNA from hair found in the house. They also said the knife could be the same one that had killed the girl, but they would know for sure when they did further tests.

* * *

The home secretary sat at his desk, opposite the commissioner and Assistant Commissioner Crick.

"Thank you for coming to this meeting at such short notice, Commissioner. I have to speak to you about one of your most senior officers, who I believe has been running a corrupt operation against certain members of the police force and myself. I have invited Assistant Commissioner Crick here as he has information that shows involvement by this officer in the planting of evidence, namely drugs and firearms, to implicate another officer in crimes and corruption – the officer being Chief Superintendent Smith of the Serious Crime Squad."

The commissioner spoke, "That's strange, as I have been informed today that the Police Complaints Division were planning an investigation into Chief Superintendent Smith on information they had received – in fact, they were going to raid his house this evening. I was planning on getting AC Crick to my office to discuss it before I got the call to come to this meeting. Who is the officer you say has been carrying out these corrupt acts?"

"Assistant Commissioner Walker," the home secretary said.

The commissioner was taken aback. "Surely your information is wrong. He's the head of the Anti-Terrorism Squad and there has been no rumour or word of anything being wrong in his department."

"I don't know about rumour," the home secretary said, "but we have clear evidence that senior officers on his staff have carried out criminal offences. What I want you to do now, Commissioner, is ring up whoever is in charge of the investigation into Chief Superintendent Smith, ask them to cancel it and join us right away, and I mean right away – in the next fifteen minutes."

The commissioner made the phone call and when he was finished, he said, "They are on their way over to your office now, Sir."

"While we are waiting, Commissioner," the home secretary said, "I want you to read this." He handed over some files to the commissioner. "When you have finished reading them, we have a couple of CDs for you to watch and AC Crick has a couple of items to show you."

Crick took the handgun and the package of drugs, which were in evidence bags, and put them on the table. As the commissioner started to read the files, the home secretary picked up his phone and asked his assistant to put a call through to the prime minister's office and arrange for him to have an urgent meeting.

***

Charlie returned to the station, after visiting Oscar's parents. He told Harry how upset they had been and how he would call in again tomorrow to see them.

"Never an easy thing to do, boss," Harry said, "but let's hope we catch the person who did it and it may give them some comfort."

"We will do that, Harry," Charlie said. "Now, what have we got?"

Harry went through all that they had gathered and laid the Ordnance Survey map of the farm out on the table. "Call the rest of the team back to the office, Harry. I want everyone here before we get stuck into this, so that we plan it right. I will see Caroline now about back-up."

Charlie went into Caroline's office and explained to her what he needed. She said he could use all the available officers he wanted.

He then called Crick, who said he was in a meeting with the home secretary, but listened as Charlie explained that Crick needed to contact the Chief Constable of Surrey, as they would be conducting an operation in Leatherhead early tomorrow morning and needed someone from SCO19 – the firearm boys – to contact him. Crick said he would do that and get back to him later. Charlie asked how the meeting was going and Crick confirmed it was going well.

Charlie went back to the office, where Harry was seated with Manjitt and Jordan. Manjitt held up a picture and Charlie took it from her.

"That's Shiza Akmal; you can see how much she looks like Ashadieeyah Khan," Manjitt said.

"Yes, they could have been sisters," Charlie said. "Harry, do you know anyone on the Surrey force? I have Crick contacting the chief constable, but if you know someone, it could smooth the way."

Harry picked up the phone, took his diary from his pocket and thumbed through it. "I think I have a mate here who's on the Surrey force and owes me a couple of favours," he said and dialled a number.

"How does he get all these people who owe him favours?" Jordan said.

"Just hope you're never one of them," Charlie said.

Danny and West arrived back at the office just as Harry got off the phone. "Sorted, boss. He said to ring him when we are ready to roll and he will make sure all of their people stay out the way until we call them in."

"Good. Now, everyone, I intend to raid this farm in the morning," Charlie said. He pointed to the map. "We need to have some idea if anyone's there, so I want Jordan and Danny to scout the place out. Be careful; we don't want to spook them. They are probably on their guard after what's happened, so just see if the BMW is there and how many people are wandering around. Make sure you don't get seen. You might need to get some night-vision binoculars. Harry, can we put our hands on some?"

Harry nodded yes.

"Then come back here. No one is going home tonight. Manjitt, I want you and Inspector West to go and visit all the other farms around and ask any neighbours about the people on the farm. If they ask why, tell them it's a suspected drug gang using it. Now, get going."

They all got up to leave the office. Harry gave Jordan a number to call for the binoculars.

"Be careful, everyone," he said.

"Make some tea, Harry. It's going to be a long night," Charlie said, looking at the map.

***

The home secretary sat quietly as he waited for the commissioner to make a comment after reading and watching the CD evidence. Instead, it was AC Crick who broke the silence.

"I have done some checking of my own," he said, "and the man my staff has known as Jamie Grant is, in fact, a detective sergeant called Michael Folds. He has worked in the Anti-Terrorism Squad for five years. The other man seen with him at Chief

Superintendent Smith's house is also a detective sergeant, who is called Donald Adams. He has been with the Anti-Terrorism Squad for three years. I have two teams of officers waiting near their home addresses for an order from me to go and arrest them."

The home secretary's phone rang. He picked it up and said, "Send them in."

A man and a woman entered.

"Please take a seat," the home secretary said. They both sat down. "Would you like to introduce yourself to me?" he asked, slightly raising his voice.

The woman spoke first, "Sorry, Sir, I am Chief Inspector Scanlon and this is Inspector Lees. We both work in police complaints."

"Thank you, Chief Inspector. I understand you were going to raid the house of Chief Superintendent Smith from Serious Crimes. Would you like to tell us on what evidence?"

"Sir, I don't think it would be appropriate to say, so as not to alert anyone should any information leak out," she answered.

The home secretary looked at her for a full minute before replying, "Chief Inspector, I take it from your answer that you want to take up a career in comedy. Sitting next to you is the highest-ranking policeman in the country and sitting in front of you is the home secretary, why do you think we got you here? Why do you think your operation was cancelled by the commissioner? If you do not answer my question, you will be looking for a new career."

The chief inspector looked to her left, where the commissioner was now staring at her. He said, "Would you please tell the home secretary the answer to that question?"

Before she could speak, the home secretary said, "I know, let me guess, was it Assistant Commissioner Walker?"

"Yes, Sir," she said.

"Now, Chief Inspector, you might realise we did not get you here to grill you, but to stop you making fools of yourselves. Commissioner, I have got to go now to a meeting with the prime minister," the home secretary said, "but I would hope this is all cleared up by the morning. I will expect you back in my office at nine with an update of what action has been taken. Take this with you, Commissioner."

He pushed all the files and evidence across the desk. They all stood and the commissioner led the way out of the home secretary's office. He turned to Crick and said, "Tell your teams to go ahead with the arrests."

As they walked out into Whitehall, Crick made a phone call, "Proceed with the operation and there must be no word getting out. Bring them back to Scotland Yard to the commissioner's office."

The commissioner nodded and said, "Chief Inspector Scanlon, follow us back to Scotland Yard and come to my office. Do not call anyone."

He and Crick climbed into the commissioner's car and sped down Whitehall towards Victoria and Scotland Yard.

* * *

When the home secretary reached Downing Street, his car dropped him outside Number Ten. The door was opened as he approached it and he walked through the hall to the prime minister's office.

The prime minister was sitting behind his desk, with the cabinet secretary, chief whip and party chairman also there.

"Take a seat," the prime minister said. "Now, your phone call earlier about a possible scandal had us worried. The chief whip was telling us about your problems and I am sure we can find a solution to them."

The home secretary looked at the prime minister, then turned to look at the chief whip, and said, "I don't have any problems. I have just been with the commissioner trying to clear up what could have been a big scandal. It seems some senior police officers have been running a campaign to discredit me."

"Who were they?" the prime minister asked.

"An Assistant Commissioner Walker of the Anti-Terrorism Squad and a number of his officers. They have been caught planting evidence against innocent police officers and briefing false rumours to the press about me. I have checked with some journalist friends and the funny thing is that they said they had also had stories given to them by members of the government."

"I am sure that's not true; it's just the press trying to stir things up," the prime minister said.

"The chief whip might be able to enlighten us," the home secretary said. "He had a private meeting with this corrupt officer yesterday in his office and my friends in the press said his staff had given them stories about me."

They all turned to look at the chief whip.

***

Danny and Jordan made their way to the farm, parked their car in a lane and walked about a mile across fields to a small group of trees a short distance from the farmhouse. The trees were on a slight rise, so they could look down on the farm and the surrounding buildings. Jordan put the night-vision binoculars up to his eyes, panning across the house and the surrounding area.

"Lights on upstairs and down," he said, "but no one moving around. I can't see any cars parked, but the doors on the barns are all closed."

"Well, looks like we will be here for a few hours. I should have brought some food," Danny said.

"I don't know how you're so skinny, you never stop stuffing your face," Jordan replied.

"You know, I'm going to miss Oscar. He was a good bloke; I always had a laugh with him when we were working together. He was always trying to get me to dance the samba and laughed when I did," Danny said.

"Yes, he was a good one," Jordan replied, "but let's hope the people responsible are down in that farmhouse and we can nick them."

Jordan put the binoculars back to his eyes, but there was still no movement.

★ ★ ★

Manjitt and Inspector West had been to three farms in the area, but no one had seen anything of the people who owned the farm in question. One had seen a few lorries and vans coming or going, but not much work seemed to be going on.

Manjitt laid the map Harry had given her on the bonnet of the car. "Where to next, Inspector?" she said.

West looked at the map. "We have covered all the farms to the south. It only shows one to the north, but there are a couple of houses on here we can visit before we go there."

"Whoever it is at our farm, they don't seem to have been very sociable." Manjitt folded the map up. "Let's get going. You never know, someone might have seen something."

She and West climbed back into the car and set off.

★ ★ ★

"The door's just opened," Jordan said, as light flooded the darkness of the farmyard.

Jordan watched as a man stepped out. He seemed to look around, before heading back to the house. He stopped at the entrance, appearing to say something, and then went off towards one of the barns, leaving the door to the farmhouse open.

"Keep your eyes on the doorway, Danny, while I watch our friend," Jordan said.

The man reached the barn, pulled one of the doors open slightly and slipped inside. Jordan kept the binoculars trained on the barn and, after a couple of minutes; the man appeared again, shut the door and walked towards the second barn. He was nearly there when he stopped, turned and walked back to the farmhouse. When he reached the door, he went in but left the door open.

"Could you make him out?" Danny asked.

"No, not clearly enough to be definite," Jordan said. "Hold on, there's more movement."

The man reappeared at the door, stepped out and went towards the second barn. This time, he was followed by another figure.

"It's a woman," Jordan said. He watched as they made their way to the barn and disappeared inside. "Well, we have two people here at least. I can't say if it's our suspect, though."

"It could just be some old farmer and his wife," Danny replied.

The pair stayed in the barn for five minutes before they reappeared, the man was carrying a box, while the woman shut the barn door. They made their way back to the house and went inside, closing the door. It was dark again in the farmyard. "Give Harry a ring and let him know what's happening," Jordan said.

★★★

Manjitt and West stopped the car in front of three small cottages that looked like they had been set down in the middle of nowhere, but were probably old farmworkers' houses.

"I'll do this end one," Manjitt said. "You do that end one and we'll meet in the middle."

They each knocked on the doors of the houses, spent a few minutes talking to the occupants, but had no luck with their enquiries. At the middle house, it was the same story.

As they reached the car, West said, "I think it's the invisible man that owns that farm – no one has ever seen him."

"All we can hope is that the last farm might be able to help us," Manjitt said.

It took them about ten minutes to find their way to the last farmhouse on the map. They parked the car next to a large tractor and walked across the yard to knock on the door. It was opened by a woman, to who Manjitt explained what they were doing there. The woman said she couldn't help but her husband might be able to. She called out and a large man appeared behind her.

Manjitt asked him the same questions and the man said he had been down to the farm to speak to them about a damaged fence that marked the barrier of his land and theirs, and how it was their responsibility to get it fixed. He told Manjitt and West that he had seen only one man, who was foreign and spoke with an Indian or Pakistani accent. He didn't know if anyone else was there, but they still hadn't fixed the fence. West thanked him for his help, and he and Manjitt returned to the car.

"Could be our man from the phone shop, but also could be anybody," West said. "Let's head back to base."

* * *

AC Crick was sitting in his office, when Chief Inspector Scanlon and Inspector Lees arrived. The commissioner told them "to sit down and read this", pushing some files across to them. "There are some pictures that go with it and I will also show you a couple of CDs when you have finished."

Scanlon started reading, passing each page across to Lees as she finished it.

After reading and watching the CDs, Crick asked what she thought.

"It would seem to be a clear case of police malpractice or corruption," Scanlon said.

Crick hated listening to politically correct jargon, but didn't say anything.

The Commissioner said that Crick had two of the officers being brought in and they would be charged with deception just to hold them for now. He told Scanlon to go ahead and arrest Walker and bring him in, but to make sure she questioned the junior officers first to firm up the case against Walker. He then asked them to keep him up to date every few hours on any progress, which he would then report to the home secretary.

Scanlon and Lees got up and left the office.

"This is going to cause a stink in the press," Crick muttered.

* * *

Assistant Commissioner Walker was sitting at home watching the end of the news, when he heard the doorbell go.

"I'll get it," he heard his wife call out.

He could hear voices coming from the hall and had just stood up when a man and woman entered the room. He could also see a uniformed police officer behind them, standing next to his wife.

It was the woman who first spoke, "Assistant Commissioner Walker, I am Chief Inspector Scanlon from police complaints. I am arresting you on suspicion of conspiracy to corrupt public officials. You do not have to say anything, but whatever…"

Walker didn't hear much of what else was said to him, but eventually pulled himself together to say, "You have made a mistake; you know who I am, don't you?"

Scanlon advised him not to speak until they were at the Yard for his own sake. She told him that his house and his office would be searched and the offices of his staff were being searched at this moment.

He was led away still trying to work out what was going on.

* * *

Manjitt and West got back to the office and went over what they had learnt.

"With what you have told us and the information Danny has phoned in, it has to be taken on trust that the people we want are at the farm," Harry said.

"It's all we have, Harry," Charlie said, "and my gut tells me they are there. Give Danny and Jordan a ring and tell them to stay on watch. We will pick them up when we get to the farm."

Harry phoned Danny and told him that he and Jordan should stay on watch, and he would call them when they were near the farm to join up.

***

A short while later, everyone was crammed into the meeting room on the ground floor of the police station. Charlie and Harry were standing by the large map of the farm, while West, Manjitt, the firearms team and thirty local officers that Caroline and West had made available were seated in front of them.

"Listen up, everyone," Charlie said, "this is the farm we are going to be raiding." He pointed to the map. "I want everybody to have a look at it before we go. We know there are at least two people at the farm, but there could be more and we have to assume there are. We have photographs of two suspects who we believe are at the farm – you can all take pictures of them from Chief Inspector Davis." Charlie pointed at Harry.

"When we get to the farm and I will give the order to begin the raid, the firearms team will go into the house first, followed by my officers. There are a number of barns and outbuildings – Inspector West and his team will secure those and the perimeter. Make sure you all have your stab vests on – two people have been killed already, possibly by somebody in that house and I don't want anyone else hurt. Now, study the map and photographs. It will still be dark when we go in and I don't want any mistakes. Grab some breakfast; we will be leaving the station at 4.15am."

Charlie went and spoke to the officer in charge of the firearms team, while Harry worked with West and Manjitt to give out photographs and brief the local officers on what they expected them to do.

★★★

At exactly 4.15am, the cars and vans filled with the raid team left the police station car park, while Charlie had Harry, West and Manjitt in the Bentley with him. The roads were pretty much deserted as they made their way towards Leatherhead and the farm. Harry had phoned Danny and told him that he and Jordan should meet them by the main road that led to the farm entrance.

It took about twenty-five minutes to reach the farm. As they parked up, Charlie told West to get a couple of his officers and get the road closed off from both directions and stressed the need for silence to the others. They all climbed out of the car and saw Jordan and Danny approach them through the darkness.

"Any change?" Harry asked.

"No movement since I last spoke to you," Danny said.

West came back and said, "The roads are closed off."

Charlie went and spoke to the officer in charge of the firearms team. When he came back, he told everyone they were going to start to approach the house.

The firearms team led the way, climbing silently over the gate at the entrance in case it made a noise when opened. Everyone else followed suit. About a quarter of a mile along the drive from the main road to the farmhouse, Charlie saw the firearms team split up. One group went off to cover the back, while the other led the rest of the team to the front. When in place, the firearms officer approached Charlie and told him his officers were in position and ready to go. Charlie checked that everybody else was in position.

Charlie took the radio from his pocket and gave the order to go. The area around them suddenly seemed to come alive with noise; the splintering of the door could be heard at the front of the farmhouse, with the same noise coming from the back. Charlie heard cries of "Armed police; stand still!" from inside the house and the screech of barn doors being pulled open, while torches lit up the courtyard of the farm.

Charlie and Harry went through the smashed front door, while Jordan and Manjitt ran up the stairs following the armed officers. Charlie could hear scuffling and people falling around from the floor above. After a couple of minutes, cries of "Room clear" could be heard.

Charlie and Harry made their way into the front room of the farmhouse. The table in the centre of the room was covered in maps, books, reels of electrical wire and tools. They turned as they heard people being brought down the staircase from upstairs. Manjitt and Jordan brought a woman, who had been handcuffed, into the room; they were followed by two other handcuffed men held by firearms officers.

Charlie said to Jordan, "Tell them their rights, and then get them straight into separate cars back to the station. Get them booked in and into the cells. We can question them later."

Jordan and Manjitt took the prisoners out of the house.

Charlie turned to Harry. "That's her, Harry, and I think we have our phone buyer, too."

Danny came into the house, "You better come and see this, boss."

Charlie and Harry followed Danny out of the house and across the farmyard into one of the barns. A black BMW was parked beside a large lorry.

"I want forensics all over that car," Charlie said.

"Boss, you better see this first," Danny said.

Danny led them to the back of the lorry, whose back doors were open. West was standing by the lorry with one of his officers. Charlie looked through the open doors.

"Is that what I think it is?" Harry said.

Danny and West both nodded.

"There's another lorry in the other barn, but its doors are locked," West said. "I told everyone not to touch it."

"Get everyone back up to the main road now," Charlie said, "and clear the whole area. Harry, you ring the Bomb Disposal Squad; tell them what we have found and that we suspect there might be two."

Harry got on the phone straightaway.

They had been standing on the point of the road where they had parked up earlier that morning. It had been forty five minutes since Charlie had told everyone to evacuate the farm, the bomb disposal team had arrived and Harry had West brief them on what they had discovered and where it was.

Charlie then phoned Assistant Commissioner Crick and told him they had arrested three people and that they thought two bombs had been discovered at the farm. He asked him to inform the Anti-Terrorist Squad, but he would be questioning the prisoners first. Crick told Charlie about the arrests of Walker and his officers, so he could expect someone new coming over. Crick said he would find out who it was and get them to ask for Charlie.

When he got off the phone to Crick, he told Danny and West to stay at the farm to make sure forensics did a good job on the BMW and the house as soon as they got the all-clear from bomb disposal.

* * *

Charlie parked the Bentley in the police station car park. He and Harry got out and made their way up the stairs to the office. As they reached the first floor, Chief Superintendent Myles met them.

"Hello, Charlie, I understand you had a successful raid this morning. You have three in custody?"

"Yes, it went great. We also found a lorry with what we think is a bomb in it and there could be another in the lorry that was in the barn next door – bomb disposal are there now. We recovered a black BMW, too, which might be the car we have been searching for. There is one thing you could help me with, however. The press will be buzzing round sooner rather than later, so could I leave you to fend them off? If you contact my boss, AC Crick, at the Yard, he will give you any help you need."

"Yes, that not a problem," Caroline said. "Pop in to my office later to let me know how the questioning is going."

They carried on up the stairs to the office and found Jordan and Manjitt sitting chatting.

"Well, you two," Harry asked. "How were the prisoners when you got them back here?"

"None of them said a word. We have them in cells seperate from each other," Jordan replied.

Harry turned to Charlie, "How shall we play this, boss?"

"You and I will question the girl first," Charlie said. "Get everything we know about her together and we will see how she reacts. You two," Charlie spoke to Jordan and Manjitt, "see what you can find out about the two men. Run their prints through the system and see what turns up."

* * *

The door opened and a constable escorted a woman into the interview room. He led her to a chair and she sat down, looking across the table at Harry and Charlie, who sat at each corner of the table with a 3-feet gap between them. It was something they always did, as it meant that whoever they interviewed would have to keep turning from one to the other to answer questions or to look at them.

The constable went and stood by the door, while Harry flicked a switch on the tape recorder.

"Interview with suspect. Present: Chief Superintendent Smith and Chief Inspector Davis," Harry said.

Charlie watched the woman. She showed no emotion and stared straight ahead.

"Would you like to tell us your name?" Charlie said.

He waited, but the woman said nothing.

"What were you doing at the farm?"

Again, she made no reply. Her dark eyes looked ahead and she showed no acknowledgement of Charlie's questions.

"Would you like a drink?" Harry said.

The woman's eyes turned to look at Harry, but she still made no reply. Charlie and Harry sat and watched her for five minutes.

"Would you tell us your name?" Charlie asked.

She turned and looked at Charlie. He thought he saw contempt and hatred in her eyes, but she sat quietly and made no attempt to answer. They sat in silence for another few minutes.

"You are in serious trouble – you know that, don't you?" Harry said. "I don't think you're stupid. It would be best if you just told us what has been going on."

Charlie saw a slight smile flicker, then disappear from her face.

"Let's get back to your name," Charlie said. "The BMW we found at the farm, is that yours?" The woman said nothing; her eyes, unblinking, stared at Charlie. "The car was registered to a Mirla Fournier, is that you?"

A smile came to her lips.

"This is going to be a long interview if you won't even confirm your name," Harry said, "but we will call you Mirla as you have not denied it. Mirla, is that a French name? Are you French?"

Charlie saw her smile as she turned to look at Harry, but she still remained silent.

Harry opened a file in front of him. "The BMW we found at the farm was registered to a Mirla Fournier. We had been looking for the car in connection to the murder of a policeman, who was stabbed to death at a house in New Malden."

Harry looked at the woman, who said nothing. The silence went on for a minute.

"Do you know anything about the murder of the policeman? Were you living at the house in New Malden? The rent for the house was paid by a Mirla Fournier."

Still no answer came.

"Well, let me help you a little to try and jog your memory. We have DNA and fingerprints from the house and car; do you think they will match yours?"

Charlie saw the first flicker of recognition come across her face, before she returned to staring ahead.

Harry continued, "I think we both know they will." Harry turned the page in the file and looked back at the woman. "When did you come to England, Mirla?"

She turned to him. For a second, it looked like she was going to answer, but she continued her silence. Harry and Charlie both sat quietly, looking at her for a further few minutes.

"How do you think you will be spending the next forty years?" Charlie asked.

She turned to look at him. Charlie stared back.

"I reckon you will have lots of high walls and a small cell as your home, which must be an attractive outlook for you."

"Did you kill the policeman or was it one of the men we found at the farm with you?" Harry asked.

"It's not a nice thought, is it? The next forty years in a small cell, in a prison, with only high walls to see from your window," Charlie said.

The woman looked at Charlie and her eyes showed hatred. It seemed she wanted to say something, but she turned away and continued to look straight ahead again.

"Mirla, if it wasn't you, who killed the police officer?" Harry asked. "You should tell us now. It would make things better for you."

"You will be aged around sixty when you can get out of prison," Charlie said. "Just think of that – sixty and all those wasted years. You could probably do some university courses to keep you busy, but you will be too old to use them when you get out."

She looked back at Charlie, who saw her eyes narrow. It was pure hatred.

Good, Charlie thought, *I'm getting under your skin.*

"Let's get back to the BMW," Harry said. The woman turned to Harry, with confusion showing for a second on her face. "Now, we know the car is registered to you, but did you let anyone else drive it?"

She continued to say nothing.

"Mirla, you really should think about answering our questions," Charlie said. "Are there any family you would like me to contact for you?"

The woman turned again to look at Charlie. He smiled at her.

"I can tell them that they might not see you for the next forty years."

They sat silently for a few minutes.

"Which one of the men lived with you at the house in New Malden? Or did they both live there?" Harry asked.

Silence.

After a few minutes, Charlie said, "Well, I have enjoyed our first chat, Mirla, but we have to make some more enquiries. I am terminating this interview."

"Constable, take her back to her cell," Charlie said.

The constable came and took the woman's arm, helping her from the chair. As she reached the door, Charlie said, "Look at those four walls when you get back to the cell and imagine the next forty years." She turned her head to look at Charlie, who smiled back at her. "I look forward to continuing our chat later."

After she was gone, Charlie asked, "What do you think, Harry?"

"She's putting on a good show, but we nearly had her a couple of times. Let's give her a few hours and then have another go. We could drop some more of her life on her and see how she reacts," Harry answered.

"Good, let's check in with the team to see how they are getting on."

They both stood and left the room, heading back to the office.

* * *

Danny and West had returned to the office and were sitting talking to Manjitt and Jordan about the raid and what had been found. Charlie and Harry came in.

"How did you get on at the farm?" Harry asked.

Danny pulled a number of exhibit bags from under the desk. "We got some gold, Harry." He held up a clear plastic evidence tube with a knife inside. "This was found in a handbag, along with a passport in the name of Mirla Fournier. It was in the room where the woman was sleeping." He put it on the desk. "We also got this." Danny held up a bag; inside was a mobile phone. "I called it and it's our pay-as-you go-phone we've been looking for. It was found in a coat hanging up behind the door."

"Well done, just what we needed," Harry said.

"Manjitt, get the knife and phone to Doctor Taylor at forensics," Charlie said. "Ask him if the knife is the one used to kill Ashadieeyah Khan and if it was the same one that was used to kill Oscar. See if we can get some DNA or fingerprints off the phone. Also take the jacket the phone was found in, as there might be some DNA on that too, so we can put the phone in someone's possession. Jordan, go and check if the information has come back on the two men we have in custody downstairs. If not, chase it up as a priority."

"The anti-terrorism boys turned up at the farm before we left,"

West said. "We gave them your name, boss, if they needed to speak about the case."

"Okay, you two, grab something to eat and then come back here," Charlie said.

West and Danny got up.

"Do you want us to bring anything back for you?" Danny asked.

Harry shook his head.

"No, nothing for me," Charlie said.

Charlie picked the phone up on the desk and phoned AC Crick at the Yard. He told him how things were progressing and what evidence they had gathered so far. Crick told him that AC Walker's two junior officers had made full statements and Walker was going to be interviewed later in the day. He would let Charlie know how things had gone when they spoke again. He said the commissioner had heard about the finding of the bombs at the farmhouse and sent his congratulations. Charlie said he hoped this didn't mean he would get invited to the swanky parties at the Yard. Crick assured him there was no chance of that.

Putting down the phone, Charlie said, "Let's have some tea, Harry." As he switched the kettle in the corner of the office on, he told Harry of his conversation with Crick.

"Well, I guess you might get invited to all the best parties," Harry said. "Still, you can always ask Caroline along if you need a partner."

Charlie looked at Harry. "Do you want the tea in your lap?" he asked and Harry laughed. "Let's get back to the real world. When we restart the interview, how long do you want to go before we tell her we know who she is?"

"I think we let her carry on thinking we don't know her real name. She seems pleased with herself," Harry said. "Then we can let her know and see how she reacts. I get the impression she's no fan of yours, though."

Charlie put a cup of tea down in front of Harry. "I guess I will have to learn to live with that," he said.

Jordan came into the office, "I have the name for one of the men. His fingerprints match those we got from the farmhouse. His name is Rashid Butt, aged twenty-eight from Leeds. He got arrested for threatening someone with a knife about five years ago. He got twelve months probation, but there's nothing else on file."

"That's good," Charlie said. "You question him and take West with you when he gets back. Don't mention the bombs – we will leave that to the Anti-Terrorism Squad – just stick to the murders. Go over the files with Harry and you can work out a questioning strategy before you go in." Charlie stood up. "I am going down to see Chief Superintendent Myles." Harry looked up. "Not a word, Harry."

Harry smiled and stretched out his arms, "Boss, I wasn't going to say anything."

Charlie turned and walked to the door. As he went through it, Harry said, "Don't forget to tell Caroline about your congratulations from the commissioner."

***

Charlie was sitting with Caroline in her office, going over what they had on the case and how the questioning was going.

"I have had a couple of calls from the press about bombs being found at the farm," Caroline said. "I spoke to someone from the Anti-Terrorism Squad and they are getting back to me with a line to take with the press for the time being. However, we already have some press outside the station."

"I expect the officer in charge of the Anti-Terrorism Squad to be here soon, so we can sit down and have a chat with him," Charlie said.

"When do you expect a solicitor to turn up for your suspects?" Caroline asked.

"Not too long I think, but we will continue to hold them for as long as we are allowed, then go to a magistrate if we have to for an extension," Charlie said. "I had a call from my boss and they have arrested three policemen on corruption charges over the interference in our case – two have made full statements admitting their part and the other is being interviewed later."

"That might cause a bit of a stink at Scotland Yard," Caroline said. "Do you think there could be more than just those three?"

"Probably a couple more, but the main players have been caught," Charlie said. "By the way, next Sunday I am inviting all the team to my house for dinner, as a sort of get-together for a well-run operation. I wondered if you would like to join us, seeing as you have done your part and put up with my team coming and going."

"Next Sunday? Yes, I would," said Caroline.

"I will drop you off my address later," Charlie said, as he stood up. "If the anti-terrorism boys turn up while I am interviewing the suspects, can you sort them out and send a message to me?"

"Of course Charlie, I hope you get your breakthrough," Caroline said.

⋆⋆⋆

Charlie went back to the office, where he found all of his team seated round the table listening to Harry, who looked up when he saw Charlie come in.

"Boss, Jordan has got everything on the man he is going to question. We have been going over how they should play the questioning."

"That's good for me, Harry, if you're happy with things," Charlie said. "Jordan, you and West get off and start the interview. Good luck."

Jordan and West left the office.

"Manjitt, did you get everything over to Doctor Taylor?" Charlie asked.

"Yes, he has everything. He said he would put all his staff on it and get back to us as soon as he has something," she said.

"Danny, chase up what's been found on the second man we have in custody. I think Jordan left how far he had got and who he spoke to on his desk, but we need a name," Charlie said.

Danny got up and went into the office next door.

The phone on Harry's desk rang. Harry picked it up, listened for a moment and asked the caller to hold.

"I have the German boy, Karl Bauer, on the phone."

"Manjitt, you deal with him. Get a statement off him, question him about Ashadieeyah and their walking holiday, find out where he's been and when he's going to go back to Oxford so we can get a written statement off him," Charlie said.

Harry passed the phone to Manjitt.

"Come on, Harry," Charlie continued, "let's go and start round two with our friend."

⋆ ⋆ ⋆

Charlie and Harry were seated in the same chairs as before, when the woman was brought into the interview room. She sat down, not making any comment or showing any acknowledgement of them. Harry started the recorder and repeated who was there and the time.

"Now, Mirla, before we start questioning you, would you like a drink of water or something else?" Harry said.

She made no answer.

"Okay, would you like to tell us what happened in the house with the policeman?"

They all sat quietly.

"We recovered a knife from the farm, which was found in a handbag along with a passport in the name of Mirla Fournier. It's your picture." Harry held up the passport. "Look at the picture, is that you?"

The woman glanced at the passport, but said nothing.

Harry passed the passport to Charlie, who flicked through it and said, "I have to say it looks like you. According to your passport, you went to Egypt. Was that for a holiday or for business?"

Charlie thought he saw confusion in her face.

Harry held up the handbag. "Is this yours?"

No answer.

"Well, it probably has your fingerprints inside and out. We also found some make up, lipstick and things, inside, so I'm sure that the DNA from that will confirm it's yours. Could you tell us how the knife got into your bag?"

"It would do you some good if you answered," Charlie said. "We are questioning the two men found with you at the farm; what are their names?" She looked at Charlie and smiled. "So you don't think they will say anything either? What makes you think that? Perhaps they don't want to spend forty years in prison."

She still said nothing.

"How long have you been in the country, Mirla? Did you always live at the house in New Malden?" Harry asked. "Is one of the men your boyfriend or husband? Is that why you don't want to say anything?"

There was a knock at the door. Manjitt put her head around and signalled to them. Harry said the interview was being stopped now, and he and Charlie got up and went out of the door, leaving the woman in the room.

Outside, Manjitt said, "Doctor Taylor called and the knife was the one used to kill both Oscar and Ashadieeyah. He also found Ashadieeyah Khan's blood all over the passenger seat and floor of the car. The evidence is consistent with her being killed in the car. Also, the phone has our suspect's fingerprints on it, along with the man Jordan is questioning. As soon as they get the DNA evidence, they will be straight in touch with us."

"What about the German boy?" Charlie asked.

"He confirms he was with Ashadieeyah walking for two weeks. He's coming back to Oxford in a week, so we can get a full statement then. Oh, and Chief Superintendent Myles said to tell you the Anti-Terrorism Squad boss is here. He's in her office," Manjitt replied.

"Harry, I am going up to Caroline's office. Take Manjitt back into the interview room with you and keep nibbling away at our suspect. Manjitt, follow Harry's lead and remember: no mention that we know her name yet."

Harry and Manjitt went back into the interview room.

* * *

Charlie got to Caroline's office, where she introduced him to Commander Flynn.

"Hello, Sir, nice to meet you," Charlie said.

"And you, Chief Superintendent," Flynn said. "How are you progressing with the case? The Commissioner has told me about the trouble you have had, so I want to make clear that we will do everything we can to aid you."

"Thank you, Sir, we have just begun the questioning," Charlie said. "We are not raising the terrorist angle yet, as we will leave that to you. We have got the name of one of the men, Rashid Butt, from Leeds – you might want to look into his background. The other one, we are still looking to trace something on him, and I will get one of my officers to give you all we have gathered on the girl."

"We have recovered some good intelligence from the farm," Flynn said, "paperwork, maps and some contact details. We never knew the farm existed, but the two lorries were packed with explosives and were ready to be moved. I think an imminent plot was foiled; they would have been massive explosions. I am going back to the farm again, but could I have a couple of my officers come over and get briefed on what you have so we can start digging?"

"Yes, Sir, if they ask for Chief Inspector Davis, he will give them everything we know. There is one other thing, though: the press are starting to ask questions and have turned up outside the station. Is it possible that they are told the suspects have been taken to the high security station at Paddington Green, so they will stay out of our hair?" Charlie asked.

"I think that can be arranged," Flynn said.

They exchanged phone numbers, before Flynn said he was going back to the farm to have a look around.

Charlie then returned to the office to see how Danny was getting on with his enquiries. Danny said he was still trying to track down the identities of the second man, but forensics had been onto him as there was another set of prints in the house and in both lorries.

Charlie phoned Flynn to let him know, who said he would get a couple of officers over straightaway to help find out who they belonged to.

★★★

Harry and Manjitt returned from questioning the woman.

"She's still playing dumb. Not a word. We've put her back in her cell," Harry said.

"I have some officers from the Anti–Terrorism Squad coming over – good ones this time," Charlie said. "It appears there are a fourth set of prints at the farm and in the lorries, which they are going to find out who they belong to. Manjitt, I want you to go over to the Khan's house and let them know we have someone in custody who we think is their daughter's killer. Stay there for a while, talk to them and explain that we are doing everything to ensure they won't get away with it."

Manjitt got up and left.

About twenty minutes later, Danny brought two men into the office.

"Boss, these two are from the Anti-Terrorism Squad," Danny said.

Charlie introduced himself, explained where they were with the case, and told them to go next door with Danny as he had all the information on the people that were being held. Charlie told them to see what they could find out using their contacts.

Charlie took a phone call from Commander Flynn, who told him he had had Rashid Butt's family home in Leeds raided and they had recovered some items that might be interesting, along with a laptop that was being looked at. If anything turned up, he promised to be back in touch.

Jordan and West came back into the office.

"How did you get on with your man?" Harry asked.

"He didn't say much, only confirmed his name and where he came from. I reckon if we give him a bit more thinking-time in his cell, he will crack. He doesn't seem to me to be the sort who likes being alone," Jordan said.

"In about an hour's time, go to his cell and ask if he wants a drink or bite to eat. Get chatty about anything except the case, and then leave him for another hour, before bringing him up for another interview. He might be friendlier and come across with some information," Charlie said. "In the meantime, go and get yourselves something to eat."

Jordan smiled, saying, "Those are words I love to hear. Come on, Inspector; let's go before he changes his mind."

"Harry, I will go and pick us up a sandwich," Charlie said. "I don't know what time it is in Australia, but get onto the officers that Manjitt spoke to and let them know we have Shiza Akmal in custody and what she's been up to over here. They might want to raid any address she lived at out there, but ask them to keep things quiet. If they turn anything up, tell them to let us know."

Ten minutes later, when Charlie had returned to the office, Harry told him he had been onto the Australians and they had sounded more than happy to go and knock a few doors down. They would be in touch about anything they found.

Danny popped his head round the door and told them the anti-terrorism boys had got a hit on the other man. His name was Mohamed Atif, who was from London. He was already known to them, from mixing with radical groups, but had disappeared from view about a year ago. Danny said that everything they had on him would be sent over.

Charlie finished his sandwich, threw the empty wrapping into the bin and said, "Let's go and have another crack at our ice queen, shall we, Harry?"

Harry phoned down to custody to get her taken to the interview room.

***

They were again seated in chairs when the woman was brought in. She sat down and stared ahead, not making eye contact. Harry switched on the tape and went over who was present and the time.

"Do you want a drink?" Harry asked.

The woman said nothing, but nodded.

That's a start, Harry thought.

"I hope you have had time to think since we last spoke," Charlie said. "I know you think you're doing something worthwhile by not saying anything, but really you're not."

She looked at Charlie and smiled.

He continued, "Let's see, you were going to tell us who killed the police officer in the house. If not, I think your friend, who is being interviewed now, will."

She still said nothing, staring blankly ahead.

"Why don't we go back to the beginning?" Harry said. "Let's start with your name. You don't want to tell us, but we believe it's Mirla Fournier."

She looked at Harry with just a smile on her face.

"Are you sure that's right, Chief Inspector?" Charlie asked. "Perhaps she won't answer because that's not her name."

She turned back to Charlie, who smiled at her now.

"If we call you Shiza Akmal, will you talk to us?"

Charlie noticed her face stiffen.

"Did you murder your old school friend Ashadieeyah Khan?" Harry asked.

Charlie saw her face change and he noticed her confusion. *She's wondering how we know.* Charlie exaggerated looking at his watch.

"I don't know what time it is in Australia, but I think they will be knocking on all your family's doors right now," Charlie said.

"Why did you murder Ashadieeyah? She let you borrow her passport to take your trip to Pakistan," Harry said.

"Your friends, Rashid Butt and Mohamed Atif," Charlie said, "will be telling us lots of stories."

"Did you kill her in the car? Why would you do that?" Harry asked. "She thought of you as a friend."

Her face now looked very confused. Charlie noticed she was sweating and he watched as a bead ran down the side of her face. They sat silent for five minutes, though she shifted in her seat a number of times.

"Would you like a drink of water?" Harry asked.

She nodded. Charlie told the constable by the door to go and get one, sitting in silence until he came back. She drank half the cup in one go and placed it down on the table, but still they sat in silence for a further few minutes.

"Shiza," Harry said, using her real name, which Charlie noticed made her jump. "What was it Ashadieeyah discovered that made you murder her? She was an old school friend who was happy to see you and we know she was doing you a favour by lending you her passport, because you told her about your family and an arranged marriage. It was kind of her to worry about you like that, but then you go and murder her – or was it Rashid or Mohamed?"

Charlie saw she was now starting to lose her hard face and her eyes were watering. They sat quietly again.

"Shiza, you must know we have lots of information that we could go through, but don't you want to put Ashadieeyah's mother and father at ease? They want to know their daughter was not mixed up in anything bad. Her mother is brokenhearted."

She reached for the cup and drank the rest of the water.

Suddenly she said, "I just wanted to give her passport back, but she saw the stamps inside and started asking questions. Rashid panicked and grabbed her neck. She started to struggle and I just stabbed her."

It was like a dam had been broken. She talked for two hours, giving all the details of what had happened to Ashadieeyah and Oscar, as well as the bomb plots.

★★★

When they got back to the office, Danny, Jordan and West were there.

"Rashid gave us a full statement," Jordan said.

"Shiza Akmal has confessed to the two murders and Harry has charged her," Charlie said.

Charlie phoned Commander Flynn and told him he could have the three prisoners now, explaining how they had charged Shiza Akmal and Rashid Butt with the murders. Flynn said he would come to the station and take the prisoners away to Paddington Green.

"That went well, Harry. You've still got your interviewing technique," Charlie said.

"I was worried at one point that she was just going to sit there and say nothing," Harry said.

"It was the family that cracked her," Charlie said. "I don't know why, but I could see her soften at that point. The only thing worrying me now is that when she got up to go back to her cell, she said it's not over yet."

"Well, we know there was a fourth set of prints at the farm," Harry said. He turned to Danny and asked, "Are the anti-terrorism boys still trying to get a match on them?" Danny nodded. "Maybe she was referring to that."

"Listen, Harry, I am going to go and see Oscar's parents," Charlie said, "to let them know we have charged someone with Oscar's murder. You start getting all the paperwork sorted out."

Charlie left the office.

Harry turned to the others. "You heard the boss, let's start getting all the loose ends sorted out. Danny, you get me some tea – and I noticed you still haven't got your hair cut."

★★★

Sometime later, Charlie returned to the office. He found the team completing reports and pulling all the paperwork together for the case.

"Manjitt has been on to me, boss," Harry said. "Mrs Khan has asked her to stay for dinner."

"Did you bring her up to speed on everything?" Charlie asked.

"Yes, told her all about it," Harry said.

"How are the anti-terrorism boys doing with the fourth set of prints that were found at the farm?"

"They've had no luck, yet," Harry said

Charlie's phone rang and he spoke to the caller for a minute.

"Commander Flynn is here and he will be taking the prisoners away with him to Paddington Green. I am just going downstairs to see him now."

Charlie met Flynn in the custody area, where there were about fifteen officers standing around – half of them armed. The custody sergeant was signing some paperwork and passing it to one of the anti-terrorism officers.

"Everything going alright, sergeant?" Charlie asked.

"Yes, Sir, just finishing the release papers to hand the prisoners over," the sergeant replied.

Charlie watched with Flynn as the prisoners were brought out one at a time and taken to separate police vans outside.

"Thanks for your help, Chief Superintendent. They could have caused a lot of harm," Flynn said.

"It was just a bonus for us; we were just chasing the girl's murderer when we fell onto the farm," Charlie said.

"I got word from my men up in Leeds that might interest you," Flynn said. "They have had a look at the laptop we recovered from Rashid Butt's home and it would appear that he was in email contact with someone who was giving him details of your murdered girl's movements. The other worrying thing is that there was mention of an attack on the home secretary. It wasn't with the bombs we found at the farm; however, as we know they were destined for other targets. I have put extra security around the home secretary and we are doing all we can to trace the email account the messages came from. We know there was a fourth set of fingerprints found at the farm, so whoever it is could have explosives. I will keep you up to date if we get any more information."

"Could you send me over copies of the messages?" Charlie said. "We might be able to piece something together from our end."

"I will get someone to do that right away," Flynn said.

They watched as Shiza Akmal left the police station and was escorted to the waiting police vans.

Flynn turned to Charlie, "Thanks for all your help."

They shook hands and Flynn followed the last of the officers outside.

★★★

Walking back into the office, Charlie explained to the team what Flynn had told him about someone passing on Ashadieeyah's movements.

"He is going to send us over the email exchanges, but until they arrive, let's look at her movements. Get Shiza Akmal's statement, see which dates she said they met and check it against Ashadieeyah Khan's diary. Recheck all her friends and family again; let's see if we can get an idea of who knew where she would be on the days she had meetings with Shiza Akmal. It must have been planned that she was able to bump into Ashadieeyah again after all those years of not seeing each other."

"Come on then, let's get on to it," Harry said to the squad. "No loose ends; someone is just as culpable as the person who killed Ashadieeyah."

Danny, Jordan and Inspector West started to go through all the paperwork, pulling out reports and statements ready to cross-check against Ashadieeyah's movements. Charlie pulled Harry to one side.

"Commander Flynn told me about some information they got from Rashid Butt's laptop about an attack on the home secretary. He was worried, as whoever the other person was at the farm might have explosives. He is putting extra security around the home secretary. I think you should get hold of Manjitt and bring her up to speed, ask her to have a quiet word with Mr and Mrs Khan about Ashadieeyah's movements and who might have known."

"I will call her now; you don't think it was one of the family?" Harry asked.

"Stranger things have happened, Harry," Charlie said.

* * *

Manjitt had taken the call from Harry and was sitting with Mrs Khan, who had been telling her how the family would still be taking the holiday to Pakistan that Ashadieeyah had been looking forward to. Her son had said that his sister would be traveling with them in their hearts, and Mrs Khan said she liked to think that was so.

Mrs Khan had also told Manjitt that her husband was very upset about his daughter's death and though he put on a brave face when people were around, he had broken down in tears many times when they were alone together.

Mr Khan suddenly entered the room and joined them, sitting next to his wife.

He spoke to Manjitt, "I have just got off the phone speaking to my brother, Mahbeer."

"That's the home secretary to you," Mrs Khan interrupted.

"Yes, sorry, the home secretary," Mr Khan continued. "He is going to join us for dinner this evening and he said he has some exciting news to tell us. He was pleased to hear about Ashadieeyah's case being solved, too. I told him you would be here and he looks forward to hearing about it."

"I spoke to one of my superior officers earlier and there are a couple of small points we still have to clear up," Manjitt said.

"You don't mean they could get off?" Mrs Khan asked.

"No, we have the right people," Manjitt replied. "It's just that we are trying to get to the bottom of how they knew where Ashadieeyah would be. We know they only phoned her a few times, but they met her on a number of occasions, so someone must have been passing on information of her movements."

"You don't think it was one of the family, do you?" Mr Khan asked.

"I am hoping it's not, but what do you think?" Manjitt said.

"No, never, none of my family would do anything like that," Mr Khan said. "They all loved Ashadieeyah as much as us."

"We have to check all these things out," Manjitt said, "because someone put your daughter in harm's way and that led to her death. We want to catch them, as they are just as responsible as the killers."

"We understand, but I don't believe one of the family would do something like that," Mrs Khan said. "Now, I am going to prepare dinner. Would you like to join me in the kitchen, Officer Virdee, and we can continue our chat."

Manjitt and Mrs Khan got up to go off to the kitchen.

"Ask Raju to bring me some tea in," Mr Khan said, as he picked up a newspaper and began to read.

* * *

The team had received the copies of the email exchanges between Rashid Butt and the mystery person who was supplying Ashadieeyah's movements. They were cross-checking dates and times. Harry was writing on the whiteboard as each one of the team called a possible link, before drawing a line to connect it to a possible source. They had been going over it for an hour, when Harry sat back down. All of them stared at the whiteboard.

"I think it's pretty clear it's not at the university end," Jordan said.

Harry looked over at Charlie, "Jordan's right, boss, we can rule out all her friends at university, as the meetings and times were when she was at home. It has to be someone in the family."

"Manjitt questioned the family," Charlie said. "Get all their statements out and we can go through them to see if there's anything that gives us a hint."

"Hippie," Harry asked, "you took statements from the son and the butler – what's his name?"

"Raju," Danny said.

"Yes, Raju, get those out, too," Harry said. "Now, everybody have a read and pass them round. Let's see if anything shows up."

They all began reading. When they had finished a statement, it was passed to the person next to them to read.

After all the statements had been read by everybody, Harry said, "Did anybody spot something?"

Everyone agreed there wasn't anything in the statements that gave rise to suspect any of the family.

"Well, no one is going to tell us they were tipping off her killers, are they?" Harry said.

"Could it have been someone we don't know about?" Inspector West asked.

"There is that possibility," Charlie said, "but they would have to know when she was going to be back at her home from university and when she would be leaving the house to go out." Charlie looked at Harry, "It could only be someone who is in the house all the time."

"Rule out her mum and dad," Harry said.

"Her brother idolised her, so I also wouldn't put him in the frame," Danny said.

"So, we are left with our friend Raju – his statement was pretty vague. Give Manjitt another call, Harry, and get her to find out a bit more about him from the Khans," Charlie said. "Jordan, get in touch with the anti-terrorism boys and see if they have had any luck matching those fingerprints they found at the farm. Danny, you run him through the system to see if anything comes up. What was his surname?"

Danny picked up Raju's statement. "Hassan; I will see if he pops up, boss," Danny said.

Jordan and Danny got up and left to do the checking.

"Boss, there is a way we could be certain – one way or the other. We could get Raju's fingerprints and check them against the ones we have," Harry said.

"We can't go and ask him to be fingerprinted," West said.

"That's true, but if something came into our hands with his prints on that he didn't know we had…" Harry said.

"Let's play this carefully, Harry," Charlie said. "If it is him, we don't want to tip him off. When you call Manjitt, fill her in and tell her to get something he has handled. Forget telling her to ask the

Khans about him; we don't want them to change their attitude, as he might get suspicious. Tell her that Inspector West will call by in the next half hour to pick it up off her. We can make up an excuse that she has papers he needs."

Harry rang Manjitt and told her what they suspected, arranging that West would call round at the house in the next half hour. She said she would find an excuse for Raju to handle something, keep it and pass it on to West when he arrived.

Harry got off the phone and said, "Manjitt will get us something, boss."

"Inspector, do you have a fingerprint scanner in the custody suite?" Charlie asked.

"Yes, they have one in the sergeant's office," West replied.

"Good, now you get over to the house and take this," Charlie picked up some blank sheets of paper, put them in a folder and gave it to West. "Give this to Manjitt and be careful with what she gives you. Get it straight back here – put your emergency lights on when you're away from the house. I want you back as soon as possible."

Inspector West got up and left to go to the house, just as Danny and Jordan came back into the office. Jordan said nothing had been found to match the prints yet and Danny told them that Raju hadn't come up anywhere on the police system. Harry told them what they had planned to help identify him.

"Harry, give Doctor Taylor a ring. Tell him I want a fingerprint expert over here now," Charlie said, as he stood up. "Let's go and wait downstairs in the custody suite for West to get back."

★★★

Manjitt was in the kitchen with Mrs Khan, helping her to finish off preparing the dinner. Everything was nearly ready. They were just chopping up onions and peppers to put into small dishes at the kitchen table, when Raju came into the kitchen with a teacup.

"Raju, when you have washed that up, could you make sure there is enough cold bottled water for the meal in the fridge? If not, get some more from the store and put it in to chill," Mrs Khan said.

Raju nodded and went to the sink to wash the cup and saucer up. Manjitt watched him finish drying it and put it back in a cupboard. As he turned to go to the fridge, Manjitt asked him, "Could you pass me a small glass, please?"

Raju looked at her, went to another cupboard, pulled open the door and turning his head to Manjitt, he asked, "Which size would you like?"

"Oh, only a small one – that one," she said, pointing.

Raju reached into the cupboard and picked up the glass Manjitt had pointed at. He went to hand it to Manjitt.

"Put it down here while I wash the onion off my hands," she said.

Raju placed the glass on the table beside her, walked to the fridge, looked inside and said he would get a few more bottles of water from the store for later.

When he had left the kitchen, Manjitt said to Mrs Khan, "One of my colleagues is calling by to pick up some paperwork I have; do you have a plastic bag that I could put it in?"

Mrs Khan said she did and went to a cupboard under the sink to retrieve a plastic bag. She passed it to Manjitt, who placed it on the table beside her.

"I am going to take some of these," Mrs Khan said, pointing to the small dishes filled with onions, peppers and assorted dips, "into the front room and get the table ready. When you have finished washing your hands, could you bring the rest in for me? There's a tray on the side."

"Yes, of course," Manjitt said.

She watched Mrs Khan leave the kitchen, quickly washed her

hands, took the plastic bag and put it over the glass. Picking it up without touching the glass herself, she carefully folded the bag round it, so that the bag looked as if it was screwed into a ball. She placed it on the tray along with the rest of the bowls and walked through to the front room.

Mrs Khan was at the table telling Mr Khan to get some better placemats from the cupboard. Manjitt placed the tray on the table.

Picking up the plastic bag from the tray, she said, "I am just going to get the paperwork my colleague is collecting from my bag."

She walked out into the hall and slipped the glass into her bag, before returning to the front room.

"I think the table looks lovely," Mrs Khan said. "Thank you for your help."

"I enjoyed it. I don't get up to see my family as much as I would like," Manjitt said, "so it was nice to be in a kitchen and have a chat with someone."

"You are not married, yet?" Mrs Khan asked.

"No, not yet. You sound like my mother saying that," Manjitt replied, smiling.

Mrs Khan laughed, "That's what we mothers are like."

Mr Khan asked if anyone would like some juice or water to drink.

"Get Raju to bring some orange juice in," Mrs Khan said.

Mr Khan pressed the button by the fireplace and Raju came in within a minute.

"Could you bring a jug of orange juice in please, Raju," Mr Khan said.

"Has Raju worked for you for long?" Manjitt asked.

"Over a year now. He is very good and gets everything done without fuss," Mrs Khan replied.

They heard the doorbell sound. A moment later, Raju came in with the orange juice.

"There is a policeman at the door to see you," he said to Manjitt, as he placed the juice on the table.

Manjitt went into the hallway, picked up her bag and went to the front door where Inspector West was waiting. She slipped her hand in the bag and gave him the plastic bag. He passed her the folder and turned quickly to return to his car. Manjitt turned and found Raju standing behind her.

"I will close the door," he said.

Manjitt placed her bag back down and walked into the front room with the folder.

"I hope that's not more work you have to do," Mr Khan said.

"Nothing I can't leave until after dinner," Manjitt said, as she placed it on one of the small tables.

* * *

As Inspector West was about to pull out of the Khan's drive, he saw three cars coming along the road: two marked police cars and a dark Jaguar between them. They signalled to turn into the drive as West pulled out. Glancing into the back of the Jaguar, he saw the home secretary.

He immediately put a call through to Harry, letting him know Manjitt had passed him the glass. West then drove to the end of the Khan's road, accelerated and put on his emergency lights and siren.

* * *

Raju showed the home secretary into the front room. He said hello to his brother and sister in-law, and Mrs Khan reminded him he had met Manjitt before.

"Yes, Officer Virdee, I remember. How are you?"

He shook hands with Manjitt.

"Come on, everyone, let's sit at the table. Safwan, tell our son to come and join us," Mrs Khan said. Mr Khan left the room to get their son. "Mahbeer, if you turn up with so many cars, we will have to get a bigger drive."

"It's just security; it has been raised recently," the home secretary said. He looked at Manjitt, "I am sure Officer Virdee would understand."

"Yes, Sir, with the situation as it is," Manjitt said.

Mr Khan came back into the front room with his son.

"Come on, everyone, let's sit down and eat. Mahbeer, you can tell us the news you have and I am sure Officer Virdee will tell you about her investigation," said Mrs Khan.

* * *

The squad were standing in the custody suite. A fingerprint specialist had come over from Doctor Taylor's team and was being told by Charlie what they needed.

Danny was standing with Jordan and Harry, explaining why he thought they needed to get more up to date with their choice of clothes. Jordan said he would pay good money to see Harry in what Danny was wearing, but Harry thought lime green dungarees might just be taking it a bit too far.

Inspector West had made good time getting back to the station. When he walked into the custody suite, he saw the rest of the team waiting for him.

"Well done, Inspector," Charlie said. "Harry, get that glass checked out now."

Harry took the plastic bag from West and went into the sergeant's office with the fingerprint specialist. The man carefully un-wrapped the plastic bag and placed the glass on the table.

"I will need to do an atmospheric superglue fuming test on the glass to get the best result," he said.

Harry looked mystified, but said, "Do whatever it takes."

The man had what looked like a goldfish tank and lifted it onto the table.

"Could someone get me a glass of boiling water, please?" the man said.

Harry called to Danny to get a glass of boiling water. "How does this work?" he asked.

"Basically, the superglue will evaporate and fume the outside of the glass and coat it. Any prints will show up clearly," the man explained.

He opened up what Harry thought was the fish tank he had brought with him and placed the glass inside. There was a small lightbulb inside the container, which he connected to a small battery. Danny came in with a glass of boiling water and the expert also placed it in the container. He then took a small tube of superglue, squeezed some into a little dish and put it next to the glass of boiling water. He closed the container lid, pushing down the catches to make sure it was tightly shut, and flicked a small switch on the side. A lightbulb came on inside.

"It will take about half an hour for the prints to appear on the glass and I can then run a match for you," he said.

Harry came out the office and said to Charlie, "Half an hour boss before he can start to run a comparison."

"Oh well, we have waited longer to get an answer," Charlie said.

***

Manjitt was seated opposite the home secretary at the dinner table and was explaining how they had captured the three suspects at the farm as they ate.

"I am sorry for your fellow officer who was killed," the home secretary said.

Manjitt nodded and said, "He was a great person, as well as a good police officer."

"Your superior officer, I forget his name?" he asked.

"Chief Superintendent Smith," Manjitt said.

"Yes, that's it; he seems a very good officer. I had a meeting with him and he was very helpful to me. I must see him again and thank him. Have you worked with him for long?" the home secretary asked.

"Yes, several years now," Manjitt said.

"I had him checked out after I spoke to him," the home secretary said. "I recieved reports that he was a good policeman, but a bit of a loner – that he didn't mix with the top brass at Scotland Yard."

"I wouldn't know about that, Sir," Manjitt said.

"I was told he drives very expensive cars, like Ferraris and Bentleys, and people often question where he gets his money from," the home secretary said, looking at Manjitt.

"He does drive nice cars, Sir, but as to where his money comes from, he has never given me any reason to think it's other than legit," Manjitt replied.

"You have never asked him or wondered?" the home secretary asked.

"I have wondered, but never asked. All I know is I could not work for a better boss," Manjitt said.

"I think you are putting Officer Virdee in an uncomfortable position, Mahbeer," Mr Khan said.

"I am sorry," the home secretary said to Manjitt, "I did not mean to. He just intrigues me. He doesn't seem bothered about what his fellow officers think of him, which is quite the opposite to us politicians."

"I have always found him very supportive when I needed his help with a case," Manjitt said.

"No, I don't mean like that. I meant with his superior officers," the home secretary said.

Smiling, Manjitt said, "Again, Sir, I would know nothing of his dealings with superior officers."

"Are all your fellow officers who work with you happy with the chief superintendent?" he asked.

"As far as I know, Sir, none of them have ever said anything bad about him in my presence. Do you know something about him that I don't, Sir?" Manjitt asked.

"No, no, nothing. I just found him interesting. He seems a very good officer," he said.

"Mahbeer, I think you have questioned Officer Virdee enough. She will think you are going to make trouble for her boss," Mrs Khan said.

"I will not be doing that, I can assure you," the home secretary said to Manjitt.

"Well, I think it's about time you told us your news, Mahbeer," Mr Khan said.

"Let us get some of the plates cleared away first," Mrs Khan said. "Would everyone like some coffee or tea?"

They all agreed on coffee. Mrs Khan rose from the table and pressed the bell, and Raju came into the room.

"You may take the dinner plates away now, please, Raju, and could you bring some coffee in?" Mrs Khan asked.

Raju nodded and started to stack the empty plates, placing knifes and forks on top, before carrying them out of the room.

The home secretary turned to Mr Khan's son and asked, "So, how are you getting on at school?"

"Very well, Uncle, I hope to get good results and go to Oxford like Ashadieeyah."

There was silence for a moment, until Mr Khan said, "She would be very proud of you if you did."

"I am sure you will get to Oxford. What are you going to study?" the home secretary asked.

"I would like to study law. I want to be a barrister," he said.

"He will do it, too," Mrs Khan said.

Raju returned with the coffee on a tray and placed it on the table next to Mrs Khan.

⋆⋆⋆

The team were standing outside the sergeant's office, talking about the case. Harry looked at his watch and went back inside the room. The fingerprint expert was seated, looking at the container, but looked up as Harry walked in.

"It's nearly done," he said. "I think I can see a couple of clear prints on your glass."

A small bell sounded and the light in the container went out. He snapped open the catches on the lid and lifted it off. He opened his bag and took out some clear tape.

"Could you switch the fingerprint scanner on?" he said.

Harry went over to the scanner and switched it on, which made a slight humming sound. The fingerprint expert lifted the glass out and carefully studied it, holding it up to the light.

"Yes, we have at least two excellent ones," he said, putting the glass on the table.

He took the clear tape and cut off two pieces, which were both about 3 inches long. He then placed each on a different part of the glass and smoothed them down. After a few seconds, he peeled them away.

"Yes, these will do," he said, as he looked at the fingerprints on the tape. "If there's a match on the system, it will show up."

He walked to the scanner and placed the two pieces of tape over the glass front, tapping a number into the keypad.

"It will take a couple of minutes," he said to Harry.

***

Mrs Khan started to pour the coffee into the cups.

"Do you want milk?" she asked Manjitt. "All my family like theirs black."

"Yes please, but not too much," Manjitt said.

Mrs Khan passed the cups around. "Now, Mahbeer, you must tell us your news."

"Well, I had a meeting with the prime minister earlier today," the home secretary said, "along with some other members of the government. He will be announcing he is going to step down tomorrow, as his illness is such that he needs to go into hospital and will need months of recuperation."

"Does that mean there will be an election?" Mr Khan asked.

"No, the party will elect a new leader and they will become prime minister," he said.

"So, I expect there will be a lot of arguments and we will see all of them parade on the television telling us why they are right for the job," Mr Khan said.

"That is how it usually is, but the party are pretty united at the moment and there are a lot of important decisions that have to be made for the country coming up," the home secretary said. "Therefore, they don't want any in-fighting that may give the opposition help in opposing the legislation we are putting forward."

"So that means there will be new people coming into the government. Will you keep your job?" Mrs Khan asked.

"That is the news. No, I won't be home secretary," he said.

"What, you are being sacked as home secretary?" Mr Khan asked.

"No, I will have a new job," he replied.

"I thought you had done a good job as home secretary," Mrs Khan said. "Why do they want to get rid of you?"

The home secretary laughed. "They are not getting rid of me; I have been asked to take over as leader of the party," he said.

"Really?" Mrs Khan exclaimed.

"Wait a minute," Mr Khan said, and he looked at his brother who was smiling back at him, "if you're leader of the party that makes you…" he stopped speaking.

Mrs Khan looked from her husband to her brother in-law, putting her hand to her mouth. "Oh my God," she said, "you are going to be prime minister."

Mr Khan stood up, went round the table and embraced his brother. "I am so proud of you," he said.

"We must ring the rest of the family," Mrs Khan said.

The home secretary laughed, saying, "You can't do that, yet. Tomorrow, after 10 o'clock, you can call them all. A press release is going out and there will be a press conference called to make the official announcement."

"Can I come to Downing Street to see inside?" Mr Khan's son asked.

"I will have all the family there for dinner and show you round," the home secretary said.

"I can't believe its true," Mr Khan said. "When we were growing up, Mother and Father would never have dreamt this. I wish they were here to see how well you have done, Mahbeer."

"You have all been part of what I have achieved," the home secretary said.

"Oh, I can't stop saying it in my head – my brother in-law, the prime minister," Mrs Khan said.

The home secretary and Mr Khan laughed at her.

Manjitt stood up. "Congratulations, Sir," she said. The home secretary shook her outstretched hand.

"Thank you, Officer, but I have to ask you not to repeat anything you have heard to anyone – well, not until after 10 o'clock tomorrow," he said.

"Of course, Sir, you have my word," Manjitt replied.

"Let us have some fresh coffee," Mr Khan said, as he pressed the bell. Raju came in. "Can you bring us a fresh pot of coffee, please, Raju?"

Raju walked to the table, picked up the empty pot and left the room.

"I think I should be going now," Manjitt said, "but if I could use your bathroom first?"

"Of course," Mrs Khan said, "when you go out of the door, turn towards the kitchen and it's the second door on the right."

Manjitt went to the door and it opened just as she got to it as Raju came in with a fresh pot of coffee. She stood aside to let him pass, then went out and turned left towards the kitchen.

* * *

"We have a hit," the fingerprint expert said.

He read the message that came through on the scanner's screen. "They are the same as the ones taken from the farmhouse and the two lorries found in the barn."

Harry quickly went out to the custody suite. "He's our man, boss," he said.

"Harry, ring Manjitt and tell her to keep him away from the family," Charlie said. "I will ring Commander Flynn."

"The home secretary is at the house, boss," Harry said. "Manjitt said he was coming to have dinner with the family."

"Get onto her now, Harry. Everyone, let's get to the house," Charlie shouted.

Charlie got hold of Flynn and told him what they had found out. Flynn said he would put an emergency call through to the team that were with the home secretary.

Outside, they climbed into the cars. Harry was in the front of the Bentley with Charlie.

"Pick up your phone," he was saying. "Manjitt, its Harry."

* * *

Manjitt had just reached the bathroom door, when her phone went off. She got it out of her pocket, but it slipped from her hand and skidded across the floor, finishing up under one of the tables in the hall. She knelt down, stretched out her hand and could just reach it. She slowly eased it towards her – it was still ringing. She stood up and answered it.

"Manjitt, it's Harry," she heard.

"Yes, Harry?" she answered.

"Raju is our man from the farm. Get the family away from him."

"I just left them in the front room with him," she said quietly into the phone.

"Go back in there. He might be armed, so be careful. We are on our way; just play it by ear until we arrive – Manjitt, please be careful," Harry repeated.

"Okay, Harry."

She placed her phone into her pocket and walked back to the front room. The home secretary was standing talking to his brother by the fireplace, while Mrs Khan was sitting with her son at the table. Raju was standing next to Mrs Khan with the coffee pot.

Manjitt was halfway across the room when a high-pitched whistle went off. Everyone froze for a second, until the home secretary shouted above the noise.

"It's okay, it's my security alarm!"

He reached inside his pocket to retrieve it. As he did so, Manjitt heard a hammering on the front doors. Voices could be heard, demanding to be let in.

"What's going on?" Mrs Khan said.

Manjitt saw Raju put the coffee pot down and move from behind Mrs Khan towards the home secretary.

"Raju, see what all that noise is at the front door," Mrs Kahn said.

The home secretary had managed to switch his alarm off, but all that could be heard was the hammering on the front door. Manjitt started to move quickly to try to intercept Raju

"Raju, go to the front door and see what the noise is," Mrs Khan said again.

Raju momentarily stopped and looked towards Mrs Khan, while Manjitt used the time to get closer to the home secretary. She saw Raju turn back and pull a large carving knife from under his jacket.

"Home secretary, look out!" Manjitt screamed.

The home secretary and Mr Khan both looked in Manjitt's direction. She was now running towards them, watching Raju raise the knife.

A cry came from Raju, "Allahu Akbar!"

The home secretary and Mr Khan turned suddenly towards Raju, while Mrs Khan screamed.

Manjitt reached the home secretary just as Raju was throwing himself forward. She shouldered the home secretary towards the wall and he cannoned into Mr Khan. Raju brought the knife down, missing the home secretary but catching Mr Khan in the arm. Mr Khan screamed in pain.

Raju raised the knife again to strike at the home secretary, but Manjitt had regained her balance. Raju was so intent on striking the home secretary that he never saw Manjitt spinning round her right leg, rising as she did until it was at head height. In an instant, the back of her heel caught Raju flush on the right side of his jaw. Though Raju's legs kept moving towards the home secretary, the rest of his body stopped dead. His legs seemed to collapse under him and he fell to the ground, unconscious before he hit it.

Manjitt heard the front doors smash open and police officers with guns drawn poured into the front room. The home secretary stood up as the officers came forward.

"You better take him away," Manjitt said, pointing to Raju.

Three officers knelt beside Raju, who was still unconscious. They pulled his hands behind his back and put handcuffs on him, lifted him up and took him away.

The home secretary said to one of the officers, "Get an ambulance here right away." He turned back to his brother, who was lying against the wall, "Stay still, Safwan, an ambulance is on its way."

Mrs Khan came over and, still crying from the shock, she held her husband's head in her hands. Manjitt grabbed a cloth off the table and wrapped it around Mr Khan's arm.

"Hold that tightly on the wound until the ambulance gets here," she said.

★★★

Harry and Charlie came into the room and saw Manjitt talking to the home secretary. Mr Khan was being placed onto a stretcher. They walked over to Manjitt.

"Is Mr Khan badly hurt?" Charlie asked.

"He has a nasty wound in the arm, but should be okay," Manjitt said.

"What about Raju?" Harry asked.

"Officer Virdee here dealt with him," the home secretary said. "I have to say, she saved our lives."

Manjitt shrugged at Charlie and Harry.

"I am sure she will put everything in her report," Harry said.

Manjitt smiled, "I won't leave a thing out, Harry."

From behind them, they heard, "Home secretary, are you alright?"

They turned and saw Commander Flynn coming into the room.

"Yes, I am fine," the home secretary said. "Can we get my brother into the ambulance?"

Flynn called two officers over, who helped to lift the stretcher up and take it from the room.

"Mahbeer," Mrs Khan said, "I will be going with the ambulance."

"Of course, ring me later and let me know how Safwan is," the home secretary said.

Flynn turned to Charlie, "That was close, but we have them all in custody now. It was a good job with the fingerprints. Well done."

"The good job was done by Manjitt. It was lucky she was here or we might be looking for a new home secretary," Charlie said.

The home secretary looked at Manjitt and smiled, "I think they still could be, don't you, Officer Virdee?"

★★★

It was Sunday afternoon and Manjitt was standing with Jordan and Danny. All three had a glass of wine in their hands and were looking out of the French windows at Charlie's greyhounds chasing each other across the lawn.

"So, you knew all along that he was going to become the prime minister?" Danny said.

"He told us over dinner that evening, but made me promise not to say anything," Manjitt replied.

"You should have whispered in my ear," Jordan said. "I could have gone to the bookies and had a few pounds on him."

"Do you know what the word 'promise' means?" Manjitt asked.

Harry and Charlie came into the dining room. They stopped by the door and Harry pointed to Danny, who was wearing a two-piece, dark orange suit with thin, green stripes running through it.

"Hippie, if you're wearing Sunday best, I would hate to see you when it's a dress-down day," Harry said.

The three of them turned.

"Harry, my mother thought I looked smarter than ever. I think she was quite proud of me wearing a suit."

Harry shook his head from side to side, "One of you get a glass of wine for me – it might help me get used to that suit."

Danny went to the table to get Harry a drink.

Meanwhile, Inspector West pulled up at the gates, with Chief Superintendent Myles in the car with him.

"I am sure this is the place; Harry gave me directions," West said.

They saw a man come from the cottage 50 yards further up the drive. He looked in their direction and walked towards them. As he got close, the gates started to open. They drove in and stopped beside him.

West said, "We have come to have dinner with Chief Superintendent Smith."

"Just follow the drive up to the main house," the man told them.

They drove onwards, coming round a curve in the road and saw the house come into view.

"Jesus," West said, "can you get one of those on your salary, Ma'am?"

"Not on my salary, you can't," she said.

They parked the car next to the others and walked to the large front door. It opened and Charlie stood there, smiling.

"Welcome to my little place in the country," he said.

Not long after, they were all seated round the table chatting and drinking. Maggie had placed a large leg of lamb in the centre of the table, along with dishes of different vegetables. Charlie stood up.

"Can I just make a toast before we tuck into dinner?" He held up his glass, "To Oscar; the finest samba dancer the metropolitan police has ever seen."

"To Oscar," they all said.